The Unwelcome Guest

Cori Nevruz

Contents

Dedicated to all of my reader friends who, given a dream vacation to a luxurious mansion on a private island, would spend most of their time in the fairy-tale library.

CHAPTER ONE

The End

He watched her body cut through the water with effortless grace, each movement a fluid dance that seemed almost otherworldly. The sleek arch of her back, the slight tension in her arms as they sliced through the water, and the rhythmic pulse of her legs—every stroke was smooth, powerful, a silent testament to the years of training behind her. Her hands cupped the surface with the precision of a seasoned swimmer while the briefest gasp of air, barely a whisper, broke the surface as she turned her head. It was hypnotic, a perfect cadence as if the water and she were one. The stillness of the pool around her seemed to magnify her presence—calm, controlled—while the ripples she left behind rolled gently, undulating like a slow-moving tide, graceful and serene.

For a moment, he felt his pulse slow. The anger that had once burned with an almost consuming heat had dulled to a faint ember; its intensity faded to a distant memory. The tightness in his chest loosened as he exhaled, the tension unwinding from his muscles with a slow, deliberate release. Even the faint hum of the pool cover motor, its drone more calming than intrusive, could not shatter the tranquility of his focus.

He stepped closer to the edge, the concrete cool beneath his bare feet, the pool-skimmer pole in his hands like an extension of his own body—steady, unwavering. Her strokes brought her nearer, each pull of her arms inching her toward him, drawing her closer to the edge of his trap. He adjusted his grip, angling the pole with the precision of a predator. He slid his left hand down the pole, shifting his fingers to a lower, firmer grip. A deep, measured breath filled his lungs, the moment stretching, hanging in the balance. As she neared, his breath stilled.

With chilling aggression, he pressed the net down over her head. Her body jerked, panic flaring in her eyes as instinct took over. But he held firm, every motion calculated to keep her from breaking free, the pole held just off-center to avoid triggering the pool cover's safety mechanism. He pushed her at an angle, forcing her under, a slow, deliberate descent into the water. The struggle was brief, a fight that fizzled out in the face of his iron grip.

One final, relentless push, and she sank beneath the surface. The water stilled for a fleeting moment, as though holding its breath in the following silence. He yanked the pole free just in time for the pool cover to slide into place, a smooth, efficient barrier, sealing her beneath it.

He let go, the skimmer clattering against the concrete deck like a church bell dropped onto a stone floor, sharp and reverberating with a hollow finality. It echoed loudly over the sudden silence that took hold as the motor whirred to a stop. A slow smile spread across his face, his lips curling with satisfaction as the enormity of the moment washed over him. The months of meticulous planning, the careful orchestration of every detail, had paid off.

The internet had been his silent accomplice. Every piece of information he needed, every scrap of knowledge to execute the perfect crime had been there, laid out for him like a banquet. It had all started with a spark, a post, an idle boast—an opportunity too perfect to ignore. The vacation listing had been a treasure trove: photographs detailing every corner of the private island, the layout of the rental house, even the number of rooms. GPS coordinates had been tucked away like breadcrumbs for anyone daring enough to follow.

Social media had filled in the gaps, and the posts were practically begging for attention. Like so many, the brazen exposure of vulnerabilities—so easy to read, yet impossible to ignore. People were so eager to expose themselves, to lay bare every detail of their lives. It didn't take a genius to spot the hidden messages, the invitations disguised as innocent posts.

"Heading to Florida today!" =

I'm not home. Help yourself to what's left behind.

"I'll be walking home from class tonight" =

When it's dark, I'll be alone.

"We broke up. I'm going out." =

I'm getting drunk. Come take advantage.

And then, the post that had started it all:

"Eeeek! I'm renting a private island!"

Where others saw carefree excitement, a bit of boastful fun, he saw an opportunity.

The planning—her planning—had been nearly complete, but for him, it was just beginning.

It wasn't the act of violence that thrilled him—it was the watching, the waiting, the knowing that he was unseen, unnoticed. The voyeuristic pleasure of observing lives stripped bare of pretension when people thought no one was watching. That was what captivated him—the unguarded vulnerability, the moments when masks slipped, and true selves emerged.

This island was their paradise, their dream escape. To them, it was a place of relaxation and joy. But for him, it was a stage—a once-in-a-lifetime opportunity to indulge in his darkest obsession. And now, the curtain had fallen. All that was left was for him to bask in the applause.

Chapter Two

The Arrival

4 Days Earlier...

Crystal's heart raced as she watched the ferry edge closer to the dock, its motor rumbling low and steady, the sound echoing through the stillness of the island air. The faint tremor of the engine disrupted the otherwise serene quiet, a subtle reminder that even paradise had its undercurrents. She tightened her grip on Jonah's hand, the soothing touch of his palm grounding her as her practiced smile remained fixed, her posture impeccable as she waved at the approaching guests. The salty breeze lifted strands of her blond hair, sending them dancing in the air like stray threads from a carefully woven tapestry. It tugged at the edges of the picture she had so meticulously arranged, teasing the image of effortless perfection.

Her palm felt damp against Jonah's, the tension in her body betraying the calm she projected. She quickly released his hand, wiping it discreetly against the fabric of her sundress. Jonah glanced down at her, his steady blue eyes meeting hers with a quiet understanding. His lips curved into a loving smile, his gaze softening the sharp edges of her nerves. He followed with a quick, playful wink, a signal of reassurance. She drew in a breath, trying to center herself in the calmness he exuded. He had been her anchor since they were teenagers, the one person who could bring her back to solid ground when everything else felt fragile.

This wasn't just a vacation. Crystal had poured nearly a year into planning every detail—every flight, every meal, every room. But the idea of this trip had lived in her mind far longer, a fantasy she had been nurturing for years. It had to be perfect. The arrival, the setting, the first impressions—they all had to exude effortless beauty and flawless harmony. The island's lush green expanse, the gentle lapping of the waves against the shore, the soft whispers of palm trees swaying under the breeze—each element was a piece of the grand design she had created. The magic was in the details, in the illusion of ease. It had to appear like this was how things were meant to be.

Jonah's family had also become hers over the last sixteen years, and she wanted them to see how well she fit into their picture and how seamlessly she belonged. Even the timing of their arrival had been planned. The ferry would dock with the sun high in the sky, casting the landscape in a soft golden light that minimized shadows, making everything appear bathed in perfection. The ocean breeze rustled the palm trees gently without disrupting her perfectly arranged hair. She knew how to stage a scene. Her long legs, silky blond hair, and creamy skin—gifts of genetics rather than hard work—had launched her modeling career. In addition to her good genes, she had a natural talent for creating picture-perfect moments. Her sheer gauze sundress billowed just enough to suggest elegance, an effortless sophistication, with each movement she made adding to the tableau. She was the living embodiment of the vacation she had so carefully orchestrated.

She couldn't see it from where she stood but imagined the scene as they came closer with the ferry. With his open linen shirt and tailored khaki pants, Jonah looked casually commanding, like a well-dressed executive on island time. Together, they stood as the perfect pair, the central characters in this idyllic play.

The ferry drifted closer, the figures on board sharpening against the sunlight, their faces becoming more distinct with each passing second. Jonah's three brothers and their wives were just as she remembered them—distinct personalities wrapped in the familiar contours of their faces.

Her husband Jonah was the eldest at 34 and had always been the family's foundation, solid and steady. His presence radiated quiet authority. His polar opposite was his brother Thomas, 32, the joker who kept things light, even when things were meant to be serious. Crystal's lips twitched as she watched him feign a stumble at the bow of the ferry, arms flailing theatrically as though he might tumble into the water. The young ferry captain who looked not a day older than sixteen shot Thomas a sharp, disapproving look, his impatience cutting through the moment's levity.

Crystal's gaze shifted to Ilma, Thomas's wife of less than a year, whom she had met only once at their wedding. Ilma sat in the ferry's only shaded corner, engrossed in a book, her posture straight, her demeanor detached from Thomas's antics. The contrast between them was striking. Ilma's poise was serene, as if she inhabited a different world entirely from her husband's playfulness.

Sean, the third brother at 30, was impossible to miss. Even on the ferry, he stood like a model poised for a fitness magazine cover. His tall frame was built for attention. Beside him, his wife April matched his energy—an unstoppable force. Both were shirtless, with the exception of April's skimpy sports bra, their sculpted bodies gleaming in the sunlight, a testament to their shared dedication to fitness. Crystal's trained eye caught the sheen on their skin—sweat or oil? She suspected it was the latter, some product designed to enhance their muscles' definition under the unforgiving sun. In Crystal's world of high fashion, a suntan was something applied from a bottle. The sun was an enemy—bringing wrinkles, dark spots, and damage. But to Sean and April, the sun was their spotlight, and their bodies were the art on display.

At the helm, standing apart from the chaos of Thomas's antics, was the baby of the family. Though he had adopted the name Will in his teens, Crystal still couldn't shake the habit of calling him by his childhood nickname, Billy. At 22, he was a full twelve years younger than Jonah, but the age gap did little to weaken their bond. As Billy met Jonah's gaze, his boyish grin widened, his confidence shining as brightly as the sun overhead—youthful and unafraid.

Then, as if on cue, Thomas struck again. He wrapped his arms around Billy from behind, pretending to hurl him into the water. Billy flailed dramatically, laughing despite himself, his movements exaggerated and wild. Crystal caught the faintest twitch of Jonah's jaw, a subtle sign of irritation that she knew well.

"It's all fun and games," Jonah muttered, his voice low and firm, "until someone ends up in the ocean."

Crystal slipped her hand back into his, squeezing gently. The connection between them was steady, a small but meaningful gesture that broke her carefully held posture. She leaned her head briefly against his shoulder, savoring the quiet comfort of his presence. At that moment, Jonah's protective instincts, so familiar and comforting, pulled her closer. She loved how he always seemed to know when to stand firm, even when he needed her stability as much as she needed his.

The ferry bumped gently against the dock, the sound cutting through the air like a subtle reminder that time was moving, that the moment had arrived. The young captain began sloppily securing the lines, and Sean and April moved first, stepping onto the dock with a practiced ease that made it seem like they were navigating an obstacle course rather than just stepping ashore. Each carried a duffel bag slung over one shoulder, their toned arms flexing with every movement.

Billy followed, his enthusiasm palpable, his youthful energy a foil to Jonah's steady demeanor. Thomas brought up the rear, his energy spilling over as he reached back to help Ilma, who hesitated, her movements deliberate and careful. Her caution stood in stark contrast to his boisterousness, a silent testament to the different worlds they occupied.

The tension that had gripped Jonah's frame was now evident, and Crystal felt it too, a quiet ripple of unease threading through the moment. The island was perfect. The timing was flawless. Everything had been strategically planned to this moment. Yet, as her eyes swept over the group, as the brothers' voices carried across the dock, and as the breeze picked up just slightly, she couldn't shake the nagging feeling that something—something small, something just out of reach—wasn't right.

Perfection, no matter how carefully crafted, always had its cracks.

Jonah and Crystal had arrived via the same ferry the previous day, and as they stepped off onto the dock, Crystal's excitement bubbled to the surface. After a lifetime of dreaming of a vacation like this, and months of diligent planning, she felt like a child at a theme park, eyes wide and heart racing with anticipation. Every step felt lighter, every breath more invigorating as she looked ahead to the island that had held her imagination captive for so long.

The caretaker stood at the end of the dock to greet them, a serene yet commanding presence. She balanced a tray of two pink cocktails adorned with paper umbrellas in one hand, the other clutching a large gold binder that seemed almost too formal for the occasion. Isabella was petite, with light brown skin that seemed to glow in the sun, and short dark hair beginning to turn silver with age. Her outfit—a fitted black tank top paired with a long, billowy white skirt—flowed in the breeze as if she were part of the island itself, gracefully unfazed by the elements. Despite the weight of her responsibilities, her smile was warm, but there was an unmistakable firmness, as though her welcoming demeanor was tempered by a quiet authority. Crystal couldn't help but think of an old Italian mother, someone who would enthusiastically welcome her children home but then immediately set about insisting they eat more, put on weight, and take care of themselves.

Jonah kept his arm around Crystal's waist as they approached, steadying her as though the ferry's arrival was more significant than simply docking.

Crystal was mesmerized by the scene, her eyes scanning the island, eager to absorb every detail. But the reality of their arrival was underwhelming. Behind Isabella, the view was limited to a few palm trees clustered around a small beach, bordered by dense woods. She let out a barely audible sigh of disappointment. Bringing the palm trees indoors each winter to escape New England's harsh cold wouldn't be easy, but given the price they were paying to rent the island, surely they could afford a dozen more for the aesthetic.

Crystal felt her excitement wane just a little. She'd seen so many pictures of this place—glossy, staged shots that made the island seem like paradise—but here, it felt more isolated. Her pinky rose to her lips, itching to chew on a freshly manicured nail. But then it dawned on her: there was no salon here. She tucked her hand behind her ear, fingers brushing a strand of her wind-tousled hair. A sudden pressure on her waist reminded her that Jonah's arm was still there, grounding her as she realized her foot was nervously tapping against the boat's hull. Her impatience was tangible, and the energy inside her wanted to break free like a caged animal, ready to leap off the boat and explore the unknown.

Having secured the ferry, the captain stepped down from the bridge to help with the bags. As Crystal watched him, she blushed when she caught him glancing back into the cabin as if looking for more passengers. She had, after all, packed far more than she could possibly need for just one week. The realization brought a self-conscious chuckle.

In her room the previous night, she had spent hours laying out her vacation wardrobe, deliberating over each item, adding one more piece and then discarding it, until finally, in a last-minute flurry, she had tossed nearly everything she owned into suitcases, unsure if she would ever need it all. It was a familiar cycle—one she didn't realize had become part of her travel routine.

As they disembarked, the caretaker greeted them with a small but precise bow. "Welcome."

Her eyes met theirs when she straightened, holding their gaze with an unspoken weight. She extended the tray toward them. "My name is Isabella, and I am the island's caretaker. I apologize for the delay in your arrival. We were short on crew members and have been training a new ferry captain." She paused, her dark eyes briefly closing as she made the sign of the cross, a fleeting gesture that added an almost ritualistic tone to her words. Before Crystal could ask for more details or even show concern, Isabella held up a hand, halting her words. The older woman exhaled slowly, gathering herself before continuing, "Despite the delay, I trust your journey over was uneventful?"

Crystal savored a sip of the cocktail while Jonah stepped in. "Yes, thank you. I'm Jonah, and this is my wife, Crystal."

Isabella quickly transferred the tray to the crook of her arm, the binder tucked beneath her other arm like a secret she was prepared to share at the right moment. After shaking their hands with an almost businesslike formality, she spun on her heel and led them toward the waiting electric cart by the shore.

As Jonah and Crystal exchanged a glance, curiosity lingering in their eyes, they raised their glasses in a silent toast and followed her.

Though Crystal planned, organized, and arranged the entire vacation, she let Jonah take the passenger seat next to Isabella and deferred to the back. It would allow her to count the suitcases behind her in the flatbed. Crystal immediately regretted her decision to take the back seat when she watched, almost in slow motion, as Isabella ceremoniously handed off the gold binder she had been carrying to Jonah.

The gold binder, now in Jonah's hands, felt almost sacred as it was passed over. It was no mere guidebook—it was the key to unlocking every hidden corner of the island. The gold book was rumored to have information about every room, appliance, and activity available to them. Crystal's pulse quickened with anticipation, but her restraint held her back. This moment, this treasure would be hers to explore in time. She would not let Jonah see her dive for it just yet.

The rough-hewn but undeniably stylish cart, with rugged wheels and leather bench seats, pulled them away from the dock. It was the perfect mix of luxury and island practicality. Crystal couldn't help but admire the quality. The stitching in the seats was intricate, and the leather was smooth to the touch. Her attention to detail never faltered. She couldn't help but appreciate it, though her mind was already racing ahead to the mansion, to the allure of what lay beyond.

As Isabella expertly navigated the cart through the woods, the landscape began to shift, and Crystal's excitement returned with full force. The mansion loomed in the distance, her destiny calling out to her. Under the vast expanse of clear blue skies, the immaculately manicured lawn stretched out before her, resembling an inviting welcome mat. The house seemed to greet her with a playful glint, as sunlight danced off its spotless windows, catching her eye like a sly wink. However, Isabella's decision to circle the grounds first before showing them the heart of the estate sent a twinge of impatience through Crystal. Her mouth hung open for a few seconds before she pursed her lips closed and sat back, watching the front of the house she had longed to enter pass her by like a star-crossed lover.

Isabella's voice broke the quiet tension. "The path we're on runs around the island's perimeter," she explained. "The dock you arrived at is on the island's west side, nearest to the mainland. However, the ocean side is inaccessible due to the jagged cliffs surrounding it."

Crystal, unable to suppress her disappointment, couldn't help but mentally file away this detail as just another imperfection. But she couldn't afford to dwell on the lack of a nice beach. She'd made her peace with it. The pool would suffice.

As the cart turned, rounding the estate, the rear of the mansion came into view—grand and imposing. It felt like they were being shown the secrets of an ancient, forgotten kingdom, a treasure that was yet to be claimed.

The caretaker's voice, still steady and controlled, offered more details. "We have a tennis court, a full basketball court. And over there..." Isabella motioned toward a far corner, the narrow building beside the court, its awning offering shelter to benches beneath. "...is the shed stocked with everything you'll need for these activities—racquets, balls, even ice skates."

"Ice skates?" Jonah's curiosity piqued.

"Oh, yes," Isabella smiled with an edge of pride. "We flood the basketball court during the colder months, turning it into a skating rink. Perhaps you'll return in the winter, yes?"

Crystal, barely listening as Isabella spouted boring details of the cart garage, and turned to look out at the glistening pool, a perfect oasis in the sun. She was already feeling a mix of impatience and excitement, her eyes glued to the mansion. She didn't care about the ice skates or the cart garage. She only wanted what lay inside those doors—the mansion that had been her dream for so long.

After the tour was complete and details finalized, Isabella reassured the couple that once she left, they had the entire island to themselves. Jonah thanked her and though she offered to walk, gave her a ride back to the ferry, where she and the captain would return to the mainland and leave Crystal with her island for a glorious week.

That evening, Jonah and Crystal were finally alone. The quietness of the island and the peaceful hum of the pool pump stretched the time between moments. Crystal made her way to the bedroom, the gold binder now at her side, but she was already too weary to read. She tossed it aside with a sigh, a mental list of priorities already forming. She'd get to it eventually.

Jonah, ever restless, had already started his own list. Crystal watched him quietly from the bed, her thoughts wandering to how she could help him leave the stress behind. He was under extreme pressure at work, and though Crystal hoped he could "unplug", there truly was never a good time for him to take a vacation. And yet, the more she observed, the more she realized his anxiety was contagious, no matter how much she tried to block it out. Once it was clear that she'd never get to sleep with him rustling around, she grabbed her pill-filled baggie off the nightstand and popped half of a sleeping pill. The last thing she needed was dark, saggy circles under her eyes when her guests arrived.

The following day, waking refreshed, Crystal found Jonah's list by the bed. To her pleasant surprise, his list was more of a tangible representation of his desire to make the vacation perfect for their family than a corporate stress dump, his innocent excitement a reminder of what this trip was meant to be—a retreat, a break from everything else. But as she smiled at the handwritten notes, including the casual mention of "trampoline basketball" and "underground tunnels," her mind couldn't help but wander back to the mysteries of this island she'd read about online. There was so much more to this place than met the eye.

Crystal could feel Jonah shifting restlessly beside her, his knee bouncing subtly and fingers drumming a silent rhythm against his thigh. He was like a boy on Christmas morning, brimming with barely contained excitement, eager to unveil his carefully chosen gift. His broad shoulders, usually a bastion of confidence, were now squared with a tension she knew was born of anticipation rather than anxiety. Crystal smiled to herself, charmed by his boyish enthusiasm.

Jonah adjusted his stance, unconsciously straightening his posture. His arm tightened briefly around Crystal's waist as if to draw strength from her perceived calm.

He, too, wanted everything to be perfect—the kind of perfection that left his family marveling and etched this vacation into their memories forever. She glanced up at him and saw his jaw tighten slightly, the faintest shadow of doubt flickering in his eyes. Crystal reached for his hand, giving it a reassuring squeeze.

Who wouldn't be impressed by a week-long vacation on a rented private island? The words looped in her mind like a mantra. She looked out at the shimmering water. The island was a paradise with the verdant canopy of trees framing the paths, and the sprawling mansion perched like a jewel in the heart of the island. Crystal's heart swelled with pride, but beneath it was a flicker of uncertainty she refused to dwell on.

This was their stage, and the players had arrived. Now, it was time for the show to begin.

Chapter Three
The Bookworm

Ilma remained seated on a weathered bench in the shaded section of the ferry, pretending to be absorbed in the pages of her book. The same two sentences stared back at her for the fifth time, the words blurring into meaninglessness as her focus drifted to the cacophony of her husband Thomas's family. As the only child of two studious, introverted parents, Ilma had been steeped in a world of quiet, orderly solitude. Now, she found herself adrift in this storm of boisterous energy, unaccustomed to the sheer volume of voices and the relentless need for conversation. The sound seemed to vibrate against her skin, the chatter crawling into every available silence like ivy through cracks in stone. She swallowed hard, her throat prickling with a phantom irritation that felt as though the noise itself had lodged there.

Her gaze drifted over the rim of her sunglasses to Sean and April, Thomas's younger brother and his wife. The couple had bonded over a mutual passion for fitness, eventually turning their shared enthusiasm into a business by opening a gym. Her rare conversations with them typically revolved around the latest mundane object they had transformed into an exercise tool. Now, they were tackling the task of unloading the luggage with the intensity of contestants on a high-stakes game show. Their movements were perfectly synchronized—a seamless display of the practiced efficiency that came from being partners in both business and life. It was almost admirable, though Ilma felt drained just watching their boundless energy. Her gaze shifted to Will—the baby of the family, who still bore the traces of "Billy" in his boyish grin and unruly hair. He bounded off the ferry, arms wide open as if he intended to hug the entire island. After lingering embraces with Jonah, the eldest brother, and his composed wife, Crystal, he turned his attention back to Sean and April, wrapping them both in exaggerated hugs despite having just shared an hour-long ferry ride. Ilma couldn't decide if his affection was endearing or simply overwhelming.

A hand landed softly on her shoulder, startling her enough that her book slipped from her grasp and tumbled to the floor. She turned to see Thomas, his crooked smile as familiar as her own reflection.

"Sorry, Sidd. Didn't mean to scare you," he said, using the affectionate nickname derived from her maiden name. It was a small gesture, but one she cherished—a reminder of how Thomas embraced her Pakistani heritage, even as she had chosen to simplify her name for the world. Ilma Fullerton was leaps and bounds easier to pronounce and spell than Ilma Siddiqui.

"It's okay," Ilma replied, hastily picking up the book from the floor as she stood, smoothing the wrinkles in her cream-colored maxi dress. The fabric, light and airy, was a gentle contrast to her rich brown skin, an unintentional but pleasing harmony that Thomas often complimented.

Thomas took her hand, guiding her down from the ferry with a care that didn't escape her notice. His subtle squeeze conveyed an unspoken promise: he understood how much this world of endless conversations and competitive exuberance unnerved her, and he wasn't about to leave her adrift in it. She leaned into him briefly, her anchor in the whirlwind of chaos.

The dock was alive with activity. Crystal stood with practiced elegance, bidding a theatrical goodbye to the ferry captain as their group's belongings were efficiently packed into three electric carts. Jonah, ever the leader, climbed into the driver's seat of the first cart with the confidence of someone already well-acquainted with the island's twists and turns. Will practically leaped into the second cart, his excitement reminiscent of a child boarding an amusement park ride.

Ilma's attention was caught by a sudden burst of motion as Sean and April locked eyes in silent competition, sprinting toward the third cart like athletes racing for a finish line. April's dramatic dive into the front seat sealed her victory, leaving Sean laughing in defeat as he slid in beside her. Ilma couldn't help but marvel at their unspoken camaraderie, though it still left her feeling like an outsider in this close-knit clan.

Before she could linger too long in her thoughts, Crystal appeared, a whirlwind of perfume and hugs. The embrace came from behind, enveloping Ilma in unexpected warmth before she spun around to face Jonah's wife. Crystal's cheek kisses were as awkward as they were sudden, leaving Ilma blushing and off-balance.

"Did Jonah even say hello to you two?" Crystal asked, her tone dripping with a practiced charm that Ilma suspected masked a sharp eye for detail.

Without waiting for an answer, Crystal's gaze fell to the book in Ilma's hand, snatching it up before Ilma could protest.

"What's this? Whatcha reading?" she asked with a curiosity that felt invasive. Crystal flipped through the pages, her fingers pausing on the engraved silver bookmark.

"It's a gift," Ilma said, her voice quieter than she intended. "From Thomas." She felt the words catch in her throat, and the bookmark—a small, deeply personal token inscribed with a poem Thomas had written—suddenly exposed to scrutiny.

Crystal, however, had already moved on, handing the book back with a shrug and planting another series of cheek kisses on Thomas. She was in her element playing the role of hostess, leaving Ilma feeling more like an observer than a participant.

As they loaded into Will's cart and began the journey into the dense woods, Ilma let her imagination take over. The towering trees formed an emerald tunnel overhead, sunlight filtering through the leaves in dappled, golden bursts. The air, tinged with the faint brine of the ocean, grew quieter as they left the dock behind. She imagined herself in a storybook forest, where electric carts became gilded carriages, and shadows danced with the flicker of fairy light.

Books had provided her with a lifetime of introverted escapism, and her imagination was just a tool in her anti-social arsenal.

Her daydream was interrupted only when the woods opened to reveal a expansive groomed field. The grandeur of the mansion ahead took her breath away.

The house rose like a castle, its sheer size and intricate design exuding an undeniable extravagance. The building's silhouette blurred the lines between opulence and fantasy—a modern-day castle plucked from a fairy tale but with all the indulgences of the present day.

For a moment, Ilma forgot her anxieties, her awe overtaking everything else. As the carts slowed and the family buzzed with excitement, she felt Thomas's hand on hers once more—a grounding reminder that, in the midst of all this, she wasn't alone.

CHAPTER FOUR

The Preparation

The Unwelcome Guest arrived on the ferry several days earlier, blending into the temporary crew of employees dispatched to flip the rental property between guests. The boat was a hive of quiet efficiency, its passengers slipping into the rhythms of the routine without fuss. While most of the women from the cleaning crew headed up the well-trodden path to the house, he deliberately stayed back, gravitating toward the maintenance and landscaping teams. Their demeanor was gruff but distracted, the perfect camouflage for someone trying not to stand out.

Following the example of the men ahead of him, he grabbed a box from the stack of supplies and slung his worn backpack over one shoulder. Yet, instead of joining the orderly procession of workers loading the electric carts, he veered off course, slipping into the shadows of the woods. He crouched under the guise of tying his shoe, his pulse quickening as he glanced around to see if anyone noticed. The scene remained blissfully indifferent, the steady hum of activity continuing uninterrupted.

The path leading inland was wide and well-maintained, its compacted dirt evidence of regular use. Yet its openness felt suffocating. He stayed low, ducking behind a massive fallen tree whose gnarled roots reached skyward like skeletal fingers. His heart thumped loudly in the stillness as he waited, scanning for any sign that someone might have seen him.

The crew, a well-oiled machine, had no time for distractions. They arrived in the morning, their tasks choreographed to perfection: cleaning, pruning, fixing, and replenishing. The hours ticked by with unrelenting precision, each worker intent on completing their share before the ferry returned them to the mainland at dusk. The seamless flow of their efforts worked in his favor—no one had time to scrutinize the arrival of a new face.

On the ferry ride earlier, he'd been acutely aware of the captain's eyes following him. The old man's gaze had lingered too long, and every sidelong glance felt like a spotlight on his presence. The captain, with his deep-brown skin and stark tribal eyeliner, carried an air of quiet menace. His long, gray dreadlocks were tied into thick knots at the base of his neck, giving him an almost mythical appearance—more fearsome pirate than friendly ferryman. The occasional cadence of his Jamaican accent, though soft, carried the weight of someone who noticed more than he let on.

The Unwelcome Guest tried to blend into the crowd, but each time he raised his eyes to check if the captain's focus had shifted, their gazes met like an unspoken challenge. The other passengers seemed oblivious to the tension. Fred, the chatterbox, filled the silence with an endless stream of commentary that bounced from classic rock to shark theories. "Fred loves a good mystery," he declared to no one in particular, flashing a grin as wide as the horizon. "You think this island's haunted? Fred thinks it might be!" His self-referential monologue was met with muffled groans, but even Fred's antics couldn't distract from the captain's relentless vigilance.

Now on the island, The Unwelcome Guest remained cautious. With his backpack and mystery box in tow, he ducked low, waiting until the last cart had disappeared into the trees before standing. His stomach churned, both from hunger and the nerve-wracking possibility of discovery. The box could hold anything—liquor bottles, pool chemicals, or, if he was lucky, food. During the ferry ride, the other passengers had been better prepared, munching on dry cereal or leftovers from plastic containers. He'd brought nothing, his growling stomach a constant reminder of his oversight. Sneaking food from the house was his only option, though the dire warnings from Fred about the strict staff rules gave him pause. Getting caught would blow his cover, and failure wasn't an option.

Peeking from behind his hiding spot, he saw the captain still on the ferry. The old man reclined in his chair, his oversized cap tipped low over his face. For a tense moment, The Unwelcome Guest wondered if the captain might be feigning sleep. The shade of the hat brim cast deep shadows over his features, but the faint glimmer of what might have been the whites of his eyes set The Unwelcome Guest's nerves on edge. He waited, frozen, until he was sure no movement came from the boat before creeping into the woods.

The island matched the images he had studied online: roughly a mile long and half a mile wide, with dense woods encircling its heart. Salt-stunted trees loomed like sentinels along the shoreline, their twisted limbs thick with moss. At its center, perched on a grassy plateau, stood the mansion—a monolith of opulence hidden behind nature's thick curtains. On the ocean side, jagged cliffs plunged dramatically into the churning waves, the relentless surf spraying mist into the air. The mainland-facing side was more forgiving, with a small break in the trees leading back to the dock on the sound side.

Walking toward the cliffs, he searched for the overhang he had seen on satellite maps. As he approached, the crashing waves grew louder, their rhythm a steady roar. The wind picked up, carrying the sharp tang of salt and the faint cries of distant seabirds. With luck, he'd find shelter there—a secluded spot to regroup and bide his time until the mansion was safe to explore. His fingers tightened around the box's edges, a whisper of hope lingering in his mind: sandwiches. Just maybe, it held sandwiches.

The Unwelcome Guest smirked to himself as he returned in the late afternoon to his hideout, the thrill of anticipation humming in his veins. The cave he discovered earlier was a lucky find—a shadowy sanctuary nestled against the cliffside, its jagged mouth yawning open just wide enough to welcome him. Inside, the air was damp and cool, carrying the faint tang of saltwater and earth. The cavern stretched farther than he'd initially thought, its rocky walls offering plenty of nooks and crannies to stow supplies—or a body—if it came to that.

He planned to spend most of his time in the mansion, however. With dozens of workers scattered throughout the house during his earlier reconnaissance, sneaking around had been surprisingly easy. From the mansion's information binder, he had removed about a dozen pages—critical ones detailing the network of hidden passages behind the walls. The guests couldn't know about those. They were his secret paths, the arteries of the house through which he would move unseen. His preparation had been precise, aided by a detailed floor plan sourced from the darkest corners of the web. There, he had found not only maps but also advice from others who shared his peculiar interests: how to navigate the camouflaged doors, which shoes made the least noise, and where to find the peepholes ingeniously disguised as part of the décor.

The peepholes were works of art, blending seamlessly into wood knots, light fixtures, and power outlets. The voyeuristic touch was elevated to modern sophistication with tiny, high-definition cameras mounted within, offering zoom capabilities that could capture every detail. The public rental posting boasted not only lavish amenities, but assurances of no cameras or surveillance of any kind, whereas the deviants like himself knew the darker secrets of the house. At any time and any place, someone could be watching you.

Yet, despite his hours at the mansion earlier, attempting to hack the internal system enabling him to stream the camera feeds to his phone, he was unsuccessful. In a last ditch effort to find another option, he installed a tiny camera in the game room—a less refined solution, but sufficient for his needs. If he was successful in streaming his camera to the cave, he would return to install more later.

As he paced the cave, the weight of his inevitable failure taunted at him. He pulled up the surveillance app on his phone, muttering a silent prayer that the wifi booster he had plugged in would be strong enough to transmit a signal to the cave. Seconds stretched into agonizing minutes as the hourglass icon on his screen flipped over and over. Frustration simmered beneath his skin. To distract himself, he scrolled through the photos on his phone—images of the mansion taken from every angle. They were trophies of his access, proof of his penetration into the heart of the bunker that would shield his prey.

Checking again, his failure was confirmed; the signal was nonexistent. The booster hadn't made a difference. Zero times anything is still zero. With a sharp growl, he hurled his backpack to the ground. The bag ripped open on impact, spilling its contents across the cave floor. An extension cord flung toward the entrance, and he snatched it up, draping it over his shoulders like a noose.

"What kind of luxury rental doesn't have internet?" he muttered bitterly, turning back into the cave and kicking at the pile of useless towels he'd unpacked from the mystery box he'd hauled from the ferry.

"Hey, what's this?"

The voice echoed from the cave's entrance, sharp and unexpected. The Unwelcome Guest froze, every muscle tensing as his mind scrambled for an excuse. Without turning, he quickly scanned the cave for anything incriminating. His gaze landed on the open box of towels and his backpack, its spilled contents a damning mess of wires and gadgets.

"What are you doing in here?" The voice came again, laced with curiosity. "Fred saw you walk into the woods. Is this a fort? What's with the wires? And the towels—how'd they get here?"

The Unwelcome Guest recognized the voice instantly. The incessant chatterbox from the ferry. Of course, it had to be him. His stomach churned as irritation flared. Not only had his cameras failed, but now he'd been caught—and the guests hadn't even arrived yet.

He pocketed his phone slowly and reached for the cord around his neck, wrapping its ends around his hands. Turning, he put on a calm, disarming smile.

"Oh, I was talking to him," he said, pointing behind Fred toward the shadows through the trees just outside the cave.

Fred turned, his expression puzzled, and that moment of confusion was all The Unwelcome Guest needed. He lunged, the cord tightening around Fred's neck with practiced efficiency. Fred's initial gasp turned into a strangled choke, his arms flailing as he tried to fight back, but the surprise and force caught him off guard.

The Unwelcome Guest dragged him deeper into the cave, his grip unwavering. With one final pull, his knee braced against Fred's back; the fight drained from the man's body. Fred collapsed onto the towels, their pristine white fibers soaking up the blood from his raw, torn neck.

Breathing hard, the Unwelcome Guest surveyed the scene, unconsciously grinding his right foot into the ground like a smoker extinguishing a cigarette, leaving a small three-inch circle in the sand. The towels, the cords, the limp body staring back at him with unseeing open eyes—it was messy, but it would have to do. Time was not on his side. Grabbing his phone, he left the backpack and corpse behind, jogging back toward the ferry with calculated urgency.

Emerging from the woods, he spotted a cart carrying staff as it returned to the dock. Timing his steps, he slipped into the crowd of staff and onto the ferry unnoticed, blending into the group of weary workers. The captain, however, looked suspicious.

The Unwelcome Guest felt the weight of the captain's eyes land on him, a silent accusation hanging in the air. He straightened, suppressing the goosebumps rising on his arms. Feeling the captain's unrelenting stare, he pulled his cap down in an attempt to blend in with the other men, taking advantage of the time on the return trip to take a much needed nap.

The captain muttered something under his breath, and The Unwelcome Guest released a deep exhale as he heard the man's footsteps recede away.

As the ferry pushed off into the fading light, The Unwelcome Guest forced himself to relax, though the chill of the evening air clung to his skin. He had only just begun.

CHAPTER FIVE

The Runner

As the electric carts emerged from the shadowy embrace of the woods, April fought every instinct to press the pedal to the floor and zoom past the others. The open field before them beckoned like a raceway, its sunlit expanse a tempting challenge. She glanced at Sean, catching the faintest twitch at the corner of his mouth—he was thinking it, too. They could pass everyone, easy peasy. But this wasn't just a casual outing; it was the first reunion in years; not counting weddings and funerals. Ruffling feathers now wouldn't set the tone she wanted for the week. April's hands tightened on the steering wheel, her knuckles whitening as the strain in her shin from holding back the accelerator nagged at her resolve. Go-karts, she thought, biting back a grin. That's what this island needs—go-karts to tear through the paths in the woods. Her mind wandered briefly to memories of racing her older brother Cole at the track, a pang of nostalgia swelling in her chest.

Cole had been her world growing up, the epitome of cool with his obsession with all things cars. Seven years her senior, he'd effortlessly commanded her admiration, from tinkering with engines to designing new ways to go faster. The days spent at the go-kart track were their shared haven, where she wasn't just his little sister but his partner in crime. She could still recall the pride in his face when she finally took the wheel at twelve, the way he stuck close to her kart like a guardian angel on the track.

But those golden days were fleeting. College whisked Cole away, and adulthood widened the chasm between them. Though they never recaptured their childhood closeness, the memories of racing and his carefree laughter remained a warm ember in her heart.

The sight of the mansion jolted her from her reverie. The sprawling structure loomed before them, growing larger with every passing second, a luxurious dream carved in stone and glass.

The front drive circled a multi-tiered fountain crowned by a stone palm tree, water cascading over its fronds in shimmering arcs. Jonah volunteered to park the carts in the cavernous garage while Crystal took on the role of a giddy tour guide. Bags in tow, the group climbed the broad marble steps, their awestruck expressions as vivid as tourists at a landmark.

In her flowing and completely see-through dress, Crystal threw open the double doors with theatrical flair, spinning into the grand foyer. Her movements exuded a practiced grace; her arms spread wide as if to say, *Behold, my masterpiece.* The entryway was breathtaking—a vast, open space anchored by twin staircases curving up the walls like elegant ribs. A crystal chandelier hung from the cathedral ceiling, its countless facets scattering prisms of light across the polished floor. Even the air seemed decadent, infused with a scent that married jasmine's floral sweetness with a masculine hint of cedar.

"What do you think?" Crystal asked, her tone coy but brimming with pride.

April's gaze swept the room, taking in the lavish details. It wasn't just pristine—it was the kind of place where even the dust motes felt rarefied.

The group followed Crystal upstairs, where she paused before a door and, with a mischievous grin, announced the "honeymoon suite." She swung the door open with a flourish, revealing a room so absurdly themed it bordered on parody.

April stifled a gasp as her eyes fell on the heart-shaped bed draped in glossy red satin, its headboard crowned with an oversized mirror framed in glowing crimson lights. To one side, a heart-shaped hot tub gleamed under the gaudy glare of a disco ball. The pièce de résistance was the small circular stage beside the bed, complete with a stripper pole that gleamed in the overhead track lighting.

The cloying scent of roses suffused the air, cheap and overpowering, and April couldn't help but think of roadside motels with hourly rates. Her eyes flicked to Ilma, whose stiff posture betrayed her discomfort, and then to Thomas, whose reaction was inscrutable. April fought the urge to laugh and quickly turned her attention to a metal wall sculpture of two figures entwined—oddly tasteful amidst the kitsch.

Thomas let his bag fall to the floor in a dramatic thump. The comedic timing was enough to cause a bubble of laughter to rise in April's throat. She coughed into her hand, willing her eyes not to water, as she held back a fit of giggles.

"Next!" Crystal trilled, sweeping them back into the hall just in time before April lost her composure.

When they reached the room at the other end of the balcony, Crystal gestured grandly for Sean and April to enter, her smile smug as if she'd personally designed the space.

April stepped inside and felt her breath catch. This room was everything the other wasn't—whimsical and serene, yet undeniably fun. Where April had been amazed at just how much Crystal did *not* know Thomas and Ilma, she absolutely nailed it when it came to her and Sean's room. The lush green carpet mimicked a freshly mowed lawn, and the walls were alive with cascading plants that gave the space the feel of an enchanted forest. Life-sized stuffed animals stood sentinel in the corners, their soft fur gleaming in the sunlight streaming through large windows.

But the centerpiece stole the show. A king-sized bed hung suspended from the ceiling by thick braided ropes, its frame designed to resemble a tree fort. The entire room exuded a playful charm that resonated deeply with her adventurous spirit.

"Wow," April murmured, turning to Crystal with genuine admiration.

Crystal's proud nod was slight but triumphant. April knew that all Crystal did was show up and decide who slept where, but if she wanted credit for this sweet setup, that was okay with her.

"Next!" Crystal called, her voice echoing down the hallway as she led the group onward.

CHAPTER SIX

The Supermodel

C rystal chuckled softly, her mind drifting back to the tour with Isabella. The stern woman was a study in precision, her every move deliberate, her speech rehearsed to the last syllable.

"The master bathroom," Isabella had declared with the clipped confidence of an auctioneer, "luxury jacuzzi tub, fully enclosed shower with steam capabilities, heated floors, his and his sinks..."

Jonah's brow furrowed in a flash of confusion. His eyes darted toward Crystal, silently questioning what he thought was a glaring slip in the detail-oriented caretaker's script. Crystal smirked, relishing the moment; she already knew the owners were a gay couple. She scanned Isabella's expressionless face, hunting for even the faintest flicker of humor or cleverness, but the woman forged ahead without missing a beat.

"...towel warmers, and smart toilet."

"Oh, I've always wanted to try a smart toilet," Jonah interjected, a mix of curiosity and awe lighting up his face.

Leave it to a man, Crystal thought with an inward laugh, *to zero in on the toilet while bypassing the marvel of a private steam room.* Jonah eyed the sleek, porcelain contraption warily, as though it might spring to life unbidden.

"How do you use it?" he asked hesitantly.

"Please refer to the Gold Book," Isabella replied, her tone as sharp as a knife edge.

That refrain had punctuated nearly every question they'd posed since the tour began.

"How does the tennis ball machine work?"

"Please refer to the Gold Book."

"Can the hot tub temperature be adjusted?"

"Please refer to the Gold Book."

"Do the arcade machines in the game room need coins?"

"Please refer to the Gold Book."

The woman's patience extended only as far as the pages of her precious binder, a fact she punctuated by barking "Next!" before sweeping out of each room. At first, the abruptness of her exits startled Crystal, the tiny woman's booming voice at odds with her diminutive frame. But by the time they reached the second floor, Crystal and Jonah had started to anticipate her departures, stifling grins as they echoed the command under their breaths.

Now, as Crystal led her own tour, she felt compelled to channel Isabella's peculiar blend of authority and showmanship. Jonah would've appreciated the impression if he weren't off parking the carts. For now, she relished the private giddiness of it, even if the others likely thought she was off her rocker.

As the group filed back into the hallway, Crystal felt the heat of a gaze drilling into her back. She was no stranger to being stared at—her statuesque, nearly six-foot-tall frame ensured that—but this felt different. Turning, she found Ilma hovering too close, her uneasy expression casting a shadow over her usual poise.

"Ilma, is everything okay?" Crystal asked, softening her voice.

"Oh, um, yes," Ilma stammered, though her discomfort lingered like a ghost in the air.

Billy cut in, his boyish grin breaking the tension. "Hey, Crystal. What's your room like?"

Crystal gestured down the hall, toward the unassuming doors of her and Jonah's shared quarters. "Pretty basic—no theme, just a practical spot between the others. But I *cannot wait* to show you downstairs, Billy!"

She darted ahead, her excitement bubbling over. This was the moment she'd been waiting for. Billy, a recent culinary school graduate, would lose his mind over the kitchen—a chef's paradise with cutting-edge appliances that made her own cooking attempts feel like finger-painting compared to a Monet.

Billy had been seven when Crystal first met him, a precocious kid who spent family beach trips fashioning mud pies for her approval. Back then, he was relentless in his attention, following her around like a puppy and delivering sloppy sand cakes to her sunbathing spot. While she'd initially humored him with feigned bites and exaggerated praise, he soon became more than a tagalong. He became her little brother in spirit, their bond sealed through shared laughs and a toy oven she'd once gifted him. Though he'd long since traded plastic utensils and cooking by light bulb for chef's knives and open flames, Crystal still adored watching him chase his culinary dreams.

When Jonah rejoined the group at the base of the stairs, he leaned toward Billy with a conspiratorial grin. "Seen your room yet, Will?"

Crystal's steps slowed, her nerves gnawing at the edges of her enthusiasm. She led them past the grandeur of the great room—barely pausing to note the sprawling pool view or the mesmerizing aquarium wall—and stopped before a door tucked into an alcove. Every instinct in her body told her to skip his bedroom tour and head straight for the kitchen, but when she glanced at Jonah, who gave her an encouraging nod, she knew there was no going back.

With a deep breath, she pushed the door open.

The room's overwhelming pinkness hit like a tidal wave. From the plush carpet and the canopy bed, to the life-sized mannequins, everything was drenched in pastel hues. The garish sight would have been comical if her anticipation weren't so suffocating. Crystal kept her gaze fixed on the floor, unable to face Billy's reaction as the others erupted in varying degrees of shock and amusement.

Ilma and April exchanged wide-eyed looks, while Billy's brothers doubled over in unrestrained laughter. Crystal cringed but couldn't help stealing a glance at Billy. His expression was a mixture of disbelief and reluctant amusement.

"Well," he said dryly, "at least it's... memorable."

Crystal bit back a laugh, relief washing over her. Even in a room straight out of a dollhouse fever dream, it appeared that Billy's good humor shone through. But, his body language and abrupt exit from the hysterical group spoke louder than his insincere words.

CHAPTER SEVEN

The Short Straw

Crystal couldn't help but feel a surge of nostalgia when she first set foot in the doll room. It was as if every childhood fantasy she had ever entertained had been brought to life in a single, dazzling space. The room wasn't just decorated; it was curated. The low runway, no more than a foot off the ground, jutted out into the room like a pink satin peninsula. Its edges were trimmed in twinkling lights, while soft-colored spotlights from above bathed the area in a dreamlike glow. Crystal could easily imagine her younger self parading down the runway, practicing her model walk to the beat of imaginary applause. She may have grown into the real thing, striding on runways around the world, but this—the whimsical charm of a child's unbridled creativity—still tugged at her heart.

The giant doll box in the corner was styled to look like packaging straight from a toy store. The clear, glittering panel invited someone to step inside and strike a pose, a modern Instagram-ready twist. A corner bookshelf painted in ornate white was laden with shimmering tiaras, each catching the light like tiny bejeweled crowns. Nearby, an open wardrobe offered a rainbow of boas, their feathery textures begging to be touched.

But it wasn't just the decor that caught her eye—it was the personal touches. Amid the collection of tiaras sat a framed photograph of two men in their mid-thirties posing with a little girl no older than six. The three were resplendent in sparkling gowns, grinning from ear to ear, their joy so discernible it seemed to radiate from the frame. Crystal felt a pang of envy, not for the lavish setting but for the love captured in that single image. That little girl had something she could only dream of as a child: time, attention, and parents who could still laugh after a long day.

Crystal's own childhood was a patchwork of fleeting joys and relentless responsibility. Her parents worked nights and slept through most of her waking hours. Birthdays meant thrift-store treasures, like the secondhand doll she named Bambi after her mother's co-worker. Crystal loved that doll fiercely, even after a disastrous attempt at hairstyling left Bambi with a patchy buzz cut and permanent marker makeup. By the time she was old enough to realize the doll's hair wouldn't grow back, Bambi was already a battered but cherished relic of a girlhood spent longing for connection.

Now, standing in the doll room, Crystal's heart twisted with a mixture of gratitude and guilt. It wasn't her room; it was Billy's. And while the thought of him in this saccharine wonderland might amuse their siblings, she couldn't shake the feeling that he deserved better—or at least different.

If only she could pull Billy aside and let him know that although it may not be *his* dream room, she felt thankful that it was he who could play in *her* dream room. She had become his playmate when he was a child, and now he could see what it would be like to play with a young Crystal.

When Billy turned on his heel and stalked out, Crystal felt a knot of guilt tighten in her stomach. Jonah followed after him, his somewhat serious demeanor giving way to concern as he jogged into the great room. Crystal hesitated, torn between chasing after them and staying with the others.

Ilma appeared suddenly, blocking her path. The petite woman stood awkwardly, her soft voice barely audible over Thomas and Sean's laughter, echoing through the room. "Crystal, can I talk to you for a second?"

Crystal forced a smile finding it hard to pull her attention from Billy. "Of course, Ilma. What's up?"

"I feel bad taking the themed room," Ilma began, glancing nervously at the floor. "It's just... you've put so much into this trip. I'd hate for you and Jonah to end up in a boring room."

Crystal's smile softened into something genuine. "Ilma, you're too sweet. Trust me, our room might not have a theme, but it's exactly what I wanted. Besides, you deserve the honeymoon suite," she added with a wink.

Ilma nodded, but her hesitation lingered. Crystal, sensing her discomfort, gestured down the hallway. "Speaking of dream rooms, Ilma, yours is just around the corner."

With Ilma occupied, Crystal entered the great room, the soft hum of tension pulling her toward the kitchen. As she approached, raised voices spilled into the open space, so she stopped short of them noticing her.

"Jonah, dude, I don't care about the room," Billy said, his tone sharp. "You guys laugh it up. While Thomas gets it on like he's staying in a brothel and Sean climbs the walls of his jungle gym, I'll be under a pink canopy surrounded by life-sized dolls. Life's more fun with an audience, right?"

"I admit the mannequins are a bit much. Did you know they actually come with their own wardrobe?" When Billy didn't answer or even blink, Jonah continued, "If you're not mad, why did you storm out?" Jonah asked.

"What? Do you want me to stand there and let everyone laugh at my expense? Who picked the room out for me anyway? Was it you or Crystal? Am I being shunned to the main floor like the help? Did you just invite me to cook for everyone? Is that it? Is that why you paid for my part of the vacation? Does everyone know I couldn't afford it?" The slight crack in Billy's voice tugged at Crystal's core.

"What? No," Jonah's voice sounded strained. "No one knows. Yes, we would love to try some of your cooking, but that has nothing to do with us paying your way. That all stays between us."

"And by us, you mean you *and* Crystal, right?" Billy scoffed.

"Crystal knows, of course. This is her show. But she won't tell anyone."

Crystal froze, guilt washing over her in waves. She didn't mean for him to feel ostracized, but his words stung nonetheless. Before she could react, the others arrived, their laughter cutting through the tension. Casually walking into the kitchen just ahead of Sean, April, and Thomas, she seized the moment to redirect the mood.

Holding up the house's hefty gold binder, she forced a grin. "This is the Gold Book. If there is anything you need to know about how something works in this house or where to find what you need, it will be in here. Not sure how to turn on that sexy hot tub in your room, Thomas? Check the Gold Book. Want to set your fireplace in your bedroom on a sleep timer so it doesn't burn all night? Check the Gold Book."

"Wait," said Sean abruptly. "Who has a fireplace in their bedroom? And who has time to read a manual on vacation?"

"Fair point," Crystal replied, altogether avoiding the question about the fireplace, clapping her hands to gather their attention. "Billy, how about some drinks? The guys can check out the game room, and April and I will catch up with Ilma."

She caught the flicker of irritation that passed between Jonah and Billy but chose not to press further. Still, as the group dispersed, the knot in her stomach refused to untangle.

Chapter Eight

The Library

The entire vacation thus far had been an exercise in discomfort. Ilma felt out of place from the moment they boarded the boat, with her head buried in a well-worn paperback to avoid the lively chatter. It wasn't just the awkward silences or the forced attempts at small talk; it was the rooms. Each one seemed to mock her with its bizarre, over-the-top decor, amplifying the sense that she didn't belong in their world. The guys might have felt at ease reconnecting after not seeing each other since her wedding day. But nothing about the vacation was going to be easy for her.

Typically the pragmatic one, she caught herself crossing the fingers of her left hand behind her back, whispering a silent wish to a fairy godmother she didn't believe in to grant her refuge behind the door at the end of the hall. Her right hand was occupied clutching the paperback, its pages softened by use and marked with faint smudges of sunscreen. It wasn't her most prized book—just one she'd chosen for its lack of value, knowing it might face salt spray or sand on this ill-advised trip. Ilma's love for books encompassed every form, from rare signed hardbacks to the audiobooks she played during her commute, but this one was meant to be thrown into a tote and forgotten after.

As she reached the room Crystal had suggested, her hand instinctively gripped the doorframe for balance. What she saw stopped her breath and scattered her thoughts like fallen leaves in a gust of wind. Her gasp turned into a raspy cough as she struggled to reconcile the vision before her with the dream she'd carried since childhood.

The room was a genuine library—not the shallow imitation often found in rental homes, where fake books and mismatched titles served more as décor than substance. No, this was a shrine to readers. The ceiling soared high above her, and the wall to her left was a glorious cascade of books. Hardcovers stood proudly with their jackets removed, their leather bindings glowing warmly under soft lamplight. Some spines were reversed, revealing intricate gilt designs along the page edges. A sturdy rolling ladder gleamed, its brass fittings polished to perfection, inviting her to climb and explore.

She hesitated, then pushed the ladder with a fingertip. It slid smoothly along its rail, the satisfying motion sending a shiver of delight down her spine. The room felt alive, humming with the stories held within its walls. The massive windows along the opposite wall flooded the space with natural light, and Ilma could already envision herself sinking into one of the overstuffed armchairs strategically placed to offer views of the books or the lush lawn outside.

But not everything in the room was perfection. A thin strip of shelves in the center was jarringly out of place. The section, about three feet wide and stretching floor to ceiling, contained a bizarre assortment of the least inviting books imaginable: outdated manuals on defunct coding languages, a how-to guide on repairing car window rollers, and a encyclopedia on identifying Norwegian flowers. As a librarian, Ilma had many book-loving friends who, like herself, enjoyed reorganizing bookshelves. Some of them would reshelve their book collections weekly or monthly. Books could be sorted alphabetically by title or author, genre, size, or her personal favorite of late, by color. It was not exactly the most organized system to locate a book, but the gradient of colors fading from one to another was aesthetically pleasing and looked terrific on her librarian social media posts. She could understand not everyone wanted to use the DEWEY Decimal system, but the random assortment of books on the tall, skinny section was odd. It felt like an inside joke, a hidden quirk only a bibliophile owners might appreciate.

She spun slowly, her gaze landing on a small table for two tucked in the far corner. It was topped with a vintage tea set, dainty and elegant as if waiting for her to pour a cup and settle in with a mystery. She smiled wistfully. Despite her countless attempts, Ilma couldn't stomach tea. She longed for the ritual, the aesthetic, but her palate stubbornly refused.

As her fingers brushed the edge of the table, her thoughts drifted to Thomas. He would love this space as much as she did, though for different reasons. While Ilma cherished the stories within the pages, Thomas would be drawn to the craftsmanship—the built-in shelves, the fine details of the ladder rail, the balance between function and beauty. He'd likely spend hours sketching ideas for their dream home, a home they couldn't afford for years after splurging on this trip.

As two public school system employees, they lived modestly, carefully saving where they could. Ilma packed lunches, brewed coffee at home, and indulged only in her one guilty pleasure—buying books. Not borrowing, but buying. Each one she brought home became part of her curated collection, a museum of her adventures and experiences. They were her trophies, physical evidence of her past lives and adventures. Ilma had been to other planets, other time periods, lived in prison, as a man, and even with animals. She had lived thousands of lives through the books she read.

This room, this perfect sanctuary, was a glimpse into her dream life. She closed her eyes, inhaling deeply as if trying to absorb the moment fully. Finally, she let the paperback slip into her tote, picked a hardcover from the nearest shelf, and sank into the plushest chair, losing herself in the magic of the written word.

The Unexpected Guest ducked behind a small hedge that stood perfectly trimmed under the library window. He was well aware that, although the books would be The Bookworm's initial interest, at some point, she would sit to read, and nearly every chair faced out of the window to the grounds.

He cautiously lifted his head a small fraction at a time until his one eye could see just over the window ledge. He looked around at the seating. Two overstuffed chairs were sitting to the side with big, puffy arms and matching ottomans. In the middle of the room sat a long, burgundy velvet couch with the fabric pulled tight over the back and no throw pillows. He glanced towards the wall of bookshelves and past the dainty tea table, but The Bookworm was nowhere to be found.

Just as he began to pull his head back, he saw her. She was standing directly on the other side of the window, looking out at the lawn. His heart raced as he fought the urge to move. *How had she not seen him? How had he not seen her?* He was too busy looking around the library through the small fragment of windowpane that he hadn't even noticed her standing right there. He knew there was more chance of her seeing him if he moved, so he stayed as still as a statue.

The Bookworm appeared to be in a trance. She stood nearly as still as he, with the exception of her fingers that were rubbing the edges of a silver bookmark that she held in her hands.

Sweat began to drip down his face, and his thighs were cramping. A bead of sweat ran between his eyes, falling into one. He squinted to fight off the burning sensation before another slid slowly down his nose. The itch was unbearable. It was going to make him sneeze. He had to get out of there, but one movement would give him away.

He silently counted backward from ten to one attempting to distract himself, then opened his eyes.

She had vanished from the window, now curled up in one of the oversized armchairs, her silhouette barely visible in the dim light. He released a shaky exhale and slipped further into the shadows, his pulse quickening. He would have to tread more carefully—being caught watching wasn't just risky; it was unthinkable.

CHAPTER NINE

The Gym

"Come on," Sean said, flashing a mischievous grin as he gently tugged April's arm. "Jonah is showing the guys around the basement. I figured you'd want to check out the gym."

"Where are Crystal and Ilma?" April asked, her tone light but curious.

"Crystal just darted upstairs to prepare for some 'private time' with Jonah—whatever that's supposed to mean—and Ilma's holed up in the library. You know how she gets when she's surrounded by books; we might not see her for hours." Sean rolled his eyes, his mock exasperation undercut by the unmistakable fondness in his voice. April knew he adored the quirks that made his brothers' wives so distinct.

Trailing behind Sean and the others, April descended the winding staircase tucked discreetly off the alcove near Will's room. The stone steps curved downward in a way that reminded her of a medieval castle, the rough, cool surface beneath her feet lending an air of mystery. Electric torches lined the walls, their flickering amber light mimicking flames, casting elongated shadows that danced as the group moved.

When they reached the bottom, the ambiance shifted sharply. The basement stretched out before them, its sleek, modern design a stark contrast to the stairwell's rustic charm. The walls were smooth and unadorned, painted in muted tones that absorbed the artificial light. The air carried the faint, sterile scent of polished floors and recycled ventilation, and the complete absence of windows made the space feel insulated—sealed off from the world above.

April hesitated for a moment, glancing back up the stairwell. Something about this level felt different, as if the walls themselves held secrets, and the weight of the earth above pressed down ever so slightly.

"To the right is the wine cellar," Jonah announced, his voice echoing faintly in the corridor. He paused by the arched door, its dark wood polished to a gleam. "Feel free to help yourselves, but just know everything is inventoried. We'll be charged at the end of our stay, so check the price list by the door before grabbing anything. If you pick a good one, we'll toast to it. But if you snag some overpriced bottle that tastes like it was brewed in a garbage bin for $400, I'll be pissed."

The group chuckled, though they all knew Jonah's bark was worse than his bite. If someone did crack open an expensive dud, he'd foot the bill without a word, his grumbles limited to empty threats. Not that it mattered; Sean's brothers weren't the wine-sipping type. They were beer guys through and through, with an occasional nod to bourbon when the mood struck. The warning, April mused silently, would be better aimed at his wife.

"To the left," Jonah continued, turning toward the next door, "is the movie room." He swung it open with a casual flourish but didn't bother stepping inside. A glimpse revealed plush recliners arranged in precise rows, their leather glistening under the recessed lights. "Cinema-quality sound, cozy seats, over a hundred preloaded movies... blah, blah, blah. Honestly, if you're spending your vacation watching movies, you've come to the wrong place."

"Come on, man," Thomas protested, his voice tinged with mock indignation as he fixed Jonah with an exaggerated puppy-dog stare. "Where's your sense of nostalgia? Don't you remember setting up the tent in the playroom and watching movies together as kids?"

Jonah's stern facade cracked as a smile tugged at the corners of his mouth, a flicker of fondness lighting his eyes.

"Every Friday night," Thomas continued, his grin widening as he nudged Jonah. "Until Will wanted in, that is."

Jonah burst into laughter just as Will stepped back with theatrical flair, clutching his chest in mock offense. "Can you blame a guy for wanting to watch R-rated movies with his big brothers? Actually, we should do that this week. Just the four of us, down here, reliving the glory days."

Jonah shook his head, though his smile lingered. "This house has way better ways to spend our time."

"Yeah," Sean chimed in, barely containing his laughter. "We've all seen Thomas' room."

The hallway buzzed with laughter and playful ribbing as Jonah led the way, his strides deliberate yet casual, as if he was both tour guide and host in a mansion that seemed built to impress. The house's vast, lavish spaces stretched endlessly around them, the weight of its grandeur offset by the warmth of their camaraderie. For a moment, it wasn't just a luxurious rental; it felt like a haven, where shared memories and present joys intertwined effortlessly.

The corridor opened up ahead, revealing two vastly different spaces that immediately vied for attention. To the left, April glimpsed what could only be the game room. It was a riot of fun, with a pool table at its center, flanked by a gleaming ping pong table and a foosball setup. Darts and air hockey awaited challengers, and a sleek bar lined the far wall, its rows of bottles glinting invitingly under ambient lights. Yet April barely had time to appreciate its playful energy because her gaze was pulled inexorably to the right.

Her breath caught. The home gym wasn't just a fitness room; it was a temple of physical achievement. Cardio machines—treadmills, ellipticals, and stationary bikes—stood ready in perfect alignment. A gleaming free-weight rack stretched across one wall, accompanied by pull-up bars of varying heights and a sophisticated resistance system designed for strength and balance training. Jump ropes, kettlebells, and medicine balls were neatly arranged, promising endless possibilities. Unlike the rest of the dimly lit basement, the gym was bathed in bright light that bounced off mirrored walls, creating an illusion of endless space.

Behind her, the brothers burst into the game room, their whoops and laughter echoing as they dove into mock competitions. April, however, moved toward the gym with a calculated nonchalance, trying to mask the excitement simmering just beneath her skin. Her heart raced—not from exertion but at the sheer thought of the workouts she could squeeze in during their stay.

"Hey, this is sick, right?" Sean's voice startled her, and she turned to see her husband standing in the doorway, his grin reflecting the awe she felt.

"Uh, yeah," she replied, her voice betraying her attempt at nonchalance as her gaze darted toward a set of sleek jump ropes and a row of medicine balls.

She mentally kicked herself for ignoring the deluge of emails Crystal had sent in the months leading up to the trip. Crystal had outlined every detail of the island and its amenities, attaching glossy photos and enthusiastic descriptions. April and Sean had barely skimmed them before clicking delete. Had she paid closer attention, she might have been even more excited about the trip.

"Run in ten?" Sean asked, pulling her attention back.

"As much as I'd love to spend every minute here," April said with a wistful glance at the equipment, "I really want to get back out on that trail we rode in on."

"Same," Sean agreed. "I'll crush a quick game with the boys and meet you out front."

April's fingers itched to test the resistance system or stretch out on the yoga mats, but she knew once she started, she'd lose all track of time. She gave a little wave toward the game room, though the brothers were too engrossed in their antics to notice her leave.

Jogging upstairs, she passed the library and caught sight of Ilma reclining on an overstuffed chair, a book resting lightly in her hands. The soft glow of the lamp cast her in a picture of serene contentment. Ilma was utterly in her element, surrounded by shelves packed with literature.

The sight made April smile. She had her dream space in the gym, and Ilma had found her sanctuary in the library. As April laced up her running shoes, she couldn't help but wonder: what corner of this island brought that same spark of joy to Crystal?

CHAPTER TEN

The Massage

Crystal pushed open the double doors to her *non-themed* bedroom, letting the subtle weight of the polished wood signal her return to solitude. As she stepped inside and softly closed the doors behind her, the tension that had clung to her all day began to ebb away. It was as though the room itself exhaled with her, absorbing her exhaustion and wrapping her in the embrace of its understated elegance.

The space was undeniably grand, yet it managed to feel personal—a balance of indulgence and intimacy. Her gaze swept across the room, lingering on the four-poster bed draped in the finest linens she'd ever rested her tight-ass upon. The silken sheets beckoned, promising respite, but tonight, they were merely a backdrop to her true sanctuary.

Crossing the room with purposeful strides, she bypassed the cozy seating area by the fireplace to the right and made her way to the professional massage table that Jonah had so thoughtfully prepared. Draped in fresh, crisp sheets and a plush blanket, it stood waiting, an invitation to unwind after the whirlwind of family reunions and diligent planning. Jonah always knew what she needed before she even asked—a trait that comforted and infuriated her in equal measure. He probably needed an escape himself, she mused, smiling softly. Reunions had a way of draining even the most patient souls.

Without sparing a thought for who might be walking outside her door, Crystal slipped the delicate spaghetti straps from her shoulders, letting the light fabric of her dress slide down in a whisper to pool at her feet. Her lace panties followed, discarded with the same grace, forming a careless puddle of fabric on the polished floor. Standing naked in the warm glow of the room, she hesitated at the massage table, then changed her mind.

The terrace called to her.

She moved toward the sliding glass doors, her bare feet savoring the cool touch of the stone floor that sent goosebumps rippling up her skin. The brisk sensation heightened her senses, and she felt the chill raise her nipples to taut peaks, the crisp air meeting her bare skin like an old, familiar friend.

As a child, she had often dreamed of living in a castle, imagining herself as a princess wandering endless stone hallways in flowing gowns, her skirts sweeping the floors before leading her to a balcony where she would meet her forbidden love under a glowing full moon. This terrace was the closest she had ever come to realizing those dreams. Its rustic stone floor and the marble-pillared railing felt timeless, evoking visions of Tuscany—a place she had never visited but often romanticized. Here, miles off the coast yet seemingly worlds away, she felt as though she stood on foreign soil, untethered from the life she knew.

Her gaze fell to the pool below, its water shimmering like liquid crystal under the fading sunlight. The gentle trickle of water flowing from the hot tub into the pool filled the air with a soothing rhythm, a lullaby for the soul. Beyond, the horizon was a masterpiece of fluffy white clouds painted against a sky so vibrantly blue it seemed almost unreal.

She leaned against the cool marble railing, letting the tranquil view wash over her. Dreams of waking up every morning to this peace felt indulgent, selfish even, but she let the fantasy linger. It was the unattainable dreams—the ones that danced just beyond her reach—that kept her motivated. They were the sparks that fueled her ambition, the whispers that reminded her why she worked so hard to turn fragments of fantasy into pieces of her reality.

Before the rhythmic sound of the water could fully lull her into a trance, Crystal turned back toward the room, her movements deliberate as though shaking off the spell of the terrace. She crossed the space with a graceful efficiency, climbing onto the oversized massage table with practiced ease. The plush surface yielded under her weight, and she settled onto her stomach, fitting her face into the cradle. Pulling the crisp sheet up to cover her bare skin, she tucked it securely around herself, a thin barrier against the lingering chill from the terrace's cool stone floor. Normally, she might have left herself more exposed—a teasing gesture Jonah always appreciated—but tonight, comfort won out over temptation.

The thought of standing to ignite the dormant fireplace flickered through her mind but was swiftly dismissed when she heard the door quietly open. The promise of Jonah's strong, familiar hands warming her body was enough. She exhaled deeply, letting her muscles loosen as the massage table cradled her, cocooning her in its soft embrace.

"Took you long enough," she murmured, her voice muffled by the padded cradle, teasing him as she let herself sink deeper into relaxation.

She felt his hands before she heard his response. They moved deliberately, sliding from her shoulders, gliding down her back, and curving around her waist with an almost reverent touch. The sheet, which had felt like a shield moments ago, was tugged downward—not folded neatly like a practiced spa therapist would do, but cast aside with a casual confidence. The fabric fluttered to the floor, forgotten, as his hands traced her contours, their slow movements growing faster, more insistent.

At first, the sensation was soothing, almost hypnotic, each stroke coaxing her muscles into submission. But as the pressure increased and his touch became more fervent, she felt her body shift from soft compliance to a growing tension, her muscles instinctively pushing back against the force.

Crystal's half-lidded eyes flew open, though her head remained cradled in the circular pillow. She parted her lips to speak, to question the sudden intensity, but just as quickly as it began, it stopped. The abruptness was disarming, the silence that followed unnerving.

A faint, almost imperceptible breeze swept across her bare back, raising goosebumps in its wake. Then, the unmistakable sound of hinges creaking reached her ears—soft but distinct. Her pulse quickened as she listened, her body frozen in place. The silence stretched, broken only by the sound of another door closing somewhere behind her. It wasn't the smooth, soundless motion of the bedroom's double doors. This was different—heavier, more deliberate.

"Jonah? Is everything okay?" Her voice wavered, though she kept her head down, her body tense beneath the pretense of calm.

His reply came, rich with warmth and familiarity. "Sorry, babe. Yes, everything's perfect. Damn, woman! Look at you."

Relief warred with lingering unease, and she forced herself to exhale slowly. His hands returned, firmer now, their pressure deep and purposeful as his thumbs pressed into the narrow groove between her shoulder blades. His fingers swept outward, tracing the line of her shoulders before curling around her neck with a possessive gentleness. Each movement was precise, his touch a blend of strength and devotion that left her body pliant and yearning.

The tension that had gripped her moments before began to dissolve under the weight of his skillful touch. Crystal's lips curved into a contented smile, her thoughts drifting. Everything was perfect. The house, the room, the family—all of it coalesced into a single, flawless moment. And Jonah's hands, oh, his hands... If this bliss didn't send her spiraling into sleep, she was certain it would lead them to the bed, where passion would take over entirely.

The Unwelcome Guest pressed his back against the cool, unyielding wall of the hidden passage, his breathing slow but deliberate, muffled by the oppressive darkness enveloping him. He had narrowly escaped the bedroom, slipping away mere seconds before The Supermodel's husband returned. The gamble had been reckless—standing there in the shadows, peering through the cleverly concealed peephole above the fireplace mantle. He'd watched her every move as she undressed with a practiced grace that bordered on exhibitionism, her confidence radiating through every fluid motion. She seemed to revel in the imagined gaze of an audience, moving as though she knew someone was watching and savoring the attention.

The hidden door, seamlessly disguised as an ornate full-length mirror with gold trim, had been his lifeline. Its clever design allowed him to enter and leave without detection, but tonight, he had tempted fate. For a fleeting moment, he couldn't resist crossing the threshold, compelled by an insatiable desire to feel her, to claim some tangible piece of her for himself. His hands had lingered on her skin—soft, supple, and impossibly smooth—before the sound of the husband's approach sent him scrambling back into the concealed passage. By sheer luck, the man's attention had been entirely consumed by his wife, sprawled naked on the massage table, her allure eclipsing any awareness of the mirrored door's imperfect closure.

Now, hidden in the narrow confines of the secret corridor, The Unwelcome Guest stood utterly still, his senses heightened to the sounds filtering through the walls. Muffled moans and gasps reached his ears, each one igniting a primal need that he could barely contain. Slowly, almost reverently, he lifted his hands to his face, inhaling deeply as if the remnants of her scent could tether him to the memory of her body. The sensation of her flawless skin beneath his fingers replayed in his mind, a tormenting echo of what he could never truly have.

Unbidden, his body betrayed him. A growing pressure in his pants made him shift his weight, the unconscious movement setting his right foot to its nervous tick, grinding of the ball of his foot into the ground. He caught himself just in time, freezing before the faint sound could betray his position. Gritting his teeth, he pressed harder against the wall, his hands trembling as he brought them closer to his face. Desperation clawed at him, driving him to push his fingers against his nose, as if embedding her scent deep within him could make her a permanent part of his world.

The mansion's design was a marvel, its hidden passages not an afterthought but an integral part of its construction. The secret corridors were expertly crafted, complete with carpeting and sophisticated locking mechanisms outside each room. This labyrinth of clandestine spaces was his domain, a place where he could exist unseen, free to indulge in his voyeuristic cravings. Yet, despite the comfort of his surroundings, he dared not move.

Dim, motion-activated lights traced the floorboards of the passage, their soft glow too faint to risk detection. Still, from the escalating sounds of passion in the bedroom, it was clear the couple was far too preoccupied to notice even a burst of light or the echo of footsteps. Their unrestrained fervor emboldened him. Though the temptation to watch the couple lost in their passion was overwhelming, he knew this was his chance to escape—and he couldn't waste it. As the intensity of their moans reached a fever pitch, he began to creep down the narrow stairway, the soft hum of lights flickering on and off with each step marking his path.

The stairs led him to the back of the butler's pantry, where the passage ended in a door cunningly disguised as shelving. Here, there were no peepholes—an oversight he mentally noted for later correction. Pressing his ear to the door, he strained to hear any sounds from the kitchen beyond. The silence reassured him.

With a cautious push, he emerged into the pantry, his movements as fluid as a shadow slipping across the room. The faint hum of the refrigerator greeted him, and he allowed himself a small smile. He reached for a snack, the mundane act juxtaposing the adrenaline still coursing through his veins. The mansion's web of secrets had once again granted him access to its unsuspecting inhabitants, and his escape had been flawless.

CHAPTER ELEVEN

The Run

They set off together, their feet hitting the path in unison. Their strides matched effortlessly, a testament to years of running side by side. For all their shared competitiveness, they'd somehow managed to avoid turning these runs into races. It was a small but essential victory—one that probably explained why they were still happily married.

The fountain disappeared behind them as they cut through the manicured grass, its fresh scent mingling with the earthy aroma of the woods ahead. The path opened before them like a natural corridor, its unpaved surface firm and ideal for running. As they entered the shade of the trees, the transition was immediate and almost magical—sunlight filtered through the dense canopy, splattering the ground with patches of light that shifted with the wind.

April's gaze followed the path as it split in two directions further ahead. "We'll have to see where that goes later," she mused to herself, mentally marking the trail for another run. For now, though, they stuck to the route toward the dock—a mile out, a mile back. Enough to shake off the stiffness of travel, with plenty of time left in the week for exploration.

The rhythmic sound of their synchronized footfalls blended with the forest's natural symphony: birdcalls, rustling leaves, and the occasional creak of branches swaying above. April's mind wandered, as it often did during these runs. "I wonder what animals are on this island," she said aloud, her voice breaking the comfortable silence.

Sean didn't answer, and she hadn't really expected him to. Their runs weren't for conversations but musings—fleeting thoughts shared like passing clouds. "Do you think the owners brought in animals? Or is everything here native to the island?" Her curiosity lingered even as her focus shifted back to the trail.

When they reached the clearing where the woods gave way to the dock, the sun glinted off the water, painting the scene in brilliant blues and golds. April slowed, her gaze drawn to the peaceful expanse of water. "Let's walk out for a bit," she suggested, already stepping toward the dock's weathered planks.

Sean shook his head, his lips curling into a sheepish grin. "You go ahead. I promised Billy I wouldn't be long. He's probably timing me right now so he can give me hell later." He began stretching again, loosening up for the return jog.

"Okay," April replied, adjusting her ponytail. "I might check out the other path when I'm done here, so don't worry if I'm not back right away."

Sean shot her a quick air kiss, which she caught with exaggerated flair, grinning as he disappeared back into the woods. Alone now, April wandered onto the dock, savoring the salty tang of the breeze as it danced over her skin. The water stretched endlessly before her, its surface so still it seemed to mirror the sky perfectly. She let herself exhale, the tranquility sinking into her.

The thickening cloud cover pressed down on the landscape, turning the world around her into a muted palette of grays. But it wasn't the ominous sky that sent a chill racing up April's spine. It was the tickle at the back of her neck—light as a whisper, yet insistent—that made her whirl around, heart hammering. She was certain someone was standing right behind her.

Nothing. The dock was empty. The woods beyond the clearing stood silent, their dark openings like vacant eyes watching her. Her pulse thrummed in her ears as she scanned the area, her breath shallow and quick. There was no one there. At least, no one she could see.

The unsettling sensation lingered, eating away at her resolve. With the sky darkening rapidly, she decided it was time to head back. The thought of being caught in these woods after sunset wasn't just unpleasant—it was unthinkable.

April stepped off the dock, her running shoes crunching against the gravel path. Picking up her pace, she jogged toward the mansion, the rhythm of her feet on the packed earth steady and familiar. But the woods seemed to close in around her, the leafy canopy above blotting out what little light remained. Her jog turned urgent, not from exertion but from a gnawing instinct—an animal-like awareness of something unseen yet present.

The woods had fallen eerily silent. No rustle of squirrels darting through underbrush, no trill of birdsong—just the pounding of her heart and the whisper of her breath. Then, a sharp crack behind her. The unmistakable sound of a branch snapping.

April froze, spinning on her heels, her eyes wide and searching. The path behind her was empty. She scanned the trees, her gaze darting from shadow to shadow, half expecting Sean to emerge with a sheepish grin.

But Sean wouldn't try to scare her. That wasn't his style. Thomas, on the other hand... April shook her head. No, not even Thomas would run this far into the woods for a prank. He preferred his jokes simple and close to home.

"Hello?" she called, her voice faltering. The sound seemed to dissolve into the oppressive quiet, swallowed whole by the trees. If someone was out there, they wouldn't answer—unless they wanted her to know they were there.

Her pulse quickened, but she forced herself to stay still, listening. Minutes stretched, long and tense, until the distant trill of a bird shattered the silence. The forest seemed to exhale, its life returning in small, hesitant bursts. April let out a shaky breath, comforted by the presence of something alive, even if it wasn't human.

But she wasn't about to tempt fate by exploring the other path. Not today. With quickened steps, she resumed her run, the mansion's silhouette etched in her mind like a beacon.

When she reached the fountain, she didn't stop to stretch. Her limbs ached, and sweat dripped from her brow, but she couldn't shake the feeling of being watched. Gravel and dirt clung to her shoes as she hurried through the foyer, not caring about the mess she left behind. She needed to see Sean.

The kitchen smelled faintly of citrus cleaner, the space lit warmly despite the gloom outside. Sean stood at the sink, filling a glass with water. Relief washed over her at the sight of him, whole and unbothered.

"Oh, good. You're here," she said, her voice breathless and tinged with an urgency she couldn't hide.

Sean glanced at her, raising an eyebrow. "Where did you think I'd be?"

If she told him what she felt—what she thought she'd heard—he'd either laugh it off or go hunting through the woods, neither of which she wanted. "Where is everyone?" she asked, pivoting to safer ground.

"I don't know. Around," Sean replied casually, taking a sip of water. "Billy's probably downstairs waiting for me to play pool. Ilma's in the library. Maybe Thomas is with her. Why?"

"No reason. Just curious." She turned away, unable to meet his eyes, afraid he'd see through the thin veneer of calm she was struggling to maintain. "I'm going to hit the exercise bike before I cool down too much."

"Here, take this," Sean said, tossing her the thick binder. April caught it instinctively, eyeing the gold cover with curiosity.

"There's no internet, remember?" he added with a smirk. "No streaming, no news, no movies. Consider it light reading."

April sighed, her watch confirming his point as it struggled to find a signal. She could grab something from the library, but the thought of running into Ilma and Thomas made her hesitate. The last thing she needed was to have her choice of reading material scrutinized by a librarian.

Clutching the binder, she left the kitchen, her steps purposeful yet unsettled. The mansion felt vast and quiet, its halls stretching endlessly before her. As she descended the stairs to the exercise room, a prickling unease lingered, an unwelcome companion that refused to be left behind.

The Unwelcome Guest slithered through the woods with practiced silence, his mind fixated on his secret stash hidden deep within the island. He needed to check on the body. He couldn't guess what feast nature's scavengers had made of the man's flesh, but he had to ensure the stench of decay wouldn't draw unwanted curiosity. The thought of human noses sniffing where they shouldn't filled him with a sharp, bubbling unease.

His earlier bravado had betrayed him. He'd let his guard slip after successfully navigating his encounter with The Supermodel and nearly collided with The Runner. He cursed his carelessness. The athletic couple had set off together, and he'd assumed their pace and path would give him more than enough time to avoid detection. But they'd split up, and the woman had almost stumbled upon him. He'd pressed himself against the coarse bark of a tree, his pulse pounding in sync with the oppressive silence of the woods.

The island's stillness unnerved him. No birds chirped. No insects droned. Even the rustle of the breeze had vanished, as if the entire forest held its breath. It was a silence that betrayed him, his every movement amplified in the unnatural quiet. He glared at the surrounding trees as if willing them to make noise, to conspire with him instead of against him. *It's us against them,* he thought bitterly. *Move, rustle, anything.*

Finally, a bird trilled, and the forest exhaled its life once more. The Unwelcome Guest took his cue, darting in the opposite direction from where The Runner had gone. He hated doubling back—it made him feel exposed, vulnerable—but he couldn't risk another near encounter. The circular path around the island offered him options, but now his detour would take twice as long.

By the time he returned to the house, his legs ached, and his shirt clung to his back, soaked through with sweat. He allowed himself only a brief moment to catch his breath, scanning the area with a predator's focus. The mansion loomed ahead, its grandeur hiding secrets as dark as his own. Satisfied he was alone, he slipped into the cart garage, the air heavy with the faint tang of gasoline and fresh-cut grass. With practiced efficiency, he pushed the riding mower forward, revealing a hidden floor latch. Beneath it lay the passage that would lead him safely back into the mansion.

He descended into the tunnel, a faint click echoing as the hatch sealed behind him. Unlike the grim, damp tunnels he'd read about in ancient European cities, these were disturbingly luxurious. Carpeted floors muffled his steps, and the lights flickered on as he moved through. The pristine space was unsettling in its perfection, and he couldn't help but feel a pang of guilt for the dirt and grass clinging to his shoes.

Just as he prepared to exit the tunnels, the faint hum of the gym's air conditioning reached his ears, and his stomach twisted. She was back. He knew it even before he edged toward the concealed peephole built into the gym's wall. The Runner was there.

The gym's mirrored wall reflected her figure, broken only by the mounted television displaying preloaded aerobics programs. The camera embedded in the TV offered him a perfect view of her, but the setup was unnerving—it felt as though the mirror eyes staring back at him could see into his own twisted soul.

She was curling free weights, her muscles contracting and releasing with mechanical precision. Beads of sweat caught the light, glistening against her tanned skin. Her reflection revealed a woman lost in focus, her gaze locked on her own movements. He took advantage of her position to zoom in on her breasts, not quite a handful, but they would do.

When she dropped the weights, she lingered in front of the mirror, flexing briefly before standing still, simply looking at herself. There was something hypnotic about her stare. It made *him* feel observed, as though she could see through the glass and into the black void of his hidden perch.

She stepped closer to the mirror. His breath caught in his throat, his pulse quickening. He knew she couldn't see him, but the illusion of her gaze stripping him bare was intoxicating. Another step, and his body responded with an involuntary intensity that made him shift uncomfortably in his hiding spot. He longed to know her scent, to take it in deeply and—

She leaned forward and popped a pimple.

The spell broke. Disgust roiled through him, and the tightness in his pants dissolved into a limp shame. He stepped back from the peephole, unable to stomach another moment of her mundane self-examination. What had once been alluring now felt banal, even grotesque.

As he retreated, his mind churned with frustration and self-loathing. He hadn't come to this island to lose focus. He had plans—carefully laid, delicately balanced. She was a distraction he couldn't afford.

CHAPTER TWELVE

The Sisters-In-Law

Ilma finally emerged from the library, her shoes tapping softly against the polished tiles as she made her way to the great room. The expansive space exuded an air of opulence, its soaring ceilings and broad windows framing a breathtaking view of the backyard. The sun had dipped below the trees, leaving behind a sky brushed with strokes of fiery pink and deepening indigo, like a watercolor masterpiece stretched across the horizon.

She hadn't taken a close look at the aquarium during the earlier house tour, but now its sheer magnificence caught her attention. Set seamlessly into the wall dividing the great room from the alcove, it was a marvel of design and engineering. The tank stretched a commanding eight feet wide and four feet high, its glass shimmering faintly in the dim light. Schools of vibrant, darting fish created a kaleidoscope of movement, their scales catching and refracting the light. Questions crowded her mind: *How was it maintained? How were the fish fed? Did someone dive into this aquatic fortress to clean it?* The practical mystery of it all tugged at her curiosity, but she pushed the thoughts aside. Tonight wasn't for pondering logistics. Tonight was for performing her role—the good sister-in-law, sharing polite conversation over wine while her husband bonded downstairs with his brothers, their laughter and raucous cheers already echoing faintly beneath her feet.

Ilma stepped toward the seating area, her navy dress brushing just below her knees as she accepted the glass of wine Crystal handed her. She took a delicate sip, the wine's subtle sweetness barely registering. Her eyes flicked toward the French doors leading to the pool deck. If it were up to her, she'd suggest moving outside, where the crisp evening air and lingering sunset would make the conversation more bearable. But Crystal lounged effortlessly across the curved white leather sofa, her glass of wine teetering on the edge of the armrest as if daring gravity to intervene. On the opposite side of the semicircle, April, with a faint sheen of post-workout glow yet impeccably composed, mirrored her relaxed posture with an ease that belied her earlier exertion. Ilma sighed inwardly. The evening sky would have to wait for when she could savor it in solitude, a book in hand and no one asking her to explain why she didn't gush over celebrities or designer handbags.

"Sooooo," Crystal began, her voice lilting like a high schooler teasing out gossip, "did you like the library?"

Ilma's heart gave a tiny flutter. At last, a topic she could embrace. While she didn't care for celebrities or the latest viral trends, she had been known to wait hours in line for a chance to meet her favorite authors. The thought of discussing the library ignited a spark of genuine enthusiasm.

"Oh, my goodness, Crystal. It's just perfect," Ilma said, her smile genuine for once. "Thank you for letting me duck in there for a while."

To escape, she added silently in her mind, though she dared not voice the thought.

A sudden roar of laughter erupted from the basement, reverberating through the floorboards and breaking the momentary peace. Ilma's brow furrowed.

"Does anyone know what they're doing down there?" she asked, trying to keep her tone light despite her unease.

Crystal waved a manicured hand dismissively, her diamond bracelet catching the light. "Last I saw, they were taking shots of tequila and having a ping pong tournament. Don't worry," she added with a grin, "I don't think they'll drink that much. Dinner's almost ready."

Ilma forced a smile, but her gaze lingered on the floor. She doubted Crystal's confidence. Something about the noise below—the rowdy cheers, the occasional thuds—felt dissonant, out of sync with the refined luxury of the house. Still, she pushed the thought aside, settling into her role for the evening, her glass of wine cradled delicately in her hand.

Right on cue, a cheerful ding from the kitchen timer cut through the murmur of voices and faint clinking of glasses.

"Billy, dinner's calling!" Crystal trilled, her voice carrying a sing-song tone that ricocheted off the high ceilings. She lounged back like a queen, her bare feet tucked beneath her, her wine glass held delicately between two perfectly manicured fingers. But even her practiced projection couldn't outmatch the booming chaos rising from the game room below.

April, ever the embodiment of casual poise, stretched languidly before taking a final sip of her wine. She placed the glass on the coffee table with deliberate grace, her recent workout lending her a sheen of vitality. "I'll run down there to let him know. I'm curious to see what they're playing anyway," she said, her voice infused with light-hearted curiosity. She disappeared down the hallway with a confident jog, her ponytail swaying in rhythm to the sound of her footsteps. The distant rumbles of competitive laughter seemed to beckon her, pulling her in like an irresistible siren call.

Crystal laughed, a melodic sound as she nestled deeper into the sofa. "Forget the movie room; someone should soundproof the game room," she joked, kicking up her immaculately pedicured feet. The metallic gleam of her toenail polish caught the dim light, glinting like tiny treasures as she strummed her long nails along the stem of her glass.

Ilma, on the other hand, perched on the very edge of the couch, her posture stiff as a rod, her back hovering inches away from the seat. She clasped her hands tightly in her lap, knuckles whitening as she fought to relax. Her eyes darted to the expansive windows where Crystal's gaze lingered, taking in the scene of the darkening horizon. The sky outside had transformed into a masterpiece, but Ilma could barely appreciate its beauty.

Silence filled the room like an unwelcome guest. It wasn't the soothing hush she relished in her library sanctuaries; this was heavy, expectant, and awkward. The kind of quiet that demanded conversation. Ilma's fingers unconsciously reached for her wine glass, the cool stem grounding her. She took a measured sip, hoping it might loosen the knot of nerves in her chest. Her hands trembled slightly as she placed the glass back on the table, wiping her clammy palms against her thighs.

She had prepared for this. She'd even made mental notes of conversation starters tailored to each person. But as Crystal's gaze shifted to her, expectant and amused, Ilma's mind blanked under the weight of unspoken pressure. *Why did April have to leave?* This was supposed to be their shared "cocktail hour," yet now Ilma was left to shoulder the burden of small talk.

"So, Crystal," Ilma began, her voice wavering. She paused, clearing her throat. A sudden, stubborn tickle seized her, and she coughed, attempting to stifle it with little success. Panic flashed across her face as she reached for her glass again, this time taking a much larger sip than before.

Crystal tilted her head, a bemused smile playing at her lips. She waited with the patience of someone who enjoyed watching others squirm, though there was no malice in her expression.

When Ilma's throat finally cooperated, she forced a smile and continued. "You really outdid yourself. This place is... amazing. Thank you so much for doing all the research and legwork." Her voice was steadier now, though she could feel the heat creeping up her neck.

Crystal laughed lightly, tipping back her glass to finish her wine. "Oh, it was my pleasure. What's more fun than planning a dream vacation with an unlimited budget?" she replied, her tone breezy and self-assured.

Unlimited budget? The words struck Ilma like a slap. She blinked rapidly, her throat tightening as if she might start coughing again. This vacation had drained her and Thomas's savings—a painstakingly built fund accumulated over years of frugality and compromise. The idea of an unlimited budget was as alien to her as the thought of renting an entire private island.

Her stomach churned as she thought back to the conversation she and Thomas had about the costs. He had tried to reassure her, downplaying the financial blow and emphasizing the importance of family bonding. But even as he spoke, he had let slip a detail about Crystal—how, years ago, she had tried to dissuade him from pursuing a career in education, citing the low salary as a source of lifelong stress. The memory still stung, a lingering reminder of the disparity between their lives.

A fresh wave of laughter erupted from the basement, growing louder as it approached. April led the group upstairs, her smile radiant as if she had absorbed the infectious energy of the game room.

"Top off your glasses, ladies," Will called out, his voice commanding yet warm. "Guys, grab a beer and take a seat in the dining room. Dinner will be out in a few minutes."

Thomas appeared at Ilma's side, his steps slightly unsteady, his cheeks flushed from alcohol and exertion. His silly grin melted the tension from her shoulders. He extended a hand, pulling her up from the couch with ease, and placed a soft kiss on her temple.

She smiled, feeling her composure return. With Thomas by her side and the promise of shared conversation at the dinner table, the weight of her unease began to lift.

CHAPTER THIRTEEN

The Question

Dinner was a masterpiece, a culinary alchemy that transformed humble ingredients into an experience April could scarcely comprehend. The flavors danced on her tongue in a way she hadn't allowed herself to indulge in years. For her and Sean, meals were functional, a regimen of protein shakes, broiled fish, and endless kale—a diet as joyless as it was necessary for their brand's image. Food had long ceased to be a source of pleasure; it was merely fuel. But tonight, as she leaned back in her chair, legs stretched out and stomach blissfully full, April couldn't deny the primal satisfaction coursing through her.

She wasn't alone in her food-induced haze. Around the table, blurry-eyed guests slouched in their chairs, their contented sighs a testament to Will's culinary genius. He sat at the edge of the table closest to the kitchen, arms crossed and a self-assured grin playing on his lips. He looked every bit the benevolent king surveying his realm, though there was no head of this table to define his dominion.

Unlike traditional dining rooms with their long rectangular tables and hierarchical seating, this room was strikingly unique. A perfect square enclosed a massive circular table, its presence commanding the space. At its center, an ornate floral arrangement sprawled low and wide, ensuring unobstructed views across the table. Encircling the centerpiece was a beachy wood Lazy Susan, its smooth rotation a practical solution for passing dishes across the table's impressive span. The quartz-edged outer rim shimmered faintly in the ambient light, the placemats meticulously arranged with layered chargers and an arsenal of silverware that gleamed like miniature weapons.

As April sipped her third—or was it fourth?—glass of red wine, her mind wandered to a practical concern. With no cleaning staff, who would tackle the mountain of plates, glasses, and silverware now piled across the table? The thought flitted away, swept aside by the warm, heady haze of the wine.

Though the table's seven seats were spoken for, April couldn't shake the peculiar sense of imbalance. Seven. Not six, not eight—just seven. The exact number of guests staying on the island. It was a logical arrangement, yet the symmetry of it felt deliberate in a way that sent a faint ripple of unease through her. The feeling of absence—or worse, an unacknowledged presence—clung to her like a shadow, a remnant of the uneasiness from her morning run.

Bolstered by liquid courage and the languid atmosphere of post-dinner camaraderie, April finally broke the silence. "Crystal, are there any other people on the island?" she asked, her fingers absently tugging at the waistband of her running pants. She silently appreciated her decision to stay in her workout clothes instead of changing into something more restrictive, like jeans.

Crystal, mid-stretch with her arms reaching toward the ceiling, shook her head and laughed lightly. "Oh no, it's totally private. That's the whole point. They drop us off and leave. It's like a luxury reality show... but in a mansion... with food, electricity, and indoor plumbing," she added, her voice trailing off in lazy amusement.

"I wondered the same thing," Ilma interjected, suddenly more animated than she'd been all evening. She tucked a strand of hair behind her ear, her cheeks flushed. "I spent most of the afternoon in the library," she admitted with a sheepish smile, "and there was one time I could've sworn I saw someone outside the window. But every time I looked, no one was there. It made me wonder if they had gardeners or maintenance staff who might stop by."

Crystal's tone sharpened slightly, though her expression remained calm. "Definitely not. The contract was very clear—no one else is on the island. That's why they made the Gold Book," she explained, her voice carrying an odd finality.

April raised an eyebrow, glancing at the men at the table. Their blank expressions suggested the Gold Book hadn't made much of an impression on them. Crystal continued, "The rules are specific. If something breaks—appliances, the pool, even the power—they don't send anyone out. No exceptions. There's even an emergency protocol section since cell service is practically nonexistent here."

April stiffened. The lack of internet and cellular service had been a detail she'd overlooked—or ignored—amid Crystal's exhaustive emails.

She glanced at her watch, recalling the earlier inconvenience of disabling its GPS tracking on her run.

"April?" Crystal's voice brought her back to the table. All eyes were on her now.

"Yes?"

"Why do you ask?"

April hesitated, replaying her earlier words. She glanced down at her lap, feeling the weight of their attention. Finally, she answered, "I thought I saw someone during my run today."

The clink of wine glasses and scrape of dessert forks ceased. A heavy silence fell, charged with a mix of disbelief and suspicion. Sean, seated beside her, frowned deeply, his irritation evident. April felt a twinge of guilt at having kept the sighting from him.

"What did they look like?" Sean asked, his tone clipped.

"I didn't see anyone, not clearly," April admitted. "But it felt like someone was there."

The tension in the room deflated slightly, chairs creaking as everyone shifted back into more relaxed postures. Yet April couldn't miss the fleeting glances exchanged around the table. Though the others quickly changed the subject, diving into lighter topics, April's mind remained fixated on the unease lingering in her chest.

She tipped back her glass, finishing what was left of the wine. The group may have dismissed her concern, but the sensation of being watched had been real. She decided to let the matter drop for now—but she wouldn't forget it.

CHAPTER FOURTEEN

The Noise

"OMG, that dinner!" Crystal moaned as she and Jonah entered their room, her voice laced with satisfaction and exhaustion. "Seriously, if Billy doesn't want to stick with the restaurant industry, we should tell him we'd hire him as our personal chef in a heartbeat."

Crystal casually shed her clothes, leaving a trail of garments behind her like breadcrumbs leading to the chaise lounge by the fire. She flopped down, sighing deeply as the warmth from the fire enveloped her. Jonah, still standing, glanced her way, his brow furrowing as he weighed his next words.

"Honestly, Crys, I know you mean well, but I'm not sure Will's dream job is playing house chef for his brother and sister-in-law."

"Chef? No, more like a culinary artist with perks—free room and board, a decent salary, and just the joy of cooking. He wouldn't be a servant," she argued, her voice trailing off as she realized the implications.

"And he doesn't get to eat with us?" Jonah's gaze remained steady. "You get how that might come off, right?"

"I guess," she murmured, though she didn't fully concede. To her, it seemed like a win-win. "I just hate that he's so far away. And selfishly, I love his cooking."

Crystal stretched out on the chaise, her naked form basking in the fire's glow, hoping it would entice Jonah to join her. But Jonah had had enough. He turned hastily and disappeared into the bathroom, the door closing with a soft click. The sound of the shower starting up was her cue—he was done with her for the night.

With a resigned sigh, Crystal slid off the lounge and climbed into bed. She briefly considered grabbing Ilma for a book recommendation but decided against it, knowing she wouldn't finish any book in a week. The allure of mindless scrolling through videos won out.

She retrieved a sleeping pill from the baggie on her nightstand, popped it into her mouth, and tilted her head back, struggling to muster enough saliva to swallow it past her wine-parched throat. With a little effort, the pill went down, and she reached for her phone.

The app opened, but the videos failed to load. Frustrated, she swiped to another app, only to be met with the same unresponsive spinning graphics. With an irritated sigh, her arm fell limp beside her, phone still in hand. She hadn't paid enough attention to the caretaker's warning about the island's spotty internet.

Crystal's mind wandered back to the whirlwind of information the caretaker had bombarded them with upon arrival. The elusive Gold Book had seemed like a lifeline for all the details she had ignored. At the time, her priorities had been the pool, the hot tub, and groceries. Now, as she lay in bed, the memory of that detailed tour seemed foggy, lost to the haze of exhaustion and wine.

Her stomach turned at the memory of dinner's conversation, particularly Ilma and April's queries about other people on the island. An unsettling chill traced her spine. The unease she had felt earlier in the day resurfaced, a vague, gnawing sensation she couldn't place.

Her fingers trembled slightly as she recalled the massage, how tense she had been. For a fleeting moment, she had doubted whether it was Jonah's hands or someone else's. But when she turned to face him, it was his familiar, loving face that reassured her.

A single, soft knock jolted her from her thoughts. The sound wasn't from the hallway door but seemed to emanate from the sliding doors to the terrace—or maybe the fireplace. The noise was faint, like a foot tapping against wood and the swish of something heavy being dragged.

Crystal's heart raced. The terrace doors were wide open to the night, and the soothing sounds of the hot tub and crickets had seemed comforting moments ago. Now, they felt ominous. The lack of carpet on the terrace or near the fireplace didn't match the sound. It was closer. Much closer.

She sat up, her breath quickening. Jonah's presence behind the closed bathroom door felt distant, almost unreachable. Her voice trembled as she called out, "Thomas?" But she knew it wasn't him. Thomas would never pull such a prank, especially not in the privacy of their room.

The chill in the air bit at her skin as she threw off the covers. The room seemed darker, the shadows deeper. She swung her legs over the bed, hesitating as her imagination ran wild. Was there someone under the bed, waiting to grab her? The thought paralyzed her for a moment.

Just as she gathered the courage to move, a wave of calm washed over her, the sleeping pill taking effect. The terror that had gripped her moments ago dulled. The open terrace, the strange noises, the potential intruder—all of it faded into the background. She sank back into the bed, pulling the covers over her like a shield, and let her eyes drift shut, even as a faint unease lingered, just on the edge of her consciousness.

CHAPTER FIFTEEN

The View

Pushing open the secret door, The Unwelcome Guest slipped silently into the spacious bedroom. The dim light from the gas fireplace cast flickering shadows across the room, giving it an eerie, surreal ambiance. He paused for a moment, listening to the stillness, his heart beating with a controlled rhythm, calm and measured. He knew The Supermodel had been downing wine all evening and would likely be passed out, lost in her intoxicated slumber.

He stepped cautiously into the room, his eyes scanning the surroundings, calculating his next move. The fireplace in the corner caught his attention. Unlike a traditional hearth, this one used synthetic logs made from concrete, designed to glow softly over the gas fed flames. He mused over the possibility of rigging something with the gas, envisioning the room filling silently with an invisible, odorless danger. The Supermodel, deep in her drunken stupor, wouldn't detect the scent of propane. She wouldn't stir, wouldn't resist.

He crouched in front of the fireplace, the heat radiating off the synthetic logs, searing against his skin. A single touch confirmed the controls were too hot to handle. Instead, he flipped the wall switch to shut off the flame, allowing the logs to cool, while his mind raced with dark ingenuity.

As he straightened, his head just below the top of the chair near the fire, her voice cut through the room, soft but alert, "Thomas?"

His heart jolted, a sharp contrast to his earlier calm. She wasn't passed out after all. The sound of her voice made his pulse quicken, but he forced himself to remain still, his breathing shallow. He cursed under his breath for not being more cautious. The door to the hidden passageway remained ajar, a glaring oversight.

Peering around the chair, he noticed the thin line of light glowing beneath the bathroom door. Her husband was in there, only a few steps away. For a moment, he considered fleeing through the terrace, its open doors offering a quick escape into the night. But then he saw her again, her form settling back into stillness, and he realized she had likely drifted back to sleep.

Seizing the moment, he took two swift steps from behind the chair, moving with the stealth of a shadow. He stood by the bed, where The Supermodel lay wrapped in a blanket, her golden hair splayed across the pillow like a halo. The curve of her bare shoulder emerged from beneath the cover, revealing her nudity. She was stunning, motionless, like a masterpiece captured in a moment of repose.

Her beauty was undeniable, a silent perfection. In his twisted mind, she was more beautiful this way, her lips closed, her expression serene. He imagined her as a flawless corpse, her eyes sewn shut, her body forever at peace. The thought sent a dark thrill through him, a morbid fantasy that made him feel invincible, unnoticed, and in control once more.

CHAPTER SIXTEEN

The Toy Closet

Ilma awoke to a faint shuffling noise coming from the direction of Crystal and Jonah's room. She lay still for a moment, straining to catch any further sounds in the silence that cloaked the house. After rubbing her eyes and blinking a few times, she glanced at the clock. Its luminous digits read three in the morning. Sighing deeply, she closed her eyes again, thankful for the remaining hours of the night to drift back to sleep. She rolled over to face Thomas, who lay on his back, his mouth slightly open, emitting soft, raspy breaths punctuated by the occasional cough. For a fleeting moment, she considered the noise might have come from him, but her instincts told her otherwise. The sound had distinctly originated from the opposite direction.

As Ilma settled into a more comfortable position, the pressure in her bladder became impossible to ignore. She initially resisted the urge, hoping to fall back asleep, but the sensation grew insistent, demanding attention. With a resigned sigh, she threw off the covers and swung her legs over the edge of the bed, the cold floor pressing against her bare feet. She moved quietly, careful not to disturb Thomas, and padded toward the bathroom, navigating the room without turning on any lights.

She reached out in the darkness, fingers closing around the doorknob. Turning it gently, she slipped inside and softly shut the door behind her. It was only after she turned on the light that she realized her mistake. The harsh fluorescent glow illuminated a space that was *not* the bathroom but a small, closet-like room she hadn't noticed before.

The room was claustrophobic, barely larger than a linen closet. She stood frozen, her gaze landing on the shelves directly ahead of her. At eye level, an array of dildos and vibrators in every conceivable shape, size, and color were displayed like an exotic collection of curiosities. Ilma's mouth dropped open in shock, her breath caught in her throat. A flush of heat crept up her neck, spreading across her cheeks as she averted her eyes, her heart thudding in her chest.

Her gaze was involuntarily drawn to the left wall, where ropes, handcuffs, and leather straps hung in neat rows, each item painstakingly arranged on hooks. To the right, a series of rubber and metal balls were displayed, their purpose as alien to her as the rest of the contents in the tiny room. She felt like an intruder, stumbling into a private world that wasn't meant for her eyes, and embarrassment prickled at her skin, a sensation she hadn't felt since childhood, when she'd accidentally wandered into forbidden territory a risqué store in the mall.

Her fingers fumbled behind her, searching desperately for the doorknob as her mind raced. What if the owners knew she'd seen this? Surely, this room wasn't meant for guests. Her eyes lingered briefly on a bright pink, veiny apparatus directly in front of her, its obscene presence adding to her growing unease.

The need to escape surged through her. Her breathing quickened, her chest tightening with panic. Just as her fingers found the cool metal of the knob, the door suddenly swung open, and she stumbled backward, landing awkwardly on the carpeted floor outside the closet.

Thomas stood in the doorway, his eyes narrowed to slits against the bright light spilling from the room. "Why are you in the closet?" he asked groggily, his voice heavy with sleep.

"I was going to the bathroom," Ilma stammered, her voice barely above a whisper.

Thomas raised an eyebrow, his expression skeptical. "You were going to the bathroom in the closet?"

"No, I—" she began, but her words trailed off as Thomas's gaze shifted past her, finally registering the contents of the room.

"Holy penis closet," he murmured, a mischievous grin spreading across his face as his eyes widened in amusement.

Ilma scrambled to her feet, her face burning with humiliation. She knew that look in his eyes, a gleam of mischief she had come to recognize all too well on this trip. "No, Thomas," she said firmly, her tone as stern as a mother scolding a child. "Don't even think about it. This closet is probably supposed to be locked. We shouldn't interfere with the owners'... toys."

Thomas chuckled, his gaze still fixed on the closet's contents. "Oh, come on, Sidd. Just think of the fun I could have with all this."

Ilma flipped the switch, plunging the closet back into darkness, and closed the door, turning the lock on the inside knob for good measure. "No," she repeated firmly, watching as Thomas's shoulders sagged in exaggerated disappointment.

Reluctantly, Thomas shuffled back to bed, his steps slow and heavy. Ilma shook her head in disbelief, the absurdity of the situation sinking in. She slipped into the actual bathroom, finally finding the relief she desperately needed.

Chapter Seventeen

The Tiger

April quietly descended from the treehouse bed, every movement deliberately light to avoid rocking the platform beneath her. Sean and his brothers had been up late into the night, their laughter and chatter fading only when exhaustion overtook them. She wanted to let him sleep. He would protest later about missing their morning run, but she knew he would secretly be grateful for the extra rest.

After splashing cold water on her face and brushing her teeth with Sean's toothbrush—hers mysteriously missing—she slid into her running clothes. The idea of using his toothbrush felt odd and kind of gross, but they shared so much already. It was likely Sean himself had inadvertently sent it to an untimely end during one of his late-night bathroom trips.

She moved to the door, gripping the knob carefully to prevent even the slightest sound as she slowly began to pull it shut. The hallway behind her was eerily silent. No murmurs, no clinking of coffee cups, no soft footfalls—just an unsettling stillness that made her skin prickle. The quiet was absolute, amplifying her awareness of her own presence.

April smiled faintly as she eased the door flush with the frame, the thought of Sean's clumsy nocturnal antics softening her tension. He believed he was stealthy, but his attempts at subtlety were as disruptive as a marching band. His phone's light had pierced her closed eyelids, and he had snapped on the fan switch with a loud click that could rouse the dead.

As she released the knob and stepped turned to face the hallway, her breath caught in her throat. Less than a foot away, a tiger stood, teeth bared, its lifelike eyes gleaming in the dim light. A scream tore from her lips, a blend of shock and disbelief. Her mind raced, scrambling to make sense of the impossible sight: a tiger, on this island, inside the house. It defied logic. But adrenaline surged through her, propelling her into action. With a swift, instinctive move, she roundhouse kicked the stuffed tiger to the floor, the soft thud a stark contrast to the imagined danger.

The house's quiet shattered, April winced, expecting Sean to be roused from his slumber. She cautiously opened the door, ready to apologize for the commotion, but he remained undisturbed, sprawled across the bed with an arm dangling over the side.

Shaking her head, she closed the door once more and turned to face the fallen tiger. "Thomas," she hissed through gritted teeth. The infamous prankster of the family was at it again. She made a mental note to confront him later as she jogged down the stairs, her irritation momentarily giving way to amusement. Her gaze lingered on a large hippo propped in front of Crystal and Jonah's door, another of Thomas's playful ambushes.

Though she had rarely encountered his antics firsthand, April knew Thomas's reputation well. His pranks were legendary, often recounted with a mix of horror and hilarity by his brothers. The infamous kitchen spray hose incident, the whoopee cushion at his own wedding, and the luggage swap were tame compared to the more dangerous stunts they hinted at but never fully disclosed to her. One story stuck with her—Sean, heavy sleeper that he was, had once been moved in his sleep to the garage, rolled on a creeper under Jonah's car. It was a miracle he hadn't been seriously hurt.

She entered the kitchen quietly, seeking a glass of water, her throat scratchy from her unanticipated scream. The cabinet doors opened and closed with a soft click, their sound absorbed by the silence. It wasn't until she saw Will rising from the table that she realized she wasn't alone.

"Good morning," Will greeted her brightly, his cloth covered hands deftly removing a tray of pastries from the oven. The sweet aroma filled the room, making April wonder how she hadn't noticed it before.

"Morning," she replied, still shaken and on edge. "I didn't hear you. The house was so quiet."

"I heard a bit of a commotion upstairs," Will smirked, his eyes twinkling as they met hers. "I take it you found the tiger."

April chuckled awkwardly, shadowboxing to mask her embarrassment. "Nothing I couldn't handle. Did I wake you?"

"No, I've been up," he said, squeezing icing over the warm breakfast. His tone held a mischievous edge, reminiscent of his brother. "I don't need much sleep, and I work different hours than the rest of you. Plus, I'm a lot younger than those old guys."

His practiced movements and dismissive tone made her feel unwelcome, as though Will was more interested in his culinary tasks than conversation. She placed her glass in the sink, noting how spotless the kitchen remained from the night before. Passing through the dining room, she was struck by the immaculate table, reset as if untouched, even the flowers appeared freshly arranged. Will's energy seemed boundless, his dedication to order impressive.

Stepping outside, the morning greeted her with its ambiguous embrace. The air was cooler, the sky a canvas of muted grays hinting at rain. The dewdrops on the stone steps mirrored her thoughts, each one a tiny, fleeting moment of peace after the morning's chaos.

April bent over to stretch, her eyes catching sight of the fountain before her. Its tiers cascaded with oversized bubbles, a whimsical, surreal addition that could only be the work of one person.

"Thomas," she muttered, shaking her head with a sigh before setting off on her run, the day's absurdities trailing behind her like a mischievous shadow.

CHAPTER EIGHTEEN

The Trickster

Ilma woke relatively early, considering she read late into the night. She quietly used the bathroom and crawled back into bed next to Thomas. She knew the right thing to do was to get dressed and head downstairs to socialize with anyone else who was awake, but only one day into the vacation, she was already craving her space. So, rather than admit she was awake, she grabbed her book off the phallic-shaped nightstand, rolled onto her side, and pulled the covers up to read just like she had as a child reading way past her bedtime. Thankfully, she flipped right to the page where she had stopped reading since her bookmark was missing. She must have dropped it from her book when she was in the library, or maybe Crystal borrowed it to show to Jonah. She seemed impressed by the romantic gesture when they arrived.

She must have drifted off to sleep at some point because a scream startled her back awake.

"Thomas, you asshole!" Crystal's voice echoed down the hall.

Ilma dropped her book to the ground and jumped out of bed, running to the door where Thomas stood with his arms crossed, wearing a proud smile. When Ilma peaked around the doorway into the hallway, she saw Crystal, already decked out in her bikini, sarong, and sun hat staring face to... uh... butt with a stuffed hippopotamus. Crystal standing with her face in a hippo hiney was entertaining, but the added touch was on the hippo's head. The large stuffed animal appeared to be wearing Crystal's silk scarf and several necklaces as a headdress.

"Silly boy," Ilma said, poking Thomas in the belly. "I'm going to jump in the shower."

Thomas followed her into the room, giving her a light slap on the backside.

"How did you manage to get Crystal's scarf and jewelry?" Ilma asked, suddenly feeling a secondhand privacy breach.

He leaned forward and kissed her on the cheek hovering over her ear, and said, "If I told you, I'd have to kill you."

Ilma pulled away. Thomas had used the macabre phrase before in jest, but his voice was a low whisper which added to the creepiness of the statement.

A childlike smile crossed Thomas' face, causing her tense muscles to release. "Let's just say there are more ways to get around this place than meets the eye," he added playfully.

He winked and turned around to head downstairs.

Thomas was undeniably funny, a quality that had first drawn her to him. His humor was not merely the playful teasing or the occasional joke but a deeply embedded facet of his personality, a spontaneous charm that seemed to light up every room he entered. His mind worked in brilliant, unpredictable ways, weaving wit into everyday conversations, turning mundane moments into bursts of laughter. It was this blend of quick humor and sharp intellect that made her fall so effortlessly in love with him.

At home, Thomas rarely indulged in pranks, but she had heard enough stories to know he had a mischievous streak. To her, he was more than a jokester; he was her partner in laughter, a source of endless amusement and comfort. His humor was not the kind that sought attention but rather a genuine reflection of his playful nature. He had a childlike sense of wonder that never ceased to amaze her.

It was this same quality that made him an extraordinary teacher. In the classroom, Thomas transformed learning into an adventure, captivating his students with his unique ability to make even the most complex subjects accessible and enjoyable. He had a knack for speaking their language, breaking down barriers with humor and empathy, making every child feel seen and valued. To his students, he wasn't just a teacher; he was a hero, a role model who showed them that intelligence could be as cool as any trend. His lessons lingered long after the bell rang, leaving an indelible mark on the young minds he nurtured.

Ilma stood at the door and stared into the bathroom, taking in the features she had yet to notice. She had been so impressed with the hallway bathroom next to the library she had only used their attached bathroom to brush her teeth.

The small half bath downstairs was tucked away in the alcove between Will's room and the library, serving as a discreet retreat on the main floor. Unlike the grandiosity of the rest of the house, this space was compact but exuded an unexpectedly calming ambiance. The walls were a mesmerizing canvas of bluish-green hues, sponge-painted to create a textured effect that mimicked the shifting shades of the ocean. Soft, undulating lights cast wave-like movements across the walls, conjuring the serene illusion of sunlight dancing on a pool's surface. It felt as though one had stepped into a secret underwater sanctuary, secluded and tranquil.

Above the white pedestal sink hung a simple oval mirror, its clean design subtly enhancing the room's elegance. A single bar of seafoam-colored soap rested on the sink's edge, its fresh scent mingling with the faint aroma of eucalyptus, creating an invigorating yet soothing atmosphere.

The toilet, stark white and gleaming under the soft light, stood out as a marvel of modern luxury. Its sleek, futuristic design was anything but simple, and the array of digital buttons along its side hinted at functionalities far beyond the ordinary. Ilma approached it with a mixture of curiosity and trepidation, her fingers hesitating over the unfamiliar controls. Her apprehension melted into fascination as she discovered the bidet function, its gentle precision winning her over in an instant. She made a silent vow to acquire one of her own someday, her imagination already spinning with the possibilities, if only she could afford such an indulgence.

Finally giving her own bathroom a chance, Ilma discovered that her shower was nearly as enchanting as the high-tech toilet downstairs. The shower stretched along the entire wall, a luxurious space as expansive as her entire bathroom at home. She marveled at the external control panel that allowed her to set the water temperature without stepping inside. Just beyond the glass door, another set of matching controls awaited, ready to cater to her every whim. Ilma had never thought of reaching into a shower to adjust the water temperature as a significant inconvenience, but evidently, someone had designed this haven to eliminate even the slightest discomfort.

As she activated the square rain shower head embedded in the ceiling, water cascaded down in a soothing torrent, echoing the gentle pitter-patter of a spring rain. The sound alone was a balm to her senses, reminiscent of cozy afternoons spent with a good book on rainy days.

She hadn't even dared to dream of the aromatherapy options now at her fingertips. With a touch, she selected *lavender*, only to quickly switch to *citrus burst*, fearing the former might lull her into a sleepy haze. The room filled with a vibrant, invigorating scent, lifting her spirits and invigorating her senses.

Ilma's pajama bottoms, adorned with cartoons of sleeping sloths, pooled at her feet. She stepped out of her underwear and pulled off her tank top, her anticipation mounting as she opened the shower door. There, another marvel awaited—wall sprayers lined the shower, each nozzle adjustable to customizable pressure, pattern, and pulse. She adjusted the settings, feeling the power at her command, lowering the temperature slightly with a few taps on the control panel.

A warmth began to bloom under her feet, the tingly feeling running up her lower legs. Not even the bidet had excited her this much. She bent over to toss her clothes to the side and noticed it was the floor warming her feet. But as she moved to step into the shower, after much anticipation, a flicker of unease crept in. Her eyes caught her reflection in the mirror, and she felt a sudden, inexplicable sense of exposure, as though unseen eyes were watching her every move. The sensation was fleeting, but enough to make her fold her arms across her chest, her hand instinctively covering the most intimate part of herself. She knew it was irrational—there was no one there, just her and her reflection—but the feeling clung to her like a shadow.

Remembering Thomas's offhand comment about hidden ways to traverse the house, her mind conjured images of secret passages leading to unknown realms. The thought was both thrilling and unsettling. She smiled at her own folly but couldn't shake the goosebumps that rose on her arms. Perhaps it was just her imagination, but for a moment, she felt like a character in one of her beloved fantasy novels, on the cusp of a grand, magical adventure.

The alternative, of course, was more time spent engaging with Thomas's family. Weighing the options, she decided she would rather take her chances with imaginary eyes from another world than face the awkward reality of familial small talk. With a deep breath, she stepped into the sanctuary of the shower, letting the cascading water wash away her lingering doubts.

After luxuriating in a long shower and taking her time blow-drying her hair, Ilma finally resigned herself to the inevitable: she had to head downstairs and face the family. The scent of invigorating citrus still clung to her, a lingering pop from the aromatherapy that had brightened her spirits. As she descended the grand, sweeping staircase, her steps lightened, bolstered by the cheerful murmur of voices emanating from the kitchen below. The warm, inviting sounds mingled with the soft sunlight filtering through the tall windows, casting a golden glow over the polished wooden railings.

She reached the threshold of the kitchen, pausing for a moment as she heard bursts of laughter and the clinking of dishes. The scene she walked into was a tableau of domestic ease; Will and April perched on barstools, their coffee mugs steaming gently as they observed the antics of Sean, Jonah, and Thomas. The three brothers, still bearing the battle scars of a night poorly slept—dark circles under their eyes and pillow creases etched into their faces—were devouring pastries and fruit with a ravenous fervor.

Ilma couldn't help but smile at their disheveled state. "Help yourself," Will called out from across the room, his tone as easy and unassuming as ever.

"I'm afraid I'd lose a finger," Ilma quipped, her voice deadpan but her eyes sparkling with mischief.

The room stilled for a moment, as though the air itself held its breath. Then, the three brothers froze, exchanging wide-eyed glances before erupting into a chorus of laughter that filled the kitchen with an infectious, almost childlike joy.

"Good one, Ilma," April giggled, wiping a drop of spilled coffee from her bare leg with a napkin, her eyes crinkling at the corners with genuine amusement.

"Where's Crystal?" Ilma asked, her gaze sweeping the room.

"She's out at the pool, soaking up the rays," Jonah managed between mouthfuls of food, crumbs dotting the corners of his mouth.

Will, ever the considerate one, brought a plate to Ilma, setting it down gently on the counter in front of her. "I've got extra," he said, his voice low and kind. "You don't need to wrestle those guys for your breakfast."

The contrast between Will's thoughtful demeanor and the unruly behavior of the others was striking. Ilma found herself drawn to his quiet kindness, a balm to the playful chaos surrounding them. She ate slowly, her eyes flicking over to Jonah and Sean, who were half-heartedly pretending to help Will tidy up.

A flicker of irritation stirred within her as she noticed Thomas's absence. He had bolted off to shower, leaving Will to shoulder the burden of cleaning up. Ilma made a mental note, her brow furrowing slightly as she resolved to remind Thomas to pitch in after dinner. This was his family's vacation, after all, and he should take part in more than just the leisure.

As she chewed thoughtfully, the laughter continued to ripple through the room, but Ilma couldn't shake the simmering annoyance. She watched the scene unfold, the undercurrent of her discontent adding a subtle tension to the otherwise light-hearted moment.

Chapter Nineteen

The Burn

Crystal dipped a tentative toe into the pool, the cool water sending a shiver up her spine. The late morning sun shone brightly overhead, but the warmth had yet to fully heat the pool. She sighed deeply, her breath mingling with the gentle ripple of the pool's surface. Walking on her tiptoes, she made her way to the hot tub, savoring the stillness of the morning. It was early for a swim, which was precisely why she wanted this moment alone—to float undisturbed, free from the chaotic splashes of cannonballs or the errant throws of a football between Sean and April. She longed for the soothing sound of water cascading from the hot tub into the pool, a peaceful lullaby that drowned out the world.

Reaching the hot tub, she stepped gracefully onto the top step, both feet sinking into the inviting warmth. A sharp squeal escaped her lips as the heat seared her skin, far hotter than she had anticipated. Stumbling back with far less grace, she hopped out, her feet smarting from the scalding water. The skin below her ankles glowed an angry red, the sting intensifying with every heartbeat. Quickly, she seated herself on the pool's edge, plunging her feet into the cool embrace of the pool water, a relief that was almost euphoric.

As the chill enveloped her toes, Crystal reflected on her miscalculation. The hot tub's heat had been overwhelming, perhaps because she hadn't acclimatized her body by dipping into the pool first. She had always found the interplay between hot and cold to be jarring yet fascinating, a dance of extremes that heightened her senses. Slowly, inch by inch, she lowered herself into the shallow end of the pool, her body recoiling from the temperature shock. Goosebumps erupted across her skin, the air against her wet flesh intensifying the cold. Her teeth chattered softly as she braced against the discomfort, her body reluctantly adjusting to the water's embrace.

She allowed herself a few minutes to adapt, moving slowly around the pool's perimeter. Her mind drifted back to the tour with Isabella, the caretaker who had thoroughly explained every feature of the island's amenities. There was so much to take in, so many luxuries to explore. Crystal admired the high-quality synthetic wood furniture, each piece adorned with vibrant cushions in shades of blue, teal, and white, accented by whimsical pillows shaped like sea turtles and crabs. Despite her initial disdain for the synthetic material, Isabella's detailed explanation of its practicality and expense had impressed upon her its worth.

Crystal's gaze traveled to the retractable awning extending from the patio and the elegant umbrellas casting scalloped shadows on the pool deck. She briefly wondered if Isabella had mentioned storm precautions; retracting the awning, tying down chairs, or stowing cushions, but the with the sun burning off the morning haze, she hoped The Gold Book wouldn't need addressing. She remembered Isabella mentioning streams of water shooting upward from hidden jets in the pool corners, promising an evening of synchronized light and music. She made a mental note to explore the controls later. Yet another item to research later.

As she rounded the corner where an outdoor bar loomed just steps away from the pool ledge. She imagined the delicious meals Billy would prepare with the extensive grilling setup, her mouth watering at the thought of perfectly grilled steaks. Yet, amid the luxury, she found herself wishing for a swim-up bar, where his bartending skills could shine as much as his cooking.

The vibrant flora surrounding the patio under the pagoda was almost surreal, the riot of colors bursting from the planters like a painter's palette come to life. As Crystal returned to the cascading waterfall of the hot tub, she felt a pang of unease. She angled back towards the shallow end, seeking the solace of a bright pink raft floating nearby. Gently pulling it closer, she eased herself onto it, careful not to splash.

The raft dipped unexpectedly, and she shivered anew as her body adjusted. Her fingers brushed the cool water as she adjusted her swimsuit and hair, settling into a pose that was both comfortable and camera-ready. Crystal half-hoped someone would emerge to snap a picture for social media, capturing this perfect moment of leisure.

The sun blazed overhead as it reached it's peak, even behind her sunglasses, and she longed for a passing cloud to temper its glare. As she admired the playful reflection of sunlight off the pool onto the awning, a sudden tension crept into her limbs. The soothing water sounds reminded her of the noises she'd heard the previous night—a faint scuffling on her terrace, almost like a person moving stealthily.

Her pulse quickened, the memory now vivid and unsettling. She had brushed it off, attributing it to her imagination, dulled by sleep aids. But the sensation of being watched resurfaced, her mind racing with questions. Was there truly no one else on the island? Had the caretakers been less than forthcoming? She was accustomed to blocking out *the help*, but did not want to be surprised by their unexpected presence.

A sound—a scuff, faint but undeniable—snapped her out of her thoughts. Her heart pounded as she tried to open her eyes against the sun's glare. Just then, a cloud drifted over, casting a much-needed shadow. But when she opened her eyes fully, it wasn't a cloud that blocked her view.

It was a person, standing mere inches away, their face obscured by the blinding sunlight but unmistakably close, too close.

CHAPTER TWENTY

The Body

The lemon ricotta Danish nearly lodged in Ilma's throat when a blood-curdling scream echoed through the house. After a few quick coughs and forceful throat clearing, she ran behind the others through the great room and out to the backyard. She found herself standing on the pool patio behind April, Sean, and Will vying for the source of the cry.

Ilma peeked through the group and saw a nude blond woman floating face down in the pool. "Crystal!" Ilma gasped and pushed through the crowd, confused as to why no one was moving in to help.

Standing in waist-deep water directly next to the limp body was an uncharacteristically unkempt version of Crystal with her long platinum hair plastered across her face. A calming hand rested on Ilma's shoulder, and she turned abruptly back and forth, looking between the unmoving and seemingly unfazed group behind her and the two blond women in the pool.

It was only then that she noticed behind the Crystals, just outside the pool ledge, stood Thomas gasping for breath, not with panic but with laughter. He doubled over with his hands on his knees for a moment before reaching out into the pool and grabbing the face-down body by the foot and effortlessly pulling her out of the pool.

"Laugh it up, guys," Crystal said as she ran her fingers through her hair, trying to compose herself. "I could've drowned!"

Thomas tossed what Ilma only just realized was one of the mannequins from Will's room onto a lounge chair behind him and continued to laugh.

"*Dolly* was just trying to get a look at you. I didn't realize you would fall off your raft and scream bloody murder."

Ilma watched as Jonah stepped outside, following all the action making her wonder if he was in on the joke.

"Well, now that you're all out here, let's have a pool party," Crystal shouted like a Spring Break DJ.

Jonah worked on getting the music piped out to the pool speakers as April and Sean scurried inside to change into their swimsuits.

"Hey, Thomas," Crystal shouted. "Thanks to you, I need to pull my hair back. Where is that damn scarf you used on the Hippo?"

"I thought you took it back?" Thomas laughed. "I couldn't find it when I put the stuffed animals back in Sean and April's room."

"April," Crystal called out, snapping her fingers twice quickly as if she was summoning a servant. "Did you borrow my scarf?"

Her tone was both accusing and condescending.

"Does she look like the kind of woman who would wear a *scarf*?" Ilma answered dryly in April's absence.

While most of the group had moved on from surprise to party mode, Billy was left standing poolside with Ilma, still looking on in shock.

"Billy!" Crystal called over as she climbed back onto the raft. "How about you whip us up some daiquiris?" Ilma watched as Will turned abruptly toward the house, and she caught a glimpse of a dismissive eye roll. She would probably be irritated, too, if someone ordered her to make drinks right after an entire morning of preparing breakfast. Ilma may be unable to afford regular vacations, but she was no one's servant either. Like Thomas, Crystal didn't seem to notice that Will was the only one doing any work around the house. She had no hired cleaning crew or chef but was content relaxing and letting someone else carry the load.

Ilma had heard stories about Crystal and Jonah's wedding from Thomas and the others. They were young when they wed and didn't yet have their fortune. But Crystal wanted her fairy tale wedding, so a fairy tale wedding she would have, even if that meant skimping elsewhere. Her dress made her look like a princess with a train that dragged down the entire aisle of the church. The flower arrangements at the church and then later at the reception were huge, overflowing with giant, white hydrangeas and lilies and draped with faux pearls. Though the wedding looked grand and majestic, the guests did all the work. In addition to being the best man, Thomas was also the DJ. Groomsmen Sean and Will were in charge of photography and video. Crystal's parents rounded up guests to cook dinner and serve the bride and groom. She even tasked her maid of honor to tend the cash bar.

Crystal was a woman of exquisite taste, and that taste only grew as the couple accumulated more money. But from what Ilma had inferred from passing family conversations, she had no problem getting what she wanted off the backs of others.

Ilma stared at Crystal as her perfect body floated on the sparkling water, and despite her bitter feelings and callused assumptions about the woman, Ilma wanted her approval. She wanted to be one of those people that Crystal asked for help. How could she be drawn to someone so different from herself?

When she and Thomas were first engaged, Ilma had the overwhelming task of meeting the entire family on a video call. The brothers were all kind and welcoming, but all Crystal wanted to talk about was throwing her a lavish bridal shower followed by a wild bachelorette party. The gesture was both thoughtful and selfish. Her ideas jibed more with Crystal's ideas of a good time than Ilma's. Crystal made her disappointment well known after Ilma announced to the entire group that the couple planned to have a small wedding in the quaint beach town of Masonboro, North Carolina. It was the place where they had made their home, and with the exception of the rare murder of a stay-at-home mom the previous year, the town was perfect; great weather year-round, beautiful beaches, and good schools. Apparently, Crystal had been holding out hope that someone in the family would have a destination wedding, or at least a destination more exotic than Masonboro.

As if to further unsettle Crystal, neither Ilma nor Thomas wanted a traditional bridal shower or any wedding gifts. Instead, they desired only the presence of their loved ones for a day or weekend, sharing in the simplicity of the moment. Their modest plans reflected their humble nature, eschewing grandeur for genuine connections.

Ilma and Thomas had initially dreamed of hosting a full dinner with drinks for their reception. Yet, constrained by their limited finances, they settled on a humble lunch. The ceremony took place on a secluded beach, basking in the gentle warmth of a 70-degree March day. The ocean's rhythmic whispers and the salt-kissed breeze painted a serene backdrop for their vows.

The only open restaurant in the off-season was a local dive, notorious for its casual disregard for reservations. However, a special exception was made, the owner reserving the entire outdoor patio for the wedding party, all because his son admired Thomas as his favorite teacher. It was a gesture of community and respect, transforming the ordinary into the extraordinary for the newlyweds.

The day unfolded with an effortless charm, each moment etched in the laughter and smiles of Thomas's family as they embraced Ilma warmly. Yet, even though Ilma remembered their wedding as a day of simplicity and sincerity, perfectly mirroring the couple's character, something in her ached for more.

Maybe she felt drawn toward Crystal because a part of her wondered what it would be like to live her life. To live in a two-story apartment across from Central Park, have important and wealthy friends who could pull strings when needed, to be able to host a luxurious family weekend on a private island...but it was no more far-fetched than every little girl's dream to marry a prince and live in a castle. Sure, it sounds fun, but realistically it would never happen. At least not to her... a librarian in a small beach town. Thomas wasn't a prince and didn't live in a castle, but he was her knight in shining armor. He treated her like a princess and embraced her differences that repelled other men. The men who wanted an arm candy wife who would flirt and converse with his coworkers found her debilitatingly shy and hermit-like. Thomas, however, happily listened to podcasts through headphones while Ilma read her book beside him on the couch. He had no desire to change who she was.

Although Crystal had treated Ilma with nothing but kindness and generosity, Ilma's opinion of her was still based mainly on the assumptions she made from hearing other people's stories. It wasn't fair to judge someone so harshly, but first impressions can be tainted by rumors.

Listening intently to the lighthearted chatter of the visitors as they made their way out to the pool, The Unwelcome Guest felt the oppressive weight of the dainty scarf stuffed hastily into his pocket. The fabric's softness belied the sharp pangs of panic, the terror of discovery nearly unbearable. The circumstances of how he came to possess the scarf only amplified his dread.

Earlier, navigating the labyrinthine passages with the practiced ease of someone accustomed to moving unseen, he felt invulnerable, cloaked by the shadows and the secrets these walls harbored. No one suspected his presence; he was merely a phantom, a whisper behind the walls.

But then, in the dim light cast by the flickering floor lamps, his confidence wavered. Just behind the hidden door camouflaged within the succulent wall of The Runner's room, he spotted the scarf, delicate and out of place, resting on the ground like a ghostly reminder of a breach. He hesitated, his breath shallow, his instincts screaming at him to retreat. Yet, he knew instantly to whom it belonged—it could only be The Supermodel's, an unmistakable blend of elegance and carelessness.

This scarf hadn't been here long; he had walked these halls recently and would not have missed it sitting there out in the open, so it wasn't a remnant from a previous guest. And as The Runner had implied moments ago, neither she nor The Bookworm would be caught dead wearing such an accessory. Slowly, deliberately, The Unwelcome Guest crouched down, the polished wood cool under his fingertips as he reached for the scarf. His movements, though more confident from repeated excursions through the hidden corridors, were still deliberate, every creak of the floors beneath him a potential betrayal. He strained to suppress the mounting dread, knowing that every second he lingered, every sound he made, brought him closer to the brink of discovery.

The Unwelcome Guest fingered the scarf between his thumb and pointer fingers, rubbing back and forth, feeling the incredibly small threads wound together to make the silky soft fabric. He stared down at the scarf in his hand and thought of it as The Supermodel's skin. Both were soft and flawless, the lighting reflecting off the movement of the scarf the way the sun bounced off the curves of her body.

He was eager to pull it close, to rub it on his naked body, but the suspense was arousing. Torturing himself, he inched it closer, and closer until it was right under his nose. He let every last bit of breath go before holding it close and inhaling deeply.

Yes, it was hers. He knew the smell. He would never forget it.

He stood up suddenly, nearly hitting his head on a sconce perched on the wall. *How did the scarf get behind the walls?*

Had The Supermodel found the hidden doors, or was it someone else? Either way, he had to be more cautious. His sanctuary was no longer his alone.

CHAPTER TWENTY-ONE
The Bartender

April bounded down the stairs, her swimsuit hugging her athletic frame like a beach volleyball uniform, with a snug sports bra-style top and tiny bottoms that accentuated her toned legs and perky glutes. Each step was brisk, a testament to her boundless energy and the ease with which she moved. It was almost second nature for her to jog when walking would suffice, as if her body couldn't bear the thought of slowing down. She often marveled at the contrast between her own hurried pace and Crystal's deliberate, languid strut.

Crystal's movements were a study in elegance, her slow and sultry model walk turning even the simplest act of descending stairs into an art form. April could almost picture her now, each step measured, every motion deliberate, taking minutes to descend what she herself had covered in mere seconds. It was as if Crystal's every entrance was choreographed for maximum impact, a stark difference from April's pragmatic haste.

April smiled at the thought. The three wives couldn't be more different, but she had a soft spot for them both.

As she cut through the great room, she saw Will in the kitchen prepping a tray of fruity drinks with umbrellas and fresh fruit. April hurried over to help.

"Hey, thanks. Actually, if you could just grab some beers for the guys, that would really help," Will said as he expertly lofted the tray into the palm of his hand.

"Wow, Will. You continue to outdo yourself. Those drinks are so cute!" April commented with her head in the giant refrigerator.

She grabbed two frosty beers in each hand, the chill seeping into her fingers as she deftly popped off the caps with a quick, practiced motion. The soft hiss of escaping carbonation whispered promises of refreshment. Balancing the bottles with care, she trailed after Will, her bare feet padding lightly on the cool stone floor as they headed out to the sun-drenched pool.

Unspoken, she harbored a secret longing for one of those beers herself, craving the simplicity of the cold brew over the intricately crafted cocktails Will had painstakingly prepared. Yet, she kept that thought to herself, not wanting to diminish his effort or the care he had put into assembling the colorful, umbrella-adorned drinks. They were a testament to his thoughtfulness, and she didn't want to let on that, after all that work, she still preferred something as basic as a beer.

Besides, juggling four open bottles was already testing the limits of her dexterity. Attempting a fifth might've been pushing her luck—unless, of course, she resorted to using her mouth, an image that made her stifle a chuckle.

Crystal slid her oversized sunglasses down her nose, their reflective lenses catching the sunlight as she peered over the top at April and Will descending the stone steps toward the pool. A grin spread across her face, her excitement bubbling over as she shouted, "Oh my gosh, yes, Billy! That is exactly what we need!" Her voice was loud enough to ripple across the water, and her sudden enthusiasm nearly toppled her off the inflatable raft, the edges dipping precariously under her weight.

With a playful flick of her wrist, she paddled lazily toward the pool's edge, her other arm stretched high, fingers wiggling in anticipation. Her bright, manicured nails caught the sunlight, sparkling as she waited for her drink to be delivered.

Will, ever the gentleman, balanced the tray with practiced ease, selecting a glass with precision. As he approached, he dipped into a slow, exaggerated bow, carefully placing the cocktail into Crystal's outstretched hand. The gesture was both playful and refined, the kind of theatricality that brought a spark of joy to the scene.

"Ah-ma-zing!" Crystal sang out after a long pull on the little cocktail straw.

April strolled over to the side of the pool, where the three brothers sat shoulder to shoulder on the edge, their legs swinging lazily in the water, creating gentle ripples that shimmered under the afternoon sun. Their voices rose and fell in animated bursts, punctuated by the occasional chuckle or groan as they debated the merits of their fantasy baseball teams.

She approached quietly, not wanting to break the intensity of their discussion. The beers, cold and slick with condensation, rested comfortably in her hands. As she handed each brother a bottle, she noticed their eyes remained locked on each other, the conversation flowing uninterrupted.

The scene was a perfect blend of competition and camaraderie, the bonds of brotherhood evident in their shared passion. April smiled softly, appreciating the moment before retreating a few steps, allowing them to continue their spirited debate.

April brought the remaining beer bottle to Will, who stood silently over Ilma, who was so deep into her novel that she didn't notice him standing next to her patch of shade under the umbrella. He placed the tray on a side table between the lounge chairs and swapped drinks with April. The two lifted their cocktails to each other.

"Cheers," they said together before turning and taking in the scene before them.

Ilma moaned quietly saying something in Punjabi.

April turned to find that Ilma had taken a break from her book and was thoroughly enjoying her drink. Glancing up at Will, hoping to see a look of pride, April was surprised to find him eyeing his brothers at the edge of the pool. A brief look of longing crossed his face that made April shift uncomfortably. The poor guy was playing bartender while the rest of the crew was on vacation.

It only took one cannonball from Sean for Crystal to strut her sassy ass out of the pool and over to the lounge chairs. She pulled a towel off the back of an empty chair and laid it out over the seat before lowering herself and kicking up her feet.

"Amazing, Will. Thank you," April said after taking a sip.

"My pleasure, ladies. I made an extra batch and stored it in the freezer if you ever want to treat yourself to more. I also left some sliced pineapples, cherries, and little umbrellas for you to make the experience complete."

Sean deftly swam to the side of the pool, grabbed his beer and hoisted it in the air. "To the Four Horsemen!"

Will smiled like a child on Christmas before tossing his empty drink tray and running the ten or so steps to the pool, launching off the side, and splashing his brothers.

April was relieved to see Will finally enjoying himself. He had been taking his responsibilities too seriously, acting more like a servant than a guest. But when it came to his older brothers, he never complained—they could do no wrong in his eyes. Despite being at different stages in life, their bond remained unbreakable, and April couldn't help but feel a tinge of jealousy.

For as long as she had been part of the family, Will had been more than just a brother-in-law to April—he was her buddy, her partner in mischief. In her early twenties, she found a kindred spirit in the younger, carefree Will, whose enthusiasm for life mirrored her own, unlike the older Jonah and Thomas, who seemed perpetually consumed by their work. While they immersed themselves in the weighty topics of adult responsibilities, April and Sean would lose themselves in spirited discussions with Will about sports highlights and the latest pop culture trends.

At the beach, while Crystal reclined luxuriously under the shade of an umbrella, soaking up the heat of the sun without the harmful UV rays, Will and April would launch impromptu football games, their laughter rising above the sound of crashing waves.

Their shared creativity shone through during an LA visit when Will was in culinary school. The beach, with its endless horizon, became their playground. They'd forgotten the paddle ball paddles, but they weren't about to let that spoil their fun. With Sean flexing among the muscle beach crowd, April and Will dug shallow holes in the sand, roughly ten feet apart, and devised a game—Bowl Goal. It was an inventive mix of cornhole and bowling, where precision and flair combined in every roll of the small rubber ball as it hopped over the footprint pocked sand.

As the sun beat down on them, they perfected their rolls, cheering and groaning with each near miss and triumphant score. The friendly competition evolved into a showcase of trick shots—three-point tosses requiring pinpoint accuracy, or playful snaps of the ball through their legs like seasoned quarterbacks. Their antics drew a curious crowd, onlookers charmed by their infectious joy and the sheer absurdity of their invented game.

That's who Will was to her, always—her buddy, her playmate, the one who could turn any moment into a memorable adventure.

The last day of watching him spend most of his time in the kitchen made her sad. He was doing what he loved, and she could tell he wanted to show off his new culinary skills, but until he jumped in the pool, she hadn't seen him do a thing to entertain himself.

Without taking another sip, April sat her drink down on the side table, grabbed the volleyball from under her lounge chair, and jumped in the pool.

CHAPTER TWENTY-TWO
The Escape (Figurative)

The afternoon of hours upon hours of countless drinks left the group in the mood to continue the party. Except for Ilma. The one drink she nursed way past the phase change from semi-solid to slush and finally to the watered-down liquid left her tired and eager to have some quiet time. Maybe she should've kept drinking like everyone else, but there was no way she would catch up now. Crystal had moved on to shots while April and the guys drank beer. Ilma knew she couldn't handle straight liquor and hated beer. The daiquiris were delicious but the sweetness made her mouth go dry. She had no idea how many beers Thomas had but was surprised that he seemed totally sober when he approached her after everyone else filed back into the house to head for the game room.

"How would you like to take this party down a notch?" Thomas asked, bending over to plant a gentle kiss on her forehead. "I'm thinking the two of us should go downstairs, browse the movie selection and curl up with some popcorn while these knuckleheads party on."

"You know me so well," Ilma smiled up at him, freshly invigorated by the thought of not having to come up with an excuse to get out of late-night partying.

"You go on down and pick out a movie. I'll grab some water from the kitchen, then come down to get the popcorn machine going. From the look of everyone else, it may be a liquid dinner." He turned and walked back inside, letting their hands drop from one another in slow motion.

Butterflies tickled her insides as she watched him walk away.

By the time Ilma changed into her cozy sweats and made it down to the movie room, loud music blaring from the game room filled the basement. She slipped into the soundproof room and closed the door. The seemingly normal-looking door completely filtered out the bass of the music, the clacking of pool balls, the booming voices, and tipsy laughter.

She dragged her hand over the popcorn maker switching the power on. She had no idea how to work it, but she may as well get the system heated up. How hard could it be to work a popcorn machine? From the look of things, the prepared popcorn kits had everything she needed. All she had to do was warm it up and dump the pack into the popper.

Ilma took a deep breath and released it, thankful that April wasn't in the room to look over her shoulder. Somewhere along the line, April, being mechanically inclined, began to think of Ilma as technically challenged and clumsy. April may be able to take apart and reassemble the mechanical pool cleaner, but Ilma could read the manual and know everything about the machine from top to bottom.

She thought it stemmed from her wedding when April learned of her food allergies and spoke of them as if they made her less of a person. At the lunch following the wedding, despite the event not being an open bar, April over-imbibed. She quoted ridiculous study after offensive report about how the increase of allergies in the latest generation was due to poor nutrition.

She said, "Children in the last two decades have far more food allergies than those born before the new century. The increase of processed food in our diet as a society, as well as the processed chemicals we feed to the animals we consume, have contributed to the rising number of childhood allergies. It was proven in a study."

As if any *study* ever proved one side of a debate without question. Her *study* didn't account for the children born with a milk allergy or toddlers raised on organic food who developed peanut allergies. Thomas had argued this point to April, defending his new wife.

"The problem is that everything is tainted now. Even the so-called organic grains, fruits, and vegetables have been touched by water sources that have been polluted with undetectable forever chemicals. You can't test for something you don't even know is there?" April grew more and more passionate as the conversation continued.

Ilma kept quiet at the time, keeping her opinions to herself. However, she wondered if April ever considered what chemicals were in her protein shakes, what water source treated her kale, and what impact vodka had on her body.

When Thomas had attempted to change the subject to the new bikes they bought for themselves as a wedding present, April was surprised that Ilma could ride a bike at all.

To protect the house and defend her reputation, she had to follow the simple directions of making popcorn to a T.

The popcorn began cooking and started to pop so she felt good about taking her eyes off the machine for a minute or so. Grabbing a tablet off one of the front recliners, Ilma sat down and swiped her hand across the screen to wake it up. The screen lit up with a catalog of movies. There had to be thousands of movie titles. She narrowed down the filter to a few of her favorite genres. She loved how 80's movies made her feel nostalgic for a time she didn't even live through. She related to GenX kids way more than she did to other millennials. She yearned for the good ole days of playing outside until her mom called her in for supper and summers of exploring the neighborhood rather than staying inside on video games. Unlike most 30-somethings, most of her childhood was spent with her nose in a book, but she imagined that if she grew up in the 80's, she would have been more adventurous.

A scratching noise sounded from the door. It reminded her of when her parents' dog would scratch to come into the room, but there were no dogs in the house.

"Thomas?" Ilma called out, not even thinking that it was very unlikely that someone could hear her on the other side of that door. Maybe Thomas had his hands full and needed the door opened, so she put the iPad down and walked to the door. There was the sucking sound of a broken vacuum seal as she pushed open the door to the hallway.

The noise from the activity in the game room filled her ears, but no one was in the hall. She looked back and forth, preparing herself for a stuffed panther or some other out-of-place animal seeking revenge on Thomas, but there was nothing and no one there. As she backed into the room, once again closing the door, she heard a door slam from inside.

She turned abruptly, her heart beating through her chest surveying the room. No one was there. Nothing was out of place. Well, except for the screen hanging on the wall, which was swaying just slightly. Getting her wits about her, Ilma walked over to the movie screen and bravely peeked behind it.

There was a door.

It was the same color and texture as the rest of the walls in the room, but Ilma knew a secret door when she saw one. It was meant to look like the rest of the wall, but the cracks giving away the door were covered up by the screen, hence keeping it hidden. There was no door knob or pull bar making her think it was more of a construction error being hidden rather than a door to another world.

Just when she was about to slip behind the curtain to get a closer look, she paused.

What if it really was a door? Was that how Thomas was sneaking around? Were there other doors that were camouflaged one way or another? Or was it another toy collection that her eyes were not meant to see?

Another loud noise echoed through the room, and her ears popped.

"Movie time!" Thomas sang out as he walked into the room, pulling the door to the hallway closed with his foot.

"You scared me!" Ilma yelled back.

"Were you expecting someone else?" Thomas asked with a coy smile.

Ilma took a deep breath and removed her hand from her chest while Thomas grabbed some popcorn. "What do you think about a good 80's movie?"

"Totally," Thomas laughed at his own cheesy attempt at slang and sat in the middle row, patting the chair beside him.

A couple of hours later, as the pirate ship filled with treasure sailed away into the sunset, Ilma turned to find Thomas sound asleep. He looked peaceful yet uncomfortable, tilting his head at an unnatural angle. She straightened his head and laid it back on the headrest before clicking the off button on the tablet and picking up the popcorn remnants.

The owners of the house thought of everything a guest would need to have a memorable vacation except one thing. There was no trash can in the movie room.

Ilma grabbed the paper sleeves they had eaten their popcorn out of and walked over to the door. But, when she pushed on the door, it wouldn't open. She raised the lights just enough to see if something tricky about the knob would make it difficult to open the door. She turned the knob again, pushing harder this time, but the door didn't budge.

Thomas stirred, "What's all the banging?"

"Oh. Sorry to wake you. I can't get the door open."

Thomas stood and puffed out his chest as he walked over to Ilma, casually flipping the popcorn machine off as he passed. "Do you need some assistance, little lady?"

She giggled and moved to the side so he could access the door fully.

As expected, the door didn't open for Thomas either. He reached for his back pocket, where he usually kept his cell phone, before realizing it wasn't there. When they realized there was no service on the island, they had left their phones off and in their room.

Suddenly more frantic than before, Thomas pounded on the door.

"Hey! Not funny, guys. Come unlock the door!"

Ilma looked down at the doorknob, then turned to Thomas, "It looks like the door locks from the inside."

More door banging, "Hey! Open the door!"

She had never heard him so angry. Or was he scared?

"Let's just put on another movie. This room is completely soundproofed. They can't hear the banging. Obviously, someone knows we are in here and will let us out eventually," Ilma shrugged at her failed attempt at optimism. She had *no* faith in Thomas' family seeking them out, even the next morning. Sean and April would be hustling to get their work out, Crystal would be having a soak or relaxing by the pool, and Jonah would do whatever it is that Jonah does. She took a deep breath and forced down her feelings of resentment for Thomas' sake.

The two cuddled back up in their recliners while Ilma browsed the movie catalog again. Despite his sudden outburst, Thomas fell back to sleep before she even pulled up another selection.

Ilma yawned and set the tablet down, opting to at least try to get some sleep. She reached over to her cup holder to get a sip of water from the water bottle, but it wasn't there. Sitting up, straighter, confused, she looked over to the cup holder next to Thomas. It was also empty.

Knowing that two bottles of water couldn't have disappeared from inside a locked room, she leaned back, feeling too tired to search anymore.

CHAPTER TWENTY-THREE

The Hangover

Crystal slowly blinked her eyes open, the searing glare of the basement's fluorescent lights stabbing at her retinas like needles of pure sunlight. Every inch of her body ached as she shifted her stiff limbs, the lumpy cushions of the game room couch offering little solace. Her arms, numb from the awkward position, tingled with pins and needles as she struggled to sit up. The blinking stoplights above the bar flickered like taunting sentinels, and the garish neon beer signs cast distorted shadows that seemed to dance mockingly along the walls. She squinted, wincing at the sharpness of it all, a groan escaping her lips.

She turned her head, and there he was—Jonah. Sprawled out across the couch like a king in repose, his face serene, oblivious to the discomfort she had endured. His rhythmic breathing filled the room, a stark contrast to the thumping music still playing on loop, courtesy of their late-night revelry. It seemed everyone else had retreated to the comfort of their beds, neglecting to spare her the courtesy of dimming the lights or silencing the racket.

Crystal rubbed her temples and took a deep breath, trying to shake the remnants of sleep. As she slowly assessed herself, she let out a sigh of relief. Her hair was still intact, her clothes were unruffled, and there wasn't a single marker scribble on her face, much to her gratitude. Her reflection in the mirror above the bar confirmed her assumptions—Thomas, for all his playful antics, was no match for her ruthless college sorority sisters. He might drag out an embarrassing home video, but he wouldn't stoop to the level of their humiliating pranks.

Thomas and Ilma had wisely avoided their game of "Never Have I Ever," leaving her to battle her demons alone. That game, her ultimate nemesis, had dismantled her one secret at a time. She recalled the previous night's admissions with a shudder—skinny dipping, nude beaches, streaking. Each confession had tumbled from her lips under the haze of alcohol, a cascade of unclothed indiscretions laid bare before her husband's family. The memory made her cheeks flush with mortification. *What had she done?* She buried her face in her hands, wishing she could rewind the night or, at the very least, disappear into the worn couch cushions beneath her.

She vaguely remembered telling everyone from her sprawled-out position on the couch that she was sure one of the other guys had snuck in to massage her before Jonah arrived. At first, they laughed, thinking she was making a joke, but when she mentioned that she thought someone was watching her sleep, they chalked it up to the booze.

Crystal hadn't allowed herself to challenge her own thoughts and concerns, and she couldn't believe she had voiced them out loud. Yes, Jonah's massage seemed remarkably different when he returned to the room, but he was most likely horny. Maybe it was Jonah staring at her while she slept.

Bringing her fingers up to rub her temples, she wondered if that was what she did remember; how much didn't she remember?

Empty beer bottles, tortilla chips from Billy's nachos, and playing cards were scattered around the room. For the first time, Crystal wished the caretakers had stayed on in a cleaning capacity. One thing she knew for sure was that she wouldn't clean the mess up alone. Glancing back at Jonah, she decided to leave him to sleep. He wasn't very good at falling back to sleep once awakened. She, however, would drop onto the bed and be out before her head hit the pillow.

On her way out of the game room, she hit the light switch and saw a camera partially hidden in the corner. She didn't remember the caretaker saying anything about cameras, but with her pounding headache, she could remember very little in general. She made a mental note to find the Gold Book and look up how to check the video after she had a cup of coffee. If nothing else, watching a recap of the previous night could be entertaining.

Crystal wandered out of the room, wondering what time it was. The rooms in the basement had no windows, and without a functioning cell phone attached to her hip, she felt naked.

The sudden smell of smoke dashed her hopes for a few more hours of sleep. Billy must already be up preparing their breakfast. She'd have to get on the master chef since it smelled more like something was burning.

With her shoes left behind in the game room, Crystal noticed her feet were incredibly tender. It was not a feeling of pain so much as like she was walking on balloons. While everyone else played games all night, she lounged on the couch, so maybe it was just numbness from lack of use.

Not entirely steady on her feet—whether from lingering inebriation or the remnants of exhaustion—Crystal staggered slightly, her movements uncoordinated as she attempted the impossible task of walking while simultaneously staring down at her feet. Her toe caught on something, sending her lurching forward, but she managed to catch herself before meeting the hard floor. A quick glance behind her revealed the culprit: her foot had dislodged a door jam from under the movie room door.

She frowned, puzzled. *Why would a door jam be placed on the outside of the door?* The thought swirled in her hazy mind, an oddity that didn't quite sit right.

As she regained her balance something even more unsettling caught her eye. A thin wisp of smoke curled from beneath the door, twisting and writhing. The tendrils were faint but unmistakable, and they sent a shiver down her spine. The familiar smell of something burning now making more sense.

Crystal's breath caught in her throat, her previous clumsiness forgotten. A sense of unease wrapped around her like a suffocating blanket. She knew she had to act, but for a brief moment, she stood frozen, fear rooting her to the spot.

Chapter Twenty-Four

The Escape (Literal)

Ilma stirred from sleep, her ears attuned to the raspy, relentless sound of Thomas' coughing. His allergies often led to these nightly fits, with each open-mouthed breath harshly sucked in only to be expelled in a series of rattling coughs. It baffled her how he could produce such a racket and remain blissfully unaware in slumber.

She gently extricated herself from the weight of his arm draped over her, the fabric of her shirt clinging slightly from the warmth they shared. The room felt oddly dense, the air heavier than usual. As she resumed her search for the elusive water bottles, a cold realization gripped her. A thin, acrid fog enveloped the room, more dense near the cloud that hung just below the ceiling.

Panic surged through her veins as she spun around, the creeping smoke now unmistakable. She lunged back toward Thomas, her hands trembling as she shook him with urgent force.

"Thomas! Wake up!" Her voice, edged with terror, cut through the thickening haze.

He stirred, groggy confusion clouding his face. "Oh no. I'm sorry. Was I coughing?"

But even as he spoke, a fresh fit seized him, this time driven not by his sinuses but by the sting of the smoke. His eyes widened, taking in the smoke-laden room, and in an instant, the grogginess evaporated. He leaped up with startling speed, vaulting over the recliner seats like a man possessed, every muscle primed for flight as he made for the door, urgency sharpening his every move.

His triage of actions were smooth and analytical.

If DOOR LOCKED then

TURN ON LIGHT;

FIND SOURCE OF SMOKE;

If SOURCE FOUND (popcorn machine) then

UNPLUG;

LOOK FOR ALTERNATE ESCAPE;

Ilma watched him, afraid to interrupt his mission. Then, as the memory clicked, she hurried across the room to the movie screen shouting, "Thomas, I saw a door behind the...."

Before she could finish her thought, the door to the hallway swung open with a bang.

There, framed by the doorway and bathed in the harsh, sterile glow of the basement's fluorescent lights, stood a figure so striking she seemed almost otherworldly. The light behind her cast a stark, ethereal halo, mingling with a curling haze that lent the scene a surreal quality.

"Ilma! Thomas! What the hell are you doing in there?" Crystal yelled, yanking them both by their shirts and pulling them out.

"I turned it off, I swear," Thomas called out like a child trying to get out of trouble.

A sleepy-looking Jonah ran up behind them and directly into the room, frantically spraying the fire extinguisher inside and around the popcorn machine.

Only then did the hallway smoke alarm begin to squeal.

CHAPTER TWENTY-FIVE

The Improv

"Stupid bitch," The Unwelcome Guest seethed under his breath, his voice a venomous whisper lost in the shadows. Fury burned in his eyes as he watched her through the crack in the door, his plans unraveling with each step she took. She had ruined everything. Not only had she flung open the movie room door, releasing the two he had so craftily trapped inside, but her mere existence was a constant thorn in his side.

Yesterday, when he overheard her casual mention of "taking a soak," a sinister grin had curled his lips. The opportunity was too perfect to ignore. He had crept through the dim corridors, his heart pounding with malevolent anticipation, and tampered with the hot tub's temperature control, bypassing the safety mechanisms to crank it up to dangerous levels.

In his twisted mind, he envisioned her slow, unwitting demise, comparing her to the frog from Science class experiments, gradually boiled alive without realizing her fate. He imagined her in that moment of vulnerability, slipping into the hot tub's inviting waters, maybe in a swimsuit or, if luck favored his dark desires, without it. The thought of her dozing off as the heat stealthily escalated filled him with perverse satisfaction.

He relished the idea of her flesh blistering, the skin melting away, the agony delayed by her oblivion until it was too late. His wicked fantasy played out in vivid detail, a macabre scene crafted by his depraved mind.

He hoped she would just sit there with a blank stare as her hair caught fire and her eyeballs fell from their sockets. He imagined her flawless skin as it slipped over her perfect, completely fake set of tits. *Would the silicone bags explode like water balloons?* The thought made him smile. He hated to waste such a perfect specimen, but he had to remind himself that his main reason for him being on the ridiculous waste of an island was to get rid of her once and for all.

He found the perfect place to watch, though uncomfortably, as he tested his *exploding titties* hypothesis, crouched down behind the outdoor bar. A gap in the stonework separated the bar top from the kegerator. It was just enough space for him to see through to the hot tub yet avoid being seen.

But leave it to the diva to take a long shower and put on makeup before heading to the hot tub. *Why would someone need makeup to sit in the hot tub?*

By the time she finally made her appearance, the water was already way above a safe temperature, and all it took was one step onto the highest ledge of the hot tub for her to feel the scalding heat and get out. The top ledge was only an inch or two underwater. Except for maybe maiming her, she would be fine. At least he could take solace in the fact that she would never become a foot model.

He had expected an explosion when the popcorn machine had turned on. When the trap became more of a slow burn rather than a dramatic detonation as he had hoped, he had even gone through the trouble to block their exit and sneak in during the movie and take their waters so they couldn't use them to put the fire out. Unfortunately, it did little more than stink up the room with pungent smoke. Luckily he had prepared a plan B. Standing just on the other side of the wall, behind the drop-down screen, he had been prepared to light a Molotov cocktail in hopes of finally getting the blast he sought, when in all the chaos, he swore he heard The Bookworm approach the hidden door.

Why would she walk deeper into the room where they were trapped rather than toward the exit into the basement?

He held his breath and didn't move. With his muscles tensed, he hoped he could still his tremors. The sweat on his hands was not doing his grip any favors. If somehow The Bookworm found the door and opened it, he could hit her over the head with the bottle. That is if it didn't slip out of his hand first.

He had spent hours of his pre-island research scouring the internet for instructions on how to DIY the explosive just in case the need arose. When he had to kill Fred for not minding his business, he knew the explosive would come in handy. If not for getting rid of his body, then for blowing up the entire house. He had set to work that first day, making it out of a bottle of vodka and torn-up pieces from a small sweat towel he found in the gym.

The impact from the nearly full liquor bottle against her skull would not be as easy to explain away as the original plan of having the room catch fire, but he was on a private island and had plenty of time to stage the scene. Just when it seemed that Ilma's movements were close enough to be just on the other side of the movie screen, the hallway door slammed open, and the panicked voices of The Bookworm and her husband were replaced with the whiney high-pitched voice of The Supermodel.

Damn, he wished he had been able to burn off her flawless, soft, and supple skin. Skeletons don't whine.

CHAPTER TWENTY-SIX

The Feet

April tiptoed past the closed doors of the upstairs bedrooms. Thanks to her eye mask and ear plugs, she had been able to sleep until 7 am, but after the previous night of playing games until late, she doubted anyone else would be awake. Her assumptions were proved wrong when she heard voices in the kitchen as she jogged down the stairs.

"Well, good morning, sunshine," Sean called out to her over a mug of black coffee as she crossed the great room toward the kitchen.

Had she been so careful to creep around quietly that she hadn't even noticed that Sean was already awake? She looked around and saw Will, Jonah, and Crystal were also up, and from the looks of it, they had been for hours.

"What's going on?" she asked, confused and even slightly worried, knowing each of them had drunk way more than she did.

"While you slept like the dead, the rest of us were busy being heroes," Jonah smirked.

Crystal interrupted and told April the play-by-play of the early morning events.

Of course, Ilma blew up the popcorn machine, April thought to herself. Her sister-in-law was well-read and intelligent, but she was all thumbs when it came to anything mechanical. On the ferry ride, she ducked into the emergency bathroom to wash her hands in the pump sink, only to come out holding the handle saying, "It fell off."

"Thank goodness it wasn't a real emergency since you slept through the smoke alarm," Crystal mocked as she stood up from her chair and limped over to the coffee pot.

April looked her up and down and wondered why, if Crystal was hurt in her heroic life-saving adventures, did she not mention it. She was known to milk all the attention she could get. Surely she had already drafted a press release to boast about her bravery.

As if thinking the same, Sean asked, "Did you pull a hammy while you were updating your social media?"

Crystal ignored the jab. "Ugh, no. It's my feet. I thought I could use a nice soak yesterday morning, but the hot tub was too hot when I put my feet in. I knew it was hot, but I thought I was just being a drama queen. I felt something wasn't right, but it didn't hurt that bad. But looking at them now, I can see I have pretty bad burns. See?" Crystal leaned against the counter and lifted one of her feet for everyone to see.

Looking at anyone's feet didn't exactly help her appetite, but staring at Crystal's bright red feet with giant blisters covering every inch of skin below her ankle bone was enough to make April gag.

"Sorry," Crystal looked down at her feet, ashamed. She was not used to people looking away from her in disgust.

"How the hell did the water get hot enough to burn you?" Will asked, looking around at the others in the room. "We better check on that before anyone else gets hurt."

"How are you even walking?" Sean asked, more curious than grossed out.

"It looks worse than it feels, which is probably not good. The burns must be pretty severe since it's totally numb." Crystal averted her eyes from the others self-consciously and continued, "I actually think I should go lay down for a while. I didn't get much sleep last night on the couch, and I should probably elevate my feet. The last thing I need is for these growing blisters to pop."

April covered her mouth and turned away in an attempt to suppress another gag as Crystal waddled out of the room. Once she composed herself, she looked at the guys standing around the counter. "Where are Thomas and Ilma? Are they okay?"

"They both went up to bed. I guess the movie room recliners are even less comfortable than the game room couch," Sean answered, eyeing Jonah.

Apparently, Crystal wasn't the only one complaining about the couch.

"Ilma is pretty shaken up, but I'm sure she'll be fine. Thomas was in crisis mode. He gets like that," Will said, looking over at his brothers for confirmation. "He is the absolute best of us in an emergency. He is detached, calm, and able to process everything quickly, almost robotically. But it all hits him eventually. We need to keep an eye on him today."

"Yeah," said Jonah in agreement. "I doubt he'll make it through the day without a complete meltdown."

The brothers exchanged looks but didn't answer, and April recalled a story Sean had once told her in confidence about when they had to hospitalize Thomas in a psychiatric ward as a teen.

Back when Thomas was in high school, he had a manipulative and toxic girlfriend. She played games and made up stories to make him jealous. One day, he got so angry that he punched the bathroom door. The happy, prank-playing Thomas should have found the situation hilarious since the warped door caused him to be locked in the school bathroom until hours after school ended. Eventually, a new teacher who was staying late to get caught up, heard his cries on her way out and called for help. The doctors indicated that his short time trapped in the bathroom caused some sort of psychotic break and that he had also developed an unhealthy attachment to the teacher who, in his mind, saved his life. Therapy has helped him to control his emotions in stressful situations, but his PTSD would rear its ugly head in time. It always did.

The brothers may not be pleased that Sean shared the private family business with April, so she looked back and forth as if she was clueless.

When it was clear no one was going to say another word on the subject, April said her goodbyes and headed back upstairs for more sleep, Sean following closely behind.

The fragile-flower, Ilma, got her wish in a roundabout way. Now she had an excuse to stay in her room and read, avoiding socializing for another few hours.

CHAPTER TWENTY-SEVEN

The Reflection

Ilma opened her eyes but didn't move. She had been nestled in the crook of Thomas' arm since they fell asleep in their heart bed. The shape of the bed made sleeping awkward, with the two humps of the heart being perfect for pillows, but their feet crowded together at the bottom. It was fine for snuggling, but when she wanted to have some space, there was no escaping his touch. Thomas' skin smelled like burnt popcorn and smoke, or maybe the smell was coming from her own hair. Neither of them bothered to shower when they got up to their room. They simply stripped down and crawled under the covers wanting to escape the frightening memory on replay in their minds. Thomas had held her tight to comfort her and calm her shaking limbs. The shock of the whole situation had worn off, but the smell was a trigger. The scent causing her to relive her fear and panic on repeat.

She rolled off her side and onto her back and found herself staring up at the mirrored ceiling, debating whether rubbing chapstick under her nose would afford her more time in bed masking the offensive smell. A brief tickle of arousal ran between her legs as she thought of the shower, but was gone just as fast when she remembered the creepy feeling of being watched. When Thomas woke, she would ask him for more details about how he was sneaking around the house. She would feel less concerned about people watching her if she knew how they could do it.

She knew she should shower and change the sheets and possibly even toss out their smoky clothes, but the mirror that was once a ridiculous joke to her now brought her comfort, allowing her to watch Thomas sleep from every angle.

The reflection of a circle worn into the carpet caught her eye. It looked like a tiny dog had circled the spot, flattening the area like a nest before laying down on it. Had Thomas made that mark on the carpet while he paced around their room out of concern for her? Though it looked more like a mark created by a person spinning in one spot than pacing. Her eyes drifted back to her own reflection, but rather than staring back at herself, she found two unfamiliar eyes staring up at her from under the bed.

Ilma pulled a sudden, deep inhale and nearly choked on her spit. It only took a fraction of a second for Ilma to realize it was one of those damned life-sized dolls, but it was enough to add insult to injury after the morning they had endured. What started as panic rising in her tightening chest quickly turned to red-hot anger. She rolled over and straddled Thomas, pinning him down aggressively.

Before he knew what was happening, Ilma was pounding him in the chest with her clenched fists and stinging slaps, tears streaming down her face. "How the hell could you do this to me?" Her voice was high-pitched as she screamed.

Thomas looked shocked. Confused even, but rather than fighting back or restraining her, he simply held his hands up in surrender.

"You knew I was scared from being locked in that room all night," Ilma wailed, snot from her nose running onto her upper lip. "You knew I was afraid we would die in that smoke. And somehow, you thought this was funny?"

She stopped hitting and just sat astride him, panting and sobbing hysterically.

"What was funny?" Thomas asked and flinched as if expecting her to attack him once more.

Ilma stared down at him. Her body was awash with relief and the realization that he had nothing to do with the mannequin. She could see it on his face. He had no idea what she was talking about.

But if it wasn't Thomas, then who? It had to be April or Sean. Thomas was the trickster, but they were both competitive. Surely they saw the need to one-up Thomas' game.

Without so much as a knock, their bedroom door burst open. Ilma rolled back onto the bed and pulled the sheet up over her naked and sweaty body.

"I don't know what kind of kinky shit you two are into, but it sounded like someone was getting murdered up in here," Will stood just inside the door with Jonah and Sean right behind him.

"What's going on?" Crystal shouted from her bedroom down the hall.

"Everything's fine, dear. I'll be there in a minute," Jonah answered, turning his head toward the open door but keeping his eyes on the bed.

"Did you do this?" Ilma asked, looking over at the brothers in the doorway and pointing weakly at the doll. Her anger was gone, having taken it out on Thomas' bare chest. She was past embarrassment at being barged in on while totally nude. But the tears still fell as if from an unlimited supply. The only feeling that remained was betrayal. Someone took the joke too far.

The Bookworm had to go. She hadn't irritated him as much as the other dumb bitches. He had initially hoped to just mess with her until she snapped.

Watching her beat the shit out of her husband from behind the artwork hanging from the wall had been entertaining. The Unwelcome Guest rolled his eyes, mentally kicking himself for not figuring out a way to rig up the cameras. He could watch a recording of that display of passion, fear, and anger over and over again. But, when it was all over and the sounds of open hands slapping bare skin and screams tearing through wails of crying faded away, it wasn't satisfying.

He wanted her to crush her husband's skull with the dildo lamp and get sent to prison for the rest of her life, not curl up in a ball and sob after a few perfectly placed bitch slaps. She failed his test, and now she had to die.

CHAPTER TWENTY-EIGHT

The Storm

When they first arrived on the island, April had been thrilled about her room. In truth, her excitement wasn't limited to just the room; she was eager to explore the gym, the basketball trampoline, the carts, and the winding cart paths that promised adventure. There was so much to be excited about. Yet, despite her initial enthusiasm for the room's unique theme, a subtle unease began to creep in.

The bed, although deceptively simple with its futon mattress perched on a wooden pallet, was surprisingly comfortable. She wasn't bothered by the fact that it was lofted high above the ground or the idea of climbing up and down. The source of her discomfort lay elsewhere—on the wall.

Adorned with a lush tapestry of ivy and succulents, the wall was meant to exude natural charm. At first glance, it appeared serene, even beautiful, with cleverly integrated rock climbing holds that added a playful touch. But as she lay on her elevated bed, the wall seemed to breathe with a life of its own.

In the stillness of the room, devoid of any breeze or fan, she could swear the greenery shifted. It was subtle, almost imperceptible. A leaf would twitch, just slightly, near the center of the wall. If she didn't fix her gaze intently on that spot, she would miss it. The tiny, sporadic movements were enough to set her on edge, creating a tension that whispered of something unseen, something unsettling just beneath the surface.

"Sean, the leaves on the wall are moving," she whispered.

Sean's snoring had stopped, but he didn't move.

"Sean?" she repeated.

"So?" Sean said in reply, with a tinge of irritation in his voice.

"So, why are the leaves moving?" she asked.

"Maybe they're growing. Maybe there are bugs crawling on them."

"I don't think they are real plants, Sean. And, ew," April said in disgust, thinking of tiny little bugs crawling all over the fake plant wall.

"If it bothers you, just don't look at it." Sean adjusted his pillow and tugged up the blanket, thus ending the conversation.

April turned over and faced Sean's back, but the longer she stared at the nape of his neck, the more pressure she felt on hers.

She flipped back over, preferring to stare at something than feeling stared at.

With the uneasy feeling she had in her room and the smell of the basement, all April wanted to do was get outside.

She climbed off the bed and dressed, careful not to turn her back to the wall. After grabbing her shoes, she tiptoed down the stairs; the silence was deafening. The time on the wall clock read noon, but everyone was still sleeping. Without the sun shining through the windows and no working cell phones, they likely had no idea of the time.

When April stepped outside, she felt the temperature drop. The wind blew through her hair as she pulled it back into a ponytail.

As if the weather could mimic her mood, the dark clouds slowly crept their way overhead while she jogged along the path. The dark sky only added to the creepiness of the gnarled trees and hanging Spanish moss. April tried to listen for birds or squirrels or a late-season cicada in hopes of finding beauty in nature rather than just fear. But there were no sounds. Nature had taken shelter, sensing the storm that was brewing.

The dim woods flashed bright white briefly as lightning lit up the sky overhead. Even after being completely aware of the flash of light, April fell down hard at the giant crack of thunder that followed. She bit her lip and cursed aloud.

Pulling her knees up to her chest, she rocked back and forth, hoping beyond hope that the pain in her ankle would ebb into a bruise, strain, or scratch rather than increase in intensity, signifying something worse. The rain began to fall as if a cloud decided to dump every ounce of moisture all at once. There were no small shower holes in the cloud, just a giant gaping opening with which to dump water on her head. Another flash appeared overhead, and April spied a small cave just off the path near the cliff. With some of the pain subsiding, April stood and gingerly tested her weight on the hurt foot. It was sore, but nothing more than that. She hobbled to the cave and took a seat at the opening. She was already soaked to the core, but she might as well wait out the storm under shelter rather than risk getting flattened by a fallen tree.

The cave and all the woods surrounding it were dark enough with the clouds overhead that she couldn't clearly see if there was anything in the cave with her, so she stayed at the edge. But the echo of dripping water deep into the cave indicated that it was larger than it looked from the outside. April again pulled her knees up to her chest and wrapped her arms around tight. Her warm skin, combined with the lack of sun, wet clothes, and cold rain, made the dreary cave feel even colder. Her teeth began to chatter, and she hugged her legs tighter still. She silently wished for another flash of lightning so she could at least see the bear or boar or whatever wild animal was going to eat her cold body.

As if in answer to her wish, the lightning pulsed in rapid succession. It wasn't an animal she saw just feet into the cave, but a man sleeping on a pile of towels.

April skittered backward in shock, the rain pouring down on her head once again.

"Hello?" April called out, but her shivering voice was weak and timid under the sounds of pounding rain and booming thunder.

She stepped closer, wary of the stranger but also compassionate enough to want to help another human. After ducking into the cave, the walls created a sound vacuum where not only did the sounds from outside of the cave become muffled, but the pressure on her ears was intense.

The man stunk of his own waste and something else she had yet to identify. The putrid smell was almost enough to make her run back out into the storm, but instead, she stepped closer. The body was that of a man wearing jeans and a T-shirt. His shoes were dirty and old, with frayed laces and several holes. She tried to take in any detail without looking at the man's face. Once she finally worked up the courage, she raised her eyes to the gray, pocked skin. The offensive smell wasn't from poor hygiene after all. It was the smell of decay.

CHAPTER TWENTY-NINE
The Confined

"Finally!" Crystal exclaimed from the bed as Jonah walked hurriedly into the bedroom from the shower.

She had several pillows propped up behind her back and another one under each of her calves to raise her feet up off the surface of the bed. She sat braless in a see-through white tank top and brief-style underwear. She didn't think anyone other than Jonah would come into her room, but quite honestly, she didn't care. She'd covered herself with less.

"Do you have any idea how boring it is in here?" Crystal shouted out to Jonah as he closed the door behind him, hoping to spare everyone else from her screams. "On top of that, hearing all the noise from next door and having no idea whatsoever as to what is happening."

"When I came in, you were taking a nap. You looked so peaceful, and I didn't want to wake you, so I took the opportunity to take a quick shower," Jonah explained.

He walked over to the bed, took a deep breath of patience, and took a seat next to her feet. "Damn, Crystal. Those sores look pretty bad."

"What the hell, Jonah! I don't give a shit about my feet right now. What the fuck is happening?"

"It's nothing, really. Ilma freaked out because someone hid one of the mannequins under their bed." Jonah paused as if waiting for a follow-up question. "She could see the head... you know, in the mirror?"

"Holy shit, she saw a creepy doll in the ceiling mirror reflection? No wonder she screamed. I'd shit the bed if I saw *any* body part sticking out from under the bed."

Crystal was shocked and a little creeped out, moving a few more inches away from the side of the bed toward the middle. "I've seen Thomas pull a lot of shit, but never on Ilma."

"He says it wasn't him," Jonah confirmed.

"Of course he did," she rolled her eyes. "After a reaction like that, do you really think he's going to fess up to that?"

"No, really. You should've seen him. He was fucking clueless, and she was just wailing on him." Jonah sighed and keeping his feet on the floor allowed his upper body to fall back onto the bed.

Crystal turned her head to look out the sliding glass doors toward the terrace and muttered, "Well, this weather should cheer Ilma up."

Jonah sat up and looked outside, confused, "What? It's raining."

"She's only told me a hundred times how much she loves to read when it's raining outside," Crystal mused, taking a look at the book on her bedside table and deciding again not to open it.

Two hard and fast knocks rapped against the door, but before either Jonah or Crystal had a chance to answer, Sean burst into the room breathless.

"Dude, where are the keys to the electric carts? April is out there running in this mess."

"I'll drive you," Jonah said, standing up and heading to the door behind Sean.

When Sean left, Jonah turned his head to look at Crystal. "What can I get you? I hate that you're hurting."

"I'm fine," Crystal touted and grabbed her phone. "I may not be able to post right now, but I can still record videos on my phone. It will keep me busy."

She winked at her husband and leaned back against the pillows, hoping her lie was convincing. She tried her hardest to put on a happy face. Months and months of hard work went into her planning the vacation, and she was stuck in bed because the hot tub was hot. And as luck would have it, when Will and Sean went out to check the temperature, it had been a totally normal 100 degrees, not boiling, not scalding, just perfect for relaxing. They even found the pool supplies and tested the chlorine, wondering if the burns were somehow chemical rather than heat-related, but everything was fine. She would never escape the *dumb blonde* jokes with such occurrences.

Crystal looked down at her phone, and when she moved her finger to open her camera app, her phone slipped out of her hand and landed on the bed. Her hands were sweaty from the death grip she held on her phone, her only lifeline as she lay in her lavish prison. When she picked the phone back up after wiping her slippery hands on the bedspread, she saw that she had unintentionally opened her to-do app. In front of her, taunting her, was the long list of all her vacation tasks. With her modeling jobs drying up at the advanced age of 34, she fully immersed herself in trip planning.

Finding the island was the easiest part. She had her eyes on the luxury vacation spot for years. Crystal even had an alert set up to let her know every time a guest posted a review or photos. She had memorized the floor plan, the island location, and the bedroom themes, just waiting on the day Jonah gave her the go-ahead to book it. One big annual bonus was all she needed to feel brave enough to ask, and catching him in the afterglow of sex always made him easily pliable. The booking of the island was easy and anticlimactic, so she set to create more tasks to keep herself busy yet still with her eye on the prize.

One of her lists that had been changed more times than she would admit was the food list. Not only had she started a list of liquor, snacks, and fresh seafood to request from the caretaker to stock, she made sure to reach out to Billy for his wish list. Jonah had made arrangements to pay for Billy's portion of the vacation, so she sure as hell was going to milk him for all it was worth. Crystal was pleased that he agreed to cook meals for the group. With no hired chef on the island, the option was really that or frozen pizza since none of the others cooked. Jonah and Crystal had their own chef back in Manhattan. She wasn't full-time by any means, but she prepared all of their meals, albeit that breakfast and lunch on weekdays were packed in the refrigerator. Crystal couldn't even remember the last time she cooked for herself or if she ever had. She'd been with Jonah since college, and even when he was just starting his career and didn't have money in excess, he insisted on taking her out to dinner frequently. He had always treated her like a queen.

Sean and April were usually on some sort of cleanse and drank more smoothies from the small cafe in their gym than food from home.

Thomas and Ilma had very little money, so she imagined them packing bologna sandwiches for lunch and eating a lot of soup, but really she had no idea what the two of them did for food. Other than reaching out via email about the vacation, Crystal had very few conversations with the introverted couple.

It was a nice service that the caretaker would do all the shopping ahead of time and have the house stocked before their arrival. Obviously, they would foot the grocery bill, but that was one less thing she had to pack and lug onto the ferry. She loved that she and Jonah were able to take an early ferry over before the rest of the family. Crystal told the others it was to get all last-minute preparations ready, but truly there was nothing for her to do. With the house already scrubbed clean and the landscaping tended to before she arrived, all they had to do was walk through with the caretaker.

After their tour with Isabella, Jonah spent an hour standing on the dock trying to get enough reception to make a work call, and she grabbed a book out of the library and pretended to read it by the pool. She hated to read, but she didn't feel comfortable making videos until Isabella left the island. She was wrapping up her checklist, and the last thing Crystal wanted was Isabella in the background of a reel, rolling her eyes.

Looking back, she was thankful for the extra half day since, most likely, she and her blistered feet would be up in her room for the duration of the trip. For the first time since she started to dream of this vacation, she wished the help had stayed to wait on her. With Jonah playing host to the others, Crystal didn't want to ask too much of him. But she could really use a glass of wine and some cheese. Maybe she would get lucky, and her sweet Billy would check on her with one of his amazing charcuterie boards.

To distract herself from the gnawing hunger and creeping boredom, Crystal turned once more to her to-do lists. Her eyes flickered over the tasks until one caught her attention: **Privacy**. Intrigued, she clicked on the task and scrolled through the notes from the rental listing detailing the island and house security. As she scanned the text, a nagging itch in the back of her mind pushed her to unravel a question she couldn't quite remember.

And then she saw it:

In consideration of the privacy of our guests, there will be no monitoring or surveillance on the island whatsoever.

Right beside the pasted text was a note she had typed in bold:

NO CAMERAS.

Crystal read her own note repeatedly, each time feeling a tightening sensation in her chest. Her spine straightened, her body tensing as if reacting to an unseen force. Even through her lingering hangover, she was certain—she had seen a camera in the game room. What else could it have been?

Determined, she swung her legs over the side of the bed, ready to search her room for any hidden surveillance. But as she stood, a sharp, throbbing pain reminded her of the swelling in her feet, forcing her to reconsider. Instead, she stayed seated, her eyes slowly roaming over every detail of the room, scrutinizing each object for signs of a hidden lens.

Her first sweep revealed nothing unusual. Frustrated, she glanced down at her feet, now swollen and throbbing, and resolved to keep them elevated. As she adjusted her position, something near her dangling feet caught her eye—a small, subtle, worn circle in the carpet. It seemed out of place, unsettling in their quiet presence, as if marking where something—or someone—had once stood, watching.

CHAPTER THIRTY

The Shock

When her gaze finally registered the horrifying truth, April's breath caught in her throat. It wasn't a pile of dirty laundry. It wasn't a stranger resting in the shadows. It was a dead body, crumpled and lifeless, abandoned in the grim stillness of the cave. A sharp wave of panic surged through her, freezing her limbs momentarily, before instinct took over. Her feet stumbled backward, driven by an urgent need to escape, but the forest floor conspired against her. An exposed root snagged her heel, and she tumbled, slamming her tailbone against the sodden, unyielding ground.

Pain flared through her lower back, but adrenaline dulled the ache as she crab-crawled in a frantic scramble, her hands and feet digging into the wet earth, desperate to put distance between herself and the gruesome discovery. Her eyes, wide and unblinking, remained locked on the macabre scene, even as the rain poured harder, drenching her and blurring her vision.

Finally, her trembling legs found their strength, and she surged to her feet. Ignoring the sharp pang in her bruised tailbone and the shooting pain in her sprained ankle, she ran. Fear propelled her forward, the image of the body etched into her mind. The thought of turning her back on it, letting it vanish from view, sent a shiver down her spine that no amount of rain could wash away.

Once the cave was swallowed by the dense forest, the body out of sight, April slowed to a walk. The adrenaline that had fueled her flight waned, and the aches and pains clamored for attention. Her twisted ankle throbbed, her soaked shorts chafed against raw skin, and her body trembled from more than just the cold.

She forced herself to focus, to steady her ragged breathing, concentrating on each labored step forward. *Had the man in the cave been the person she'd seen, or at the very least felt in the woods before?* The forest seemed endless, each shadow a reminder of what she had left behind, each sound a whisper of dread and endless questions. But she pushed on, every step a defiance of the terror that clung to her like the rain-soaked clothes against her skin.

By the time Sean and Jonah found her, the storm had abated, leaving the island cloaked in a somber stillness. April limped along the path, her soaked clothes clinging to her like a second skin, each step a laborious effort. The electric cart rolled up beside her, its soft hum breaking the silence, and she slid into the back seat, shivering as she pulled the blanket Sean handed her tightly around her shoulders. The two brothers exchanged a look, their eyes reflecting a shared concern. This was not the April they knew—spirited, restless, always running, never walking.

"Are you okay?" Sean asked, his voice filled with a mixture of worry and confusion as he leaned over the seat to study her pallid face.

April's gaze was fixed on the back of his seat, her eyes glassy, unblinking. The weight of the day's events bore down on her, making her feel hollow and detached. She opened her mouth to respond, but her voice faltered, emerging as a barely audible, "No." Her eyes glistened with unshed tears, blurring her vision as she struggled to keep her composure.

Whether they heard her or not was irrelevant. The brothers were already focused on getting her home, their faces tense and unreadable, as if they carried burdens they couldn't yet share. The ride back to the house was shrouded in an oppressive silence, broken only by the soft hum of the cart's motor. April couldn't shake the ominous feeling that something lingered unsaid, a heavy secret hanging in the air between them.

When they reached the house, Jonah slowed the cart, and April slid out, her every movement betraying the pain she tried to mask. Her feet hitting the ground sent a fresh jolt of discomfort up her spine. As she hobbled toward the stairs, Sean's voice cut through the quiet.

"We need to talk," he said, his tone grave.

April paused, looking up to meet his gaze for the first time since they had found her. The intensity in his eyes sent a fresh wave of anxiety through her, and she felt the tears well up again. She clenched her jaw, refusing to let the dam break, unwilling to show just how fragile she felt.

"Take a shower," Sean instructed softly, "and warm up. Meet us in Crystal and Jonah's room when you're ready."

Without another word, he turned and followed Jonah back to the cart garage. April watched them disappear into the shadows before she kicked off her sodden shoes and socks, leaving them in a soggy heap at the foot of the stairs. Gripping the railing tightly, she hauled herself up the steps, each one shooting pain through her aching body. Her mind buzzed with unanswered questions, the weight of the impending conversation pressing down on her with every step she took.

The Unwelcome Guest knew from the terror etched across her face that The Runner had stumbled upon something she was never meant to see. She always cloaked herself in a facade of invincibility, portraying the role of the unbreakable super-athlete, the relentless badass who could weather any storm or injury without a flinch. But now, that mask was slipping. Fear had stripped away her bravado, and she wasn't bothering to hide it.

Once the coast was clear, he moved with a practiced stealth, slipping out of the house and vanishing into the shadows of the woods. He darted between the trees, his feet barely touching the ground, keenly aware of the slick wet grass beneath him and the treacherous limbs scattered by the storm. Falling here, injured and exposed, was not an option. Not with Mr. Chatterbox most likely having already been discovered.

As he neared the cave, he scanned the ground, confirming his suspicions: the rain had erased the telltale drag marks, replacing them with faint, woman-sized footprints. She hadn't ventured too close—five or six feet at most—but that distance was enough. The stench alone would have been a dead giveaway. Fred's rotting flesh could knock a buzzard off a shit wagon at fifty paces.

The Unwelcome Guest inhaled deeply to steady himself, immediately regretting it as the putrid air filled his lungs. He cursed under his breath for not bringing something to mask the smell. With a grimace, he brushed away the bugs feasting on Fred's decaying feet, then gripped the corpse and began the arduous task of dragging it out of the cave.

Fred's body, waterlogged and heavy, resisted every pull, and the wet mud clung to him relentlessly. The Unwelcome Guest struggled against the resistance, each step a battle against the slick, sodden earth. He pushed forward, muscles straining, until he finally reached the cliff's edge. There, he changed tactics, shoving the body toward the precipice. Fred's head flopped back over the rim, gravity pulling at him like a silent, relentless force.

Bugs crawled from the corpse up onto his arms, a grotesque parade of life feeding on death. The Unwelcome Guest swatted them away with disgust, focusing all his strength on one final push. The remnants of rigor mortis gave him the edge he needed, and Fred's body slid over the cliff, disappearing into the void.

He didn't bother looking down to see where the body landed. Whether it was the ocean or a ledge, it made no difference now. Fred was gone from the cave, and that was enough. Grabbing a broken branch, he methodically swept the ground, erasing the traces of his presence. Satisfied, he wiped his filthy hands on a blood-soaked towel and flung it over the edge, following Fred into oblivion.

CHAPTER THIRTY-ONE
The Doubt

After a quick, hot shower, April felt more clear-headed than ever. She dressed and walked down the hallway to Crystal's room. The double doors were open, for once, to the hallway. This was April's first glance into her sister-in-law's suite. If there was a theme to this room, it was simply *Grandiose*. Everything was big and just a bit more overdone than necessary. It was perfect for Crystal and Jonah.

As tempted as April was to take in the room's other features, she had to tell them what she found, or she would lose her nerve.

Crystal was sitting up in the bed with her back against the headboard. Jonah sat on the edge of the bed facing out to the terrace. Jonah was a tall man at over six feet, but his feet hung over the high bed and off the floor like those of a small child. Thomas and Will were sitting in big comfortable-looking chairs by the fireplace. April walked over and sat on the chaise next to Sean.

"Where is Ilma?" she asked, looking over at Thomas.

"She needs some alone time," Thomas muttered quietly, looking down and rubbing his feet together as if scratching an itch.

Sean nudged April and gave her a look that said *I'll fill you in later.*

No one said a word, yet everyone looked uncomfortable. So, April decided to get the ball rolling.

"I know I mentioned to everyone about my run the first day and feeling sure someone else was in the woods with me," April began, taking note of the rolled eyes of Thomas and Will. "My last run seemed okay, but there is no question that I have felt uncomfortable since we arrived."

Taking April's words personally, Crystal spoke up, "Oh no, honey. Is it your tree-house bed? It doesn't look comfortable, but I was sure you would love it."

Frustration overtook her body, tinting her cheeks red and making her want to run out of the room. She shook her head and continued, "No, Crystal. I feel like I'm being watched. I feel like something is wrong here. Can you honestly say that none of you have a bad feeling about this island?"

April met everyone's eyes as she looked around the room. If there hadn't been someone on the island making everyone uncomfortable, she was doing that just fine on her own. When her eyes finally landed on Crystal, she recalled their late-night tipsy conversation about feeling that someone had been watching her sleep. "I know I'm not the only one," April said boldly, not wavering. Crystal dropped her eyes to her lap but didn't say a word.

"There is someone else on the island," April blurted out, wishing she had chosen her words better.

Everyone in the room looked around at each other. Some looked shocked. Others looked doubtful. But April continued. "I saw him. It was dark in the woods during the storm, and it was hard to see in the cave I was sheltering in, but I'm sure he was dead." April paused. She wanted to kick herself. She was doing this all wrong. It sounded like she made up a new story since they ignored her first one. They must think she's crazy.

"A dead guy?" Sean asked. "You found a dead body. In a cave. And you didn't say anything to me about it before now?"

April could tell by his tone and body language that he felt as much doubt as he did betrayal and embarrassment, having heard the news with everyone else once again. He was skeptical by nature, but she never would have thought he would doubt her word.

He didn't like surprises and liked to look the part of the Alpha male around his brothers. She would have to smooth things over with him later.

"I know," she looked down, tearing her eyes away from his. "I should have told you when you picked me up in the cart, but I was in shock. Taking you and Jonah back to the cave never even crossed my mind. I just wanted to get as far away as possible."

She paused, but less for dramatic effect than to give herself time to put it into words. Her intention was not to scare them, but the situation was serious. They had to alert the authorities.

"We need to call the mainland and let them know," April spoke up confidently, taking charge and shoving down her emotions.

Crystal interjected before April could continue, "No. I mentioned this before. The caretakers were very specific. They only come between renters and never stay on the island overnight. I'm sure that's what they told me. There is no cell phone service or any other way to contact anyone on the mainland. The island is great," Crystal said as if trying to convince herself. "Everything is fine."

"Now, wait a minute," Jonah interjected, taking his wife's side. "Let's not get ahead of ourselves. I think we need to check the cave before we start to panic." He looked around the room as all but April's postures relaxed. It was as if they had just been waiting for someone else to say it.

April's back went rod straight, and her eyes bore into Jonah. "Are you implying that I am making this up?" she asked through gritted teeth.

Crystal looked back and forth between Jonah and April with her mouth agape. She looked on the verge of jumping onto Team April but relaxed back into the pillow instead.

Sean stepped in front of April, facing the group. April was unsure if he was protecting her from them or the other way around. "Let's just go check it out. It was a big storm, it was dark, you were hurt, and as you said, you may have been in shock."

"Yes, Sean!" She yelled at his back. "I was in shock because I saw a dead body."

He spun around to look at her and spoke quietly, "Let the guys check it out. You stay here with Crystal. We'll take care of it, okay?"

His voice dripped with condescension. How could he disrespect her so blatantly and in front of everyone else? Before she cried again, or more likely, punched him in the throat, she ran from the room.

CHAPTER THIRTY-TWO

The Dinner

Crystal's heavy eyes roamed sluggishly around the dining room, her gaze sliding over the dark wood panels and the flickering candlelight that barely cut through the room's dimness. Jonah had carried her downstairs, cradling her as if she were delicate china, to join the others for dinner. Her feet, swollen and blistered, pulsed with a dull, throbbing ache that reverberated up her legs. The blisters stretched taut against her skin, each step threatening to rupture them and unleash a new torrent of pain. She was grateful her nerves were working again, yet each twinge of pain was a reminder of how fragile she had become.

She slumped into her chair, the weight of her body collapsing like a puppet with its strings cut. The rest of her body felt distant, as though she were watching herself from across the room. The Valium coursing through her veins dulled her senses, wrapping her mind in a comforting fog that muted the sharp edges of her reality. The burning agony in her feet was merely a background noise compared to the drug-induced serenity enveloping her.

Through her drooping eyelids, she observed the dining room filling slowly. Jonah had slipped away to help Billy with the food, leaving her with a glass of wine and a buzz he hadn't noticed. Sean and April entered next, their faces taut and expressionless, sitting down with a palpable tension that seemed to thicken the air around them. The friction between them was almost tangible, an invisible but cutting force that Crystal could feel even through her dazed state. Their earlier argument, muted and muffled through the walls, had reached no resolution, and the storm between them lingered.

Thomas trudged in with his head bowed and shoulders slumped, a shadow of his usually boisterous self. Crystal's lips curled into a faint, secret smile as she recalled the prank—a mannequin placed strategically to startle Ilma. The memory danced in her mind, a spark of mischief amid the oppressive silence. Ilma's lack of humor had sucked the fun out of the joke, and Crystal could only imagine the fallout still brewing between her and Thomas.

Thomas sank into his chair, his gaze fixed firmly on his lap, hands fidgeting with an invisible object. The suffocating silence thickened, wrapping around them like an invisible shroud. In moments like these, Crystal thought, a smartphone would have been a lifeline—a distraction from the tension, a sanctuary for the eyes in a room charged with unspoken words.

Each creak of a chair, the clink of silverware, the hushed whispers of movements—everything was magnified in the quiet, making the air feel heavier. Crystal, lost in her medicated haze, floated on the surface of this turbulent sea, watching, waiting for the next wave to crash.

Jonah and Billy walked in and set large full bowls in front of every chair, including Ilma's which still sat empty.

"Well, now that everyone is here," Jonah began.

"Thomas," Crystal interrupted. "Where's Ilma?"

Thomas shifted his weight in his seat. She had obviously touched on a sore topic. But she knew that when she asked.

"She's in the Library. She needs some time alone. I'm sure she will be back to herself in the morning," Thomas answered with a forced smile.

April stood up as if looking for any opportunity to leave, "I'll take Ilma's dinner to her."

Thomas abruptly stood up from his seat, nearly knocking his chair over. "It's okay. I'll take it to her."

April looked over at him skeptically. "What's wrong, Thomas? What are you afraid I'm going to tell her?"

Thomas sighed while he grabbed a warm roll and warped it in a napkin. "Look, I just think it would be for the best if Ilma didn't hear about your theories."

"Theories?" April asked sharply.

Sean placed a hand on April's arm, and she shook him off, shooting him an angry stare.

Thomas took advantage of the situation, grabbing the bowl and a spoon, and bolting from the room.

Crystal pondered which fate Thomas dreaded more: braving Ilma's icy wrath or returning to the minefield of tension that was dinner. Both seemed equally unappealing, and his sagging shoulders betrayed the weight of his inner conflict.

Across the table, April sank back into her chair, her posture radiating a resigned frustration. She angled her body away from Sean, pointedly avoiding his gaze. Instead, she reached for her wine, preferring the numbing comfort of the crimson liquid over the lukewarm soup in front of her. Her stiff movements and the frequency with which she refilled her glass were not lost on Crystal, who recognized the signs of someone who felt isolated and disbelieved.

Crystal's spoon dipped into her bowl just as Jonah cleared his throat, his voice breaking the heavy silence that had settled over them. "Thomas and I took a cart out to the cave just before dinner," he began, his tone cautious, almost apologetic.

April's reaction was immediate. She lowered her glass from her lips, a faint purplish stain marking the edge of her mouth, her eyes narrowing into sharp slits as they fixed on Jonah. Her furrowed brows and tense jawline were silent accusations, demanding more from him than vague reassurances.

"We found some towels," Jonah gestured towards April but avoided her piercing gaze, "but there was no body."

April rose abruptly, her chair scraping against the floor with a sharp, grating noise that echoed through the room. Her eyes darted around the table, scanning each face as if searching for the punchline to a cruel joke. The disbelief and frustration were etched deeply into her features, her breath coming in short, shallow bursts.

"Like Sean said earlier," Jonah continued, his voice softer, almost placating, "it was stormy, you were hurt..."

"Don't patronize me, Jonah," April interrupted, her voice cutting through the air like a blade. Her chair pushed back, pressing against the back of her thighs as she leaned forward, her knuckles whitening as she gripped the edge of the table. "The towels were covered in blood. There is no way that guy just got up and walked away."

For a moment, Crystal braced for the explosion, expecting April to launch into a tirade. But instead, April's fire flickered out, and she sank back into her chair with a weariness that seemed to seep into her bones. Defeated, she reached for the bottle, her hands shaking slightly as she topped off her wine. Without pause, she downed the entire glass, the tension in her body dissolving into the alcohol's dull embrace.

The room fell silent again, the unspoken questions hanging heavy in the air, pressing down on them all. Crystal, watching from her corner, felt the weight of April's despair and the shadow of something darker lurking just beneath the surface.

Eager to move on, Jonah said, "I'm not trying to patronize. I just mean, maybe, just maybe, there is someone on the island. What if they were sleeping?" Jonah paused, hoping someone would comment or argue or say anything. When he was only met with silence, he continued, "Just before we came down for dinner, Crystal and I had a little brainstorm. She is sure the caretakers have left the island, and I wondered if someone else is here, maybe even staying in the cave. What if there is a stowaway; or what if their being here has to do with one of our own personal lives? What if their being here is a threat?"

April looked back at Sean over her shoulder, then back to Jonah in disbelief. "How?"

Jonah cleared his throat and glanced around uncomfortably. "Well, for instance, in my case, I recently had to make the tough decision to lay off employees, and even though I made the cuts to benefit the company, it could have very well angered some people."

This time it was Billy and Sean exchanging looks, mouthing the word *ego* at each other and laughing.

"We're serious," Crystal added. "Disgruntled workers can exude violent tendencies."

"Where did you get that information, Crystal? TikTok?" Billy spat.

The venom in his words was shocking and caused her to choke briefly on her soup.

Billy sighed, "Look. We get it that you have a big, important job...."

"It is a big job, Billy," Crystal cut in defensively. "And I know you are going to make fun of me for saying this, but on a similar note, I've had my share of stalkers."

April scoffed under her breath and tried to cover it up with a cough. Crystal never could understand the women who doubted one another. It was bad enough that men always accused women of lying or faking, or manipulating. April made no secret of the fact she felt Crystal's stalker claims were ludicrous.

"They are called *fans*," she had said.

Yes, she's right. Even models have fans—people who admire them, who might nervously ask for autographs or selfies with trembling hands and wide eyes. But those aren't the ones who climb fire escapes or disguise themselves as delivery men. Those are the lunatics, the stalkers whose adoration twists into something darker, more insidious.

One particular nut job had made her life a waking nightmare. He lurked near her building, watching with a predatory intensity every single day. His shadow was always near, trailing her steps like a specter whenever she dared to venture into the public eye. If she braved a walk down a crowded street, there he was, trying to steal a whiff of her scent, hoping for a fleeting brush against her skin, or to catch her eye, just for a second.

His obsession knew no bounds. He applied for a doorman job at her building, his motives as clear as the danger in his eyes. He paid a hacker to infiltrate the building's security feed, watching her every move with voyeuristic delight. The invasion of her privacy reached its grotesque peak when he was caught sifting through her trash, seeking out anything she had touched—a tissue, a discarded bandage, even a tampon. These items, tainted by her mere presence, became sacred relics in his deranged mind.

When the police finally had enough evidence to hold him, his confession chilled her to the bone: he planned to create a clone of her. A Crystal that belonged only to him. His words echoed in her nightmares, a twisted fantasy that left an indelible scar on her psyche.

Though years had passed, the terror he inflicted never fully receded. Crystal couldn't walk through a park or down a city block without her pulse quickening and her breath catching in her throat. The sweat would pool beneath her clothing, soaking through her bra as the old paranoia gripped her once more, reminding her that her world had forever changed—her freedom replaced by fear.

Billy stiffened in his chair briefly, "Okay. Relax, Tenderfoot. But let's say you have a stalker who wants to get to you or Jonah pissed off some people, and they want to exact their revenge. There is no way anyone would know how to find you, right?"

"Well," April interjected, her voice dripping with mock innocence between frequent sips of wine. "That's not exactly true," she added, her half-smile curling with the satisfaction of a seven-year-old tattletale revealing a forbidden secret.

"Crystal has been posting about the island and this trip for months now."

All heads turned in slow motion toward Crystal, who sat back in her chair, her teeth worrying her bottom lip. She glanced nervously between the accusing faces around the table, her voice barely above a murmur. "My followers like to know what I'm up to."

Billy, his breath audible as he worked to keep his composure, leaned forward. "Are you saying," he asked, each word weighted with growing irritation, "that details of our vacation, this island, are on the internet for anyone to see?"

Crystal hesitated, the tension in the room thickening like a storm cloud gathering overhead. "Well, it is a public vacation rental. Of course, it's on the internet," she said, her voice wobbling slightly as she avoided mentioning her myriad posts about the trip.

Crystal had long coveted this private island, her dream destination meticulously documented in her online world. As soon as she secured the week's rental, she flooded her social media with posts—floorpans and amenities, glowing reviews of the secluded haven, and detailed plans for their stay. Her inspiration boards overflowed with vacation outfits, packing tips, and snapshots from previous guests. Not only were these boards accessible to the public, but she amplified their visibility, linking them across all her social media platforms, inviting opinions from friends, family, and any of the 50,000 followers who trailed her digital footprints.

The enormity of her exposure dawned in the room's stifling silence. Billy's frustration boiled over. His chair scraped against the floor as he pushed back abruptly, lifting his still-untouched bowl with a deliberate hand and turning on his heel toward the kitchen, leaving a palpable void in his wake.

Unfazed by the increased tension, April spoke up, "I just remembered something else about the cave."

"Oh, please tell *all* of us about what you just remembered." Sean's words slurred as he spoke.

Sean and April rarely drank; when they did, it was always in moderation. But they both looked toasted.

April rolled her eyes at her husband's petty jealousy and continued, "I know it was stormy, and I was hurt," April said, imitating Jonah's business-like voice, "but I very clearly remember seeing little circles drawn in the dirt around the cave. It was peculiar enough that I was careful to avoid stepping on them."

"What did they look like?" Crystal blurted out.

"Circles. Just circles on the ground that someone would make with the soul of their shoe," April said, agitated. As she realized Crystal wasn't making fun of her, she asked, "Why?"

"I found a circle ground into the carpet in my room," Crystal slurred as she looked at Jonah. "One by the massage table, and in the mornings, right next to my side of the bed. I rubbed the first one out, but it was back this morning. Is there such a thing as a carpet cowlick?"

"Look, there are too many strange things happening here. We need to contact the mainland. We tried checking for service on our phones again this afternoon with no luck. After dinner, I will make my way out to the dock, try to get a signal, and if I can't get one, I'll set off the flares," Sean said definitively. "Someone can come over from the mainland and check things out. It would probably be a good idea to have someone look at Crystal's feet too."

"Oh yeah," April slurred, turning her attention towards Jonah. "One more thing. I checked while you were out at the cave, doubting my sanity. The flares are missing."

CHAPTER THIRTY-THREE

The Allergy

Ilma sank deep into the plush chair in the corner of the library, its overstuffed cushions swallowing her slight frame. The soft, ambient light from the floor lamp cast long shadows, creating a cocoon of warmth around her. Yet, inside, she was a tempest of conflicting emotions, a storm raging just beneath the surface. She loved Thomas, deeply and unequivocally, but the seed of doubt had been planted. Had he lied about the mannequin under their bed? His expression had seemed genuinely surprised, yet that could have been shock from waking to her furious pounding rather than genuine innocence. If he wasn't the culprit, wouldn't he have been more determined to root out the prankster among his siblings?

Ilma's thoughts churned like dark waters, each wave bringing a new question. Thomas had been a notorious prankster for years, yet his tricks had dwindled since their marriage—a shift she had taken as a small victory. Perhaps the mannequin was a long-overdue reprisal for his past antics, but why target her? She had never been part of the pranks, never participated in the endless game of one-upmanship. The logic frayed, unraveling her sense of safety thread by thread.

Her mind flitted to the smoke-filled movie room. The terror of being locked inside, suffocating in the acrid haze, still clawed at her nerves. Thomas's calm during the ordeal, his unwavering surety in each step he took, sent an unbidden chill up her spine. How could he be so composed in the face of such chaos? His reassurances, the tender way he held her as she trembled in the aftermath, felt comforting at the moment, but now that calm seemed unsettling, too perfect, too practiced.

Thomas hadn't protested when she sought solace in the library, hoping to lose herself in a book and escape her spiraling thoughts. He hadn't pressed her to join the family dinner, respecting her need for space. But the sanctuary she sought eluded her. The mystery of her missing bookmark gnawed at her like a persistent itch. She had scoured the room, peering into every crevice and nook where it might have fallen. The cushions revealed no hidden secrets, the tables offered no clues, and the floor lay bare of any trace. Crystal had been bewildered when Ilma questioned her about it, her blank expression suggesting their entire conversation about the bookmark had vanished into thin air.

Ilma's fingers tightened around the armrests, the plush fabric yielding beneath her grip. The library, once a haven, now felt oppressive, its silent walls pressing in with the weight of unanswered questions and the lingering scent of uncertainty.

When Thomas slipped into the library with a bowl of soup, Ilma's pulse quickened, a ripple of unease washing over her. She had only moments ago told him she would eat later, preferring to grab something after the others had finished. The sudden appearance, coupled with the fact that she had just looked up from her book to find him there, standing silently in the doorway, unsettled her deeply. How long had he been watching? Her muscles tensed, and for a fleeting second, her body betrayed her with a tiny, embarrassing trickle of fear.

Thomas's demeanor was off, his actions awkward, as though he were delivering food to a stranger. Their time together had built an intimacy she once thought unshakeable, but tonight, cracks formed under the weight of the unknown. They hadn't navigated every storm life could throw, hadn't tested each other's mettle in the crucible of crisis. She realized, with a cold, creeping dread, that she didn't know how he would act in fear's grip or where his loyalties would fall if ever forced to choose between her and his family. The hypothetical became harrowing.

"Thanks, but I'm not hungry," Ilma said, her eyes shielded by the book she held as a barrier. "I thought I told you I would just get something later."

Thomas shrugged, a petulant movement reminiscent of a child unwilling to own up to mischief. He set the bowl down on the table beside her, his body language stiff, as though bound by unseen cords. Was her mind playing tricks, or did he look… guilty?

"You can take it back with you. I don't want it," she insisted, her tone sharpening, the book rising to block him from her view once more.

"Come on, this is supposed to be a family vacation. Will's been slaving in the kitchen for us. The least we can do is pretend to eat what he makes," Thomas's voice was strained, but before Ilma could respond, he moved with unsettling swiftness. He stormed to her side, snatched the spoon, and plunged it into the soup, shoving a mouthful past his lips. Red broth spilled over, staining his chest and dotting the floor.

"Mmmmm," he groaned, the sound forced, the performance unsettling. "It's delicious. You should try it."

Ilma's breath caught in her throat as she stared at him, a stranger in her husband's skin. The shy, awkward man who had entered the room moments before had vanished, replaced by someone unsettlingly aggressive. Her instincts prickled with alarm.

Her spine straightened, and she uncrossed her legs, setting them firmly on the floor as she reached for the spoon with slow, deliberate movements. She dipped it into the red liquid, scooping up chunks and broth, and brought it to her lips, her gaze never leaving Thomas.

"No!" Thomas's exclamation shattered the tense quiet, and he lunged forward, smacking the spoon from her grip with the ferocity of a cat striking at prey.

"What the hell is wrong with you?" Ilma demanded, her anger surging as she rose to her feet, her voice a blade honed by growing fury. "One minute, I have to eat so I don't hurt Will's feelings, and the next, you're stopping me? What sick game are you playing, Thomas? What is going on?"

Thomas's face contorted in a grimace as he muttered, almost breathlessly, "I taste shrimp."

The room seemed to contract around them, the silence swelling with unspoken fears and questions, as Ilma's heart pounded in her chest, each beat echoing the growing realization that the man before her was cloaked in layers of mystery she was only beginning to unravel.

"Shrimp!" Ilma shrieked as she stormed into the dining room, her voice reverberating off the walls like a clap of thunder. She slammed the bowl of soup onto the table with such force that crimson waves of broth sloshed over the edge, spreading across the polished surface like a sinister tide.

Will appeared in the doorway, emerging from the kitchen with a look of mild curiosity masked by defensive posture. He leaned casually against the doorframe, arms crossed, but his eyes were wary.

"There is shrimp in the soup!" Ilma shouted again, her fury now directed squarely at Will.

"Yeah. It's seafood gumbo," Will responded, his tone flat, as though stating the obvious.

Ilma's breath came in short, shallow bursts, her chest heaving as tears threatened to spill from her eyes. "I am allergic to shellfish. You know that. We discussed it—emailed about it." Her voice cracked as she spoke, the weight of her emotions pulling at her words. "If I had taken just one bite..." Her sentence trailed off, her teeth sinking into her bottom lip to hold back the torrent of emotions. She turned, her eyes meeting Thomas's, the depth of her fear reflected in the shimmering surface of her tears. "You would never have been able to get help in time."

Will uncrossed his arms and lifted his hands in a placating gesture. "Relax. There was no shellfish in the soup. No clams. Clams have shells. No oysters. Oysters have shells. Just fish and shrimp. Fish don't have shells. Shrimp don't have shells. Shrimp are crustaceans."

"Fuck you, Will," Thomas snarled, his voice low and dangerous. "You're a chef. You have to know that shrimp are considered shellfish when it comes to allergies."

"And you," Ilma spat, her finger trembling as it pointed toward April. "You knew about my allergy. We had an entire conversation about how you thought my allergy was due to poor nutrition."

Ilma's voice wavered, the intensity of her anger escalating with each word. Her body quivered under the strain of her fury, her focus sharp and unforgiving as she directed her gaze around the table.

Realizing the gravity of the situation, Will stepped forward and reached out to Ilma, his hand resting gently on her arm. She recoiled at his touch, her muscles tightening beneath his fingers. "I'm so sorry. I truly had no idea. Don't you carry an epinephrine pen?"

Ilma jerked her arm away, her eyes scanning the faces around her, searching for some glimmer of remorse or understanding. Instead, she found only confusion and discomfort. "And which one of you took my bookmark?" she demanded, her voice like a whip crack in the tense silence.

The group's expressions ranged from puzzled to startled, their reactions so disparate that Ilma briefly wondered if she had inadvertently switched to speaking Punjabi. The question wasn't strange, was it? It wasn't lost. It was taken, either as a cruel joke or a malicious act.

Unable to bear the collective weight of their stares any longer, she spun around and marched out of the room, her exit punctuated by the sharp clatter of her shoes against the floor. The tension in her wake was tangible, hanging in the air like a storm cloud.

After watching The Bookworm lose her shit over the shrimp in the soup, The Unwelcome Guest leaned back in thought, a wicked grin creeping across his face. Perhaps, just perhaps, she had the potential to kill after all. Her fury had erupted with a raw, visceral intensity that sent a shiver of excitement down his spine. She wasn't entirely unhinged—no, she possessed a controlled madness, a simmering rage that could boil over in an instant. It was the kind of terror that clung to the edges of sanity, ready to strike without warning.

He couldn't help but picture the scene in his mind, the vision taking on a life of its own. The Bookworm, in a moment of pure, unbridled rage, hurling the bowl of toxic soup across the table, the ceramic shattering upon impact and showering everyone with crimson liquid. He could almost hear the gasp of surprise, the startled cries of those caught in her line of fire. But it didn't stop there. No, in his imagination, she climbed onto the table, her eyes burning with a feral intensity, and began kicking over every bowl of the lethal concoction onto the hapless guests. All the while, the room filled with the haunting strains of classical Pakistani music, a haunting juxtaposition to the chaos she unleashed, her bold red salwar-kameez dress swirling like a tempest around her as she dove at the necks of her unsuspecting victims with broken shards.

The Unwelcome Guest allowed himself a moment to savor the fantasy, his dark thoughts spiraling deeper. What would have happened if she had eaten one of those shrimp? The question lingered, enticing and macabre. Would her body betray her, swelling grotesquely like a berry about to burst? Would her eyes, wide with terror, silently plead for salvation as she realized that breath was her last, her airway sealed tight by an unseen assassin? Would she gasp for help, or would she use her final moments in a desperate, frantic attempt to uncover the truth, to identify her killer even as life slipped away?

He relished the imagined scene, each detail etched vividly in his mind, a sinister ballet of desperation and death. It was a dance he might never witness in reality, but in his mind's eye, it played out with a chilling perfection that left him both enthralled and hungry for more.

CHAPTER THIRTY-FOUR
The Night Rider

As much as he yearned to complete his dark mission, The Unwelcome Guest felt his sanity slipping through his fingers, teetering on the edge of madness amidst these insufferable people. How could they all belong to the same family? The incongruities between them were glaringly obvious, like pieces from different puzzles forced into an awkward fit. Did they truly believe that a week-long vacation together would be filled with harmonious joy? Such naïveté bordered on stupidity.

The Bookworm, cloistered in her corner with a book perpetually in hand, exuded the air of a hermit who had accidentally wandered into civilization. Somehow expecting her husband to be spineless and meek, following her lead, his attempts to normalize her reclusiveness only deepening the pitiful display. The Unwelcome Guest sneered at the thought of humiliation she lay upon him, standing by her side, emasculated before the other men.

Then there was The Supermodel, a vision of beauty when unconscious, her features serene and unmarred by the grating tone of her voice. Her allure was magnetic, and on bold days, The Unwelcome Guest indulged in stolen glances even when she was awake, recording her incessant video diaries. Her self-absorption was boundless, each word dripping with a narcissism that left no room for the reality of others. Her dream of a secluded island vacation was everyone's nightmare, a delusion she paraded shamelessly across social media. Initially, envy had clouded his judgment, fantasizing about the privileges her husband must enjoy. But as her vapid personality unfolded, desire gave way to disgust, her beauty eclipsed by her insufferable vanity.

The Runner, however, ignited a seething hatred within him. Her relentless drive, the need to outshine and dominate, grated on his nerves like nails on a chalkboard. She was the embodiment of a perpetual one-upper, her competitive nature exhausting to witness. How she managed to run a gym, a place meant to inspire and motivate, was beyond him. Her existence seemed fueled by a toxic cocktail of unmet childhood expectations or an inferiority complex bred by constant comparison. Whatever the origin, her presence was a blight he longed to erase from the world, an itch in his brain that only her absence could soothe.

Each character played their part in the grotesque symphony of dysfunction, their discordant lives grating on The Unwelcome Guest's patience. They were a cacophony he could no longer endure, their every interaction a reminder of his growing disdain and the dark urges simmering beneath his surface.

After ensuring the house was wrapped in the stillness of slumber, The Unwelcome Guest descended into the underground tunnel, his footsteps whispering against the cold stone. The tunnel led him to the garage, where he retrieved a weathered cart, its metal frame creaking softly under his touch. His destination was his secret cave, once a sanctuary of solitude but now tainted by the prying eyes of The Runner. His stomach churned with disgust at the thought of her invasion, her curiosity tearing through his privacy as if it were tissue paper—just like Fred had done.

The recent visit by the men, dismissing The Runner's tales as fanciful nonsense, brought a perverse satisfaction. It reinforced his belief that they wouldn't venture back. This island, under its mundane facade, was a voyeur's haven—a fact cleverly concealed, only revealed to those who stumbled upon the right fetish websites. He had known from the beginning that taking the Gold Book in its entirety would raise suspicion. Instead, he had only removed the pages detailing the hidden doors and secret passageways, adhering to the advice of the clandestine community on watcher forums. The thrill lay in the unsuspecting guests, oblivious to the eyes trailing their every move.

Yet, someone had pieced the puzzle together, roaming the hidden corridors. This revelation sent a chill down his spine. He had to relocate his precious collection of stolen documents, chemicals, and pills. They were no longer safe behind the walls, especially with an intruder in their midst.

The Bookworm's bookmark had been an easy target—a sentimental trinket inscribed with a syrupy note. Its theft had been intended to sting, but the chaos it sparked among the guests was an unforeseen bonus. The Runner's filthy, rain-soaked shoes were another matter. Their stench was so overpowering that even he, with his tolerance for the unpleasant, considered burning them. But the acrid smoke might attract unwanted attention.

The Supermodel's scarf, however, was a treasure of a different sort. Soft, luxurious, and steeped in her essence, it was a trophy he coveted. Her phone or wedding ring would have been ideal, but they were too difficult to procure. The scarf was a serendipitous find, its delicate fibers clinging to the faint scent of her perfume, mingled with the imagined warmth of her skin. He inhaled its fragrance sparingly, afraid to strip it of its intoxicating aroma, a reminder of his proximity to her vulnerability.

Navigating the path between the cave and the house, he moved with the stealth of a shadow. The cart, though cumbersome, was his ally in transporting his cache efficiently. He avoided flicking on the garage lights and kept the cart's headlights off until he was swallowed by the woods, enveloped in their nocturnal embrace. Caution was paramount.

Most pressing was the removal of the flares from the house. Upon learning that The Runner had discovered the body, a sense of urgency gripped him. He had to act swiftly, eliminating any means of signaling the mainland. The flares, nestled in the first aid kit, were swiftly confiscated. He ran through a mental checklist, ensuring nothing was left behind that could compromise his carefully constructed isolation. The stakes were too high for complacency.

Now that he had fully committed to what needed to be done, The Unwelcome Guest knew he couldn't squander the opportunities the island presented. Its isolation was his ally, a fortress of solitude that would unravel into chaos should any guest make it back to the mainland. If they escaped, his mission would morph into a far more complicated affair—he might even be forced to resort to the crude tactics he had used on the ferry captain, a strategy he hadn't planned to repeat.

The memory of that fateful encounter lingered vividly in his mind. The ferry captain had been watching him with a scrutinizing gaze during their last trip from the island, his eyes burning holes into the back of The

Unwelcome Guest's head. There was a tension in the air, palpable and thick, as if the captain could sense the disturbance beneath the surface. True, someone was missing, but why the captain's suspicions had landed squarely on him was a mystery. The conversations between the captain and Fred had been frequent, albeit one-sided. Still, there was no concrete reason to believe the captain had seen anything or knew too much, but leaving loose ends was a luxury he couldn't afford.

Once they docked, the maintenance workers dispersed quickly, their presence fleeting as the night swallowed them whole. The ferry captain remained, alone and vulnerable, or so it seemed. As the man made his way to his rusting truck, locking up for the night, The Unwelcome Guest seized the moment. He waited, breath held, heart pounding, and then, with a sudden burst of acceleration, he plowed into the captain from behind, just a few steps away from his old vehicle.

He had always been morbidly curious about the physics of hitting a person with a car. Would the body bounce off the hood and tumble over the roof? Would it be flung forward like a ragdoll? The reality was far less theatrical. Upon impact, the captain crumpled, dragged under the vehicle, his body folding like a marionette with its strings severed. The rear driver-side tire thudded over him with a jarring bounce, a grotesque mimicry of a speed bump.

He didn't stop. There was no need. In the rearview mirror, under the stark illumination of the parking lot lights, he caught a glimpse of the body—contorted, lifeless, with dark, viscous stains spreading across the concrete like a morbid piece of abstract art. The scene was ghastly, yet he felt no remorse, only the cold satisfaction of eliminating a threat.

Cleaning the rental car had been a bitch, each scrub reminding him of the act he had committed. Oddly enough, the vehicle bore no visible damage, as if it, too, wanted to forget the violent encounter. But he had no intention of making a habit of such methods. His purpose on the island was clear, and until he saw it through, no one would be leaving.

CHAPTER THIRTY-FIVE

The Fucking Circles

Still dressed in her worn pajama bottoms and an oversized t-shirt that hung loosely off one shoulder, April descended the stairs with deliberate caution. Each step was a careful negotiation, her hand gripping the railing as if it were the only thing anchoring her to the stairwell. The air was cool against her skin, but she barely noticed, her mind clouded with the fatigue that had settled deep in her bones.

In the dim light, she had bypassed the mirror in the bathroom, not wanting to confront the reflection that would surely betray her exhaustion. She could imagine the hollowed eyes, the lines etched deeper into her skin—a testament to the unrelenting stress of the past few days. How quickly the vitality of her daily routine had eroded in the chaos of Sean's family dynamics.

Where once she could rise with the dawn for a brisk 5 AM run, tackle the day managing their gym, and still have energy to spare for a night out at their favorite vegan spot, now she was a shell of her former self. The island, meant to be a sanctuary, had become a stage for drama she could scarcely endure. How could one family contain so much turmoil?

The kitchen, usually a bustling hub, was eerily subdued. Sean's brothers were gathered around the island, their silence deafening, heads bowed over steaming mugs as though seeking answers in the swirling depths. They looked up as she shuffled in, their expressions a mix of confusion and concern. April knew she must look a sight—disheveled, defeated, nothing like the poised and energetic woman they had come to expect. She could feel their eyes tracing the shadows under her eyes, the pallor of her skin. She had long since stopped caring about impressing them.

With a quiet resolve, she crossed the room, poured herself a mug of coffee, and inhaled the comforting aroma, savoring its warmth against her hands. The decision to stay or retreat weighed heavily, but curiosity won. What might they say, these men, without the filter of their wives present?

April settled into a chair at the kitchen table, positioning herself so she could gaze out at the lush, inviting backyard. The island was, indeed, a paradise. Had it been just her and Sean, they would have relished every luxury—exploring the grounds, challenging each other in the gym, swimming laps under the open sky. But that dream was overshadowed by the relentless pressure to play their part in this dysfunctional family tableau.

She sighed, the weight of reality pressing down. The truth was, even sharing the cost, the trip was beyond their means. Crystal's sudden adjustment of their share had been a kindness April hadn't missed, though it stung her pride. Running their gym had its perks, but wealth was not one of them. In this paradise, her financial constraints were glaringly evident.

The morning light spilled across the patio, a stark contrast to the storm brewing inside her. She stared out, her mind drifting, lost in the possibilities of what might have been—what could still be.

Sean broke the silence, his voice tinged with confusion, as he asked, "Are you planning to go for a run this morning?"

April slowly turned to face the kitchen, her expression a mask of disbelief. She stood in her rumpled pajamas, her hair a tangled mess that resembled a bird's nest, and the shadows under her eyes hinted at sleepless nights. The answer should have been evident. "I can't," she responded, her voice flat and drained.

The brothers, engrossed in their coffee, didn't even bother with a follow-up question, their silence as dismissive as it was deafening.

April, growing weary of the constant disregard, broke the quiet with a sarcastic tone. "Why, April? Why can't you go for a run today?" she asked herself aloud, her voice laden with bitterness. Her rhetorical question snapped the brothers out of their coffee-induced trance, their eyes reluctantly lifting toward her.

"Oh, I'm so glad you asked, April," she continued, answering herself in a mocking cheer. "Actually, my ankle is still tender, but it doesn't matter anyway. I can't go for a run today because someone stole my running shoes."

Will and Thomas exchanged a knowing glance, rolling their eyes as if they had just heard the latest in a long series of conspiracy theories from her.

"Stole?" Sean's laugh was strained, his discomfort palpable. "Don't you mean you just can't *find* your running shoes? Or maybe you mean that you have *misplaced* them?" He edged closer to his brothers, subtly distancing himself from April.

April's eyes narrowed, her voice sharp as she took a step toward him. "No, dear," she hissed, her words dripping with venom. "Someone stole my running shoes. I remember leaving them by the front door since they were so wet from when I was stuck in the rainstorm."

A shiver coursed through her, not from cold but from the memory of icy rain soaking her to the bone. She could almost feel the weight of the drenched fabric clinging to her skin, the relentless downpour chilling her fingers and toes. Her mind drifted dangerously close to recalling the horrifying discovery in the cave, but she forced it back into the recesses of her mind, locking it away to preserve her sanity.

Thomas, attempting to diffuse the tension, spoke up hesitantly, "Maybe someone put them in the dryer for you."

April's laugh was hollow, her contempt cutting through the air. "Yeah, Thomas. Sure. Crystal crawled down here, or wait, Ilma must have left the confines of the library to throw my wet sneakers in the dryer," she snapped, her voice laced with anger and disbelief.

Turning back around, she sank into her chair, her gaze fixed on the world outside the window. The idyllic view was lost on her, overshadowed by her frustration. She was tired of being dismissed, of their incessant need to prove her wrong rather than simply listening. How much simpler it would be to admit that perhaps, just perhaps, she was right?

April couldn't fathom why someone would take her shoes, but she was certain it wasn't one of the family members. And in her heart, she knew Ilma hadn't merely *misplaced* her bookmark, and Crystal's scarf hadn't just *vanished*. There was something more sinister at play, and she was exhausted from fighting to be heard.

Jonah cleared his throat, his voice cutting through the tense atmosphere as he abruptly changed the subject. "So, who took the cart out for a moonlit ride last night?" His gaze remained fixed on his coffee mug, deliberately avoiding eye contact as he took a slow, deliberate sip.

April, sitting by the window, shifted her attention to the brothers, her curiosity piqued by Jonah's peculiar and assumptive question. The air around the kitchen island thickened with unspoken tension as Will, Thomas, and Sean exchanged puzzled glances.

Jonah finally lifted his eyes, fixing a pointed stare at his brothers across the counter. "Well, I know for certain it wasn't Crystal. I still have to carry her to the toilet like some kind of queen," he said with a dry smirk before turning to Thomas. "And I seriously doubt Ilma went for a joyride unless she was trying to escape back to the mainland."

He tried to inject a note of humor, but the room remained silent, the joke falling flat. Thomas bristled visibly, the tension escalating with each passing second. Will stood abruptly, distancing himself by leaning against the countertop behind him, arms stubbornly crossed, disappointment etched across his face.

Jonah, baffled by the silence, scanned the room. "Seriously? None of you are going to fess up?" His eyes flicked toward April briefly. "It's not a big deal. I was up at two in the morning, saw the headlights from the cart deep in the woods. Someone took it out. Why not just admit it?"

Thomas shifted uncomfortably under Jonah's scrutiny. "Why are you looking at me?"

Sean intervened. "Maybe because you're the only one who'd set an alarm in the middle of the night just to pull a prank."

Thomas retorted, "I don't even know where those carts are kept or how to start them. I've only ever sat in the back when we were dropped off at the front of the house, remember?"

Will, still leaning, shot back, "It's an electric cart, Thomas. It's not a rocket ship."

April, sensing the rising tension, spoke up, "What if it wasn't one of us?" Her voice trembled slightly, but she steadied herself, trying to be heard.

All eyes turned to her, the weight of their collective stares pressing down on her. Will's gaze hardened as he stepped away from the counter. "You really think someone else is on the island? Someone who's hiding out, stealing flares, sabotaging the popcorn maker and the hot tub, and now joyriding with our cart? Is that what you think, April?"

His tone was harsh, his body language aggressive as he loomed over her seated form. The physical disparity made her feel small, almost insignificant.

April's cheeks flushed with heat, and her stomach churned, but she squared her shoulders, meeting his gaze. "Yes," she replied, her voice firm, though inwardly she longed for the armor of her workout gear. "I'm positive I saw a body in that cave. Someone has been in the house, watching us sleep, taking our things. Why wouldn't they use the cart?"

She turned to Jonah, her expression hardening. "Didn't Crystal say she felt like someone was watching her sleep? What about the circles on the carpet?"

Will rolled his eyes. "The fucking circles? Seriously, April? That's your big clue?"

Sean stepped in between them, his voice calm but firm. "Back off, Will."

Thomas, attempting to defuse the situation, added from behind the counter, "We're on vacation. Why does it matter who took the cart? If there's someone else here, they're probably just looking for a place to stay. No one is in danger."

Will muttered, "Maybe if you'd just admit you took the cart, Thomas, we could all move on."

April's patience snapped. The petty argument over a cart was infuriating, especially when none of them seemed to take her seriously. She hurled her coffee mug at the sink, the crash of shattering ceramic punctuating her frustration.

Without a word, she stormed out of the room, her fury evident. She knew they thought her mad, and in that moment, she didn't care. She needed allies, and she hoped Crystal and Ilma would understand. Climbing the stairs, she realized with a pang of betrayal that Sean hadn't followed her.

He had clearly chosen his side.

CHAPTER THIRTY-SIX

The Inner Circle

When April burst into the bedroom, the door swung wide, startling Crystal into tossing her phone aside as if it had burned her hands. Her cheeks flushed with embarrassment. She had been scrutinizing her reflection, searching for any telltale signs of stress—fine lines, maybe a wrinkle or two that the trip might have etched into her face. Yet, in that unguarded moment, when April barged in unannounced, Crystal had been caught in the act of practicing sultry expressions at herself.

April stormed in, looking disheveled, her face a canvas of exhaustion. Without a word, she crossed the room and collapsed into the tall chair by the fireplace with such dramatic force that for a fleeting moment, Crystal wondered if she was mocking her. It was out of character for April. She was usually composed, her appearance effortlessly sporty, often clad in high-end athletic wear and her ever-present running shoes—ready to sprint at a moment's notice. But now, she resembled a toddler rudely awakened from a too-short nap, her hair tousled, her clothes crumpled.

Crystal, ever the diplomat, called out in a tone laced with faux cheer. "Good morning," she said, her voice tinged with sarcasm.

April barely registered the greeting, her eyes fixated on the cold, dark fireplace. "Do you ever feel like you'll never get into the inner circle with those guys?"

Crystal raised an eyebrow, confused. "Why the hell would I want into their circle? I have never aspired to be one of the boys."

Abruptly, April rose from the chair and began pacing the room, her steps agitated, her movements sharp. She halted in front of Crystal's bed, her eyes locking onto Crystal's with a fierce intensity. "Do you think you'll ever be as important to Jonah as his brothers are?"

Crystal's lips curled into an involuntary smile, amusement bubbling up despite the seriousness in April's voice. She couldn't hold back her laughter any longer. It erupted, shaking her shoulders. "What the hell are you talking about? I am the *most* important person in Jonah's life. You are the most important person in Sean's life." She hesitated, mentally adding, *Well, except for Sean,* but chose not to voice it. "They're a close-knit family, but we are their foundation, their stability."

April's gaze softened, her expression shifting from tense concern to a look of awe. Crystal had always marveled at April's lack of self-assurance, finding it baffling. April was the epitome of athletic grace and competitive spirit, her beauty as undeniable as her intelligence and wit. She was the kind of woman who could lounge in her panties and one of Sean's old college shirts, devouring nachos during a game, effortlessly embodying the ideal fantasy for many. Yet, despite all her attributes, she doubted Sean's affection.

April's voice dropped, her tone vulnerable. "Maybe I'm overreacting. I just know something's wrong. It's one thing for Jonah, Thomas, or Will to ignore me, but not Sean. Sean knows I'm not dramatic. I don't crave attention."

Crystal's mind flickered back to the day they arrived, recalling April strutting around in her sports bra, her abs on full display. April might not consider herself dramatic, but she certainly enjoyed attention, whether she admitted it or not. It wasn't about seeking the spotlight; it was about owning her hard-earned achievements. Crystal held her thoughts, watching April with a mix of sympathy and understanding.

As April turned to leave, her hand reached for the door, but before she could exit, Ilma entered, her presence adding another layer to the charged atmosphere.

Rather than hide in her room—or better yet, the sanctuary of the library—all day, Ilma steeled herself to face the discomfort head-on. She walked straight through Crystal's bedroom doors with the deliberate calm of someone pretending nothing had happened. As if there had been no near-death experience in a smoke-filled room. As if a mannequin hadn't been stashed under her bed to give her a heart attack. As if her husband hadn't almost served her a deadly plate of seafood. As if she hadn't unleashed her fury on Will and the rest of the family the night before.

Ilma crossed the room and seated herself in one of the plush chairs by the fireplace, its soft cushions swallowing her weight as she feigned nonchalance. She caught the quick exchange of glances between April and Crystal but chose to ignore it, burying the haunting memories of the past days beneath a fragile veneer of composure. The morning had been suffocating, Thomas barely speaking to her before vanishing to the kitchen, despite his promise not to leave her alone. She clenched her jaw, her frustration simmering just under the surface. His abrupt departure felt like a betrayal, a crack in the fragile promise he'd made.

Will had peeked into the library earlier, his eyes downcast, apologizing in a mumbled loop, shifting nervously on the cold tiles of the hallway, afraid to step inside. Ilma replayed his awkwardness in her mind, a bitter taste left by his guilt and discomfort.

Three more days. She clung to the mantra like a lifeline, willing herself to endure just a little longer. This fancy island retreat, meant to be a dream vacation, had morphed into a slow march through quicksand. She longed for her cat, her books, the comforting cocoon of her privacy. Even the sprawling island house couldn't shield her from the invasive proximity of everyone else.

Her fingers found a loose thread on the chair, tugging at it absentmindedly, grounding herself in the small, tactile action. "I don't know what's going on," Ilma murmured, her voice barely above a whisper. Her eyes stayed fixed on the fabric beneath her fingers. "Thomas won't tell me anything. I feel like a stranger. What is everyone keeping from me?"

When she finally lifted her gaze to meet Crystal's, her eyes were brimming with unshed tears. Thomas, in his misguided attempt to shield her, had only succeeded in deepening her sense of alienation.

Crystal's expression softened, a tender resolve settling over her features. "Thomas didn't want you to know. But we'll tell you everything." She reached for April's arm, pulling her close, and patted the spot on the bed beside her, inviting Ilma to join them.

At that moment, Jonah entered the room, his brow furrowed in concern as he took in the sight of the three women sitting together. "Uh, what's going on?" he asked, his tone awkward. He turned to Crystal, his words hurried. "Do you need anything? I just grabbed a cart. The boys and I are heading to the dock to fish."

He glanced at April, adding with a touch of confusion, "To my surprise, all the carts were there."

Crystal, uninterested in Jonah's fishing plans, released April's hand and reached for her nail file on the nightstand. Jonah continued, "Billy packed a cooler and some lunch, but we won't be gone long."

"I'm fine. If I need anything, I'll scream until April or Ilma comes running," she quipped.

The joke fell flat. No one laughed.

They were all teetering on the edge, unsure when the ground would give way beneath them.

After Jonah left, they shared everything with Ilma—the cave, the body, the alleged late night cart ride, and the eerie disappearances. They spoke with honesty, their voices gentle as they laid bare the secrets Thomas had tried to shield her from. Ilma's tears fell freely. She paced the room, staring out over the terrace, wondering how she had reached this point of mistrust in her marriage.

When silence finally settled over them, it wasn't uncomfortable. It was a shared stillness, a quiet bond in their collective vulnerability.

April drifted to the terrace, the breeze playing with her hair. Ilma sat beside Crystal, watching her through a haze of unshed tears. Out of the corner of her eye, she saw Crystal's hand hover near the nightstand, almost grasping a small baggie of pills before she pulled back, resuming her task with the nail file.

April turned, her voice steady. "Why don't you two relax? I'm going to hit the gym, then maybe take a swim." After sliding the terrace doors shut, she crossed the room to the hallway uncharacteristically slow, pausing only to add, "It's not like I can go for a run without shoes."

She left without looking back.

"Go ahead," Crystal encouraged, her smile faint but reassuring. "I'll be okay."

Ilma returned the smile, rising to leave. She was surprised by April's apparent calm, but beneath the surface, she suspected even April was unraveling. As for Crystal, she clung to the illusion of a perfect vacation, her determination unyielding.

Three more days. Ilma whispered the mantra once more as she thought of the cocktails waiting in the fridge, a temporary escape from the chaos that had engulfed them all.

CHAPTER THIRTY-SEVEN

The Paranoia

For the first time in as long as she could remember, April couldn't summon the energy to drag herself into her usual workout routine. With the men all gone, the house fell into a strange quiet, one that seemed to press in on her. She'd thought about lying in bed, letting her mind wander, piecing together everything that had happened, but after hours of staring at the ivy creeping up the walls and waiting for it to move, a restless itch formed deep in her bones. She needed to get out of her room.

The stillness had settled too thick around her, and she felt trapped within her own thoughts. She needed clarity, and the best way to find it was always through movement. Yet, with her swollen ankle and no shoes, running was out of the question—thankfully, because she couldn't bring herself to face the woods again. The thought of being alone in those shadowed paths, the sensation of eyes watching, following, waiting for her to break the silence... it made her skin prickle with unease. She shuddered, unable to shake the memory of the suffocating feeling that had clung to her the last time she'd been out there.

Even in the gym, the sensation of being observed was constant. The mirrors multiplied her reflection, an unnerving reminder that she wasn't alone, no matter how hard she tried to concentrate on her workout. Every time her gaze flickered, her own image made her flinch, and that unease translated into danger—it's too easy to misstep or lose focus when the mind is clouded with fear.

Swimming, however, would be different. The rhythm of each stroke, the lap after lap, it calmed her restless mind. The sounds of the water, combined with her ear plugs, muffled everything, turning the world into a gentle hum, and she could lose herself in it.

With determination finally stirring in her, she slid into her swimsuit, the cool fabric against her skin grounding her, though the effort to move felt almost foreign. She didn't bother with a cover-up—her mind already drifting to the pool, the clarity she sought just beyond the door. Crystal was still lying in bed, Ilma was keeping to herself, and the guys were off fishing. There was a slim chance she'd run into anyone, and that thought was a comfort.

As she stepped into the hallway, she paused, her shoulders slumping under an invisible weight. She glanced at Crystal's door. For a moment, a flicker of hesitation passed through her. The truth was, she didn't want to interact, didn't want to risk her swim being interrupted. But, out of some sense of obligation, more out of habit than kindness, she poked her head into the room, the door barely cracking open as she peered inside.

Crystal was sitting up in bed, absorbed in her phone. April cleared her throat, her voice casual but with a slight edge, a polite invitation cloaked in thinly veiled reluctance. "I'm going for a swim. Need anything?"

The offer was hollow. The way her body language read: *I'm just checking, but I'm really hoping you don't ask me to stay. Please, don't ask.*

Without looking up, Crystal lazily waved a hand in dismissal, as if brushing away a fly. "Girl, I'm good. Go do your thing."

The wave was dismissive, but more than that—it was a clear signal that Crystal wasn't interested in any more socializing either, and April didn't have to fake the relief that washed over her. With a silent nod, she backed away from the door, feeling the weight in her chest lighten just a little. The swim was calling her now, the water offering a temporary reprieve from the mounting tension in the house.

April shut the door behind her with a soft click, the sound swallowed almost instantly by the cavernous silence that stretched out in every direction. The house felt empty, hollow—like an abandoned cathedral, its towering walls echoing the absence of life. She padded quietly down the stairs, her bare feet skimming the cold floor. Every footstep seemed amplified in the stillness, each one a reminder of how alone she felt within these walls.

She passed the alcove leading to the Library and Will's room, her gaze involuntarily flicking to the shadowed doorway. The temptation to sneak a peek inside the "Doll Room" was like a persistent itch, gnawing at her curiosity. But she fought it down, unwilling to cross that boundary, even if she was certain Will wouldn't mind. It wasn't his privacy she was protecting—it was the creeping sensation that she didn't want to be caught rummaging through his things by Ilma. Ilma was almost certainly in the Library, retreating from everyone, just like always.

It wasn't that April didn't feel for Ilma. The woman had had an awful couple of days—hell, she was probably still trying to find her place in this tangled family, still a recent addition, still floating on the outskirts. There was no denying it, though: awkward and uncomfortable were Ilma's default states. It was as if she carried that discomfort in her bones, like it was woven into the fabric of her personality.

With an unspoken sigh, April took lighter, more measured steps as she moved through the living room. Her eyes flickered back toward the hallway, watching for movement, but the tension in the air was thick. Then came the loud slam from the kitchen, like the sudden cracking of a distant thunderclap.

April's heart lurched in her chest, the sound crashing into her bones with a shock of adrenaline. Without thinking, she darted behind the sofa, her breath shallow and erratic. The instinct to hide, to shrink into the shadows, overwhelmed her. She couldn't remember thc last time she'd felt this paranoid—this exposed. Here she was, sneaking around in a house she thought she knew, and now it felt like a prison. A claustrophobic, dark cave pressing in on her from all sides, suffocating the very air around her. The thought of being trapped in that small, cramped cave at the end of the island sent another shiver down her spine.

She lay perfectly still, her body frozen in a tense, unnatural position, praying her rapid, panicked breathing wouldn't give her away. Her gaze landed on the tank across the room, the slow-moving, spiky fish drifting lazily through the water. For a moment, she found herself fixated on it—the creature's steady, peaceful movements, a stark contrast to the storm brewing in her own chest. But the calmness should've been soothing... and yet, it only made her more uneasy. Her heart beat in her ears, and she pulled her eyes away from the lonely fish as she contemplated being not-so-alone..

Another noise echoed through the house, this one more distant but growing louder. It sounded like something—or someone—was dragging something along the floor. April's pulse raced in response. Her mind spun wildly with possibilities. *Is it the body?* Was the dead man from the cave being dragged back inside? Her heart pounded, and her breath caught in her throat. Was someone else dragging him? Was she about to come face-to-face with something far more sinister than a mere intruder?

The sound drew closer, and the tension in the room became unbearable. She could hardly take it anymore. With every nerve screaming at her to act, April finally shoved aside the paralyzing fear long enough to peek around the side of the couch. Her muscles tensed, ready to spring into action, to fight or flee. But instead of a threat, she found herself face-to-face with... Ilma's bunny slippers.

April blinked, startled, as she looked up to see Ilma standing above her. She watched as Ilma casually lifted the entire pitcher of Will's fruity drink to her lips, took a loud, exaggerated sip, and smacked her lips with dramatic relish. All while staring at April on the floor.

"Weird," Ilma muttered, her voice flat, as if nothing at all had happened. Without missing a beat, Ilma turned and shuffled toward the Library, her plush slippers softly dragging against the floor.

April collapsed back against the sofa, her body sagging in a mix of relief and embarrassment. She couldn't believe it—*Ilma.* Out of all people, it was Ilma. Her heart was still racing, her body tense from the sudden shock, and yet, she couldn't help but feel utterly foolish. If only she knew that being scared could be such a workout. She'd have opened a haunted house instead of a gym if she had known how much cardio fear would give her.

The front door creaked open, and the loud voices of the men echoed through the house, their casual banter suddenly jolting the stillness.

"Oh, hey, Ilma," she heard Sean call out.

"Hey yourself," Ilma replied curtly, her voice becoming more distant as she made her way back to the Library. With a soft thud, the door slammed shut behind her, cutting off any further interaction.

Chapter Thirty-Eight

The Retreat

Prepared to shut herself away in the Library for the remainder of the day, Ilma had made a quick stop by the kitchen, gathering provisions as if fortifying her personal retreat. She could slip in and out of the Library to use the bathroom without anyone noticing, but traversing the entire first floor to reach the kitchen—well, that could spell socializing. And socializing was the last thing she needed. So, she grabbed the essentials: a bag of nuts, a bowl of grapes, and the entire pitcher of whatever fruity cocktail Will had concocted the day before.

By the time she neared the hallway leading to the Library, she heard the guys' boisterous chatter from outside the front door, a distant droning of noise reaching her sensitive ears. She tensed, knowing she was running out of time to make a clean getaway. She couldn't exactly sprint without risking disaster, not when she was balancing the pitcher—awkwardly by its tiny handle—along with the nuts and bowl of grapes. The pink drink sloshed dangerously over the lip, a small warning that would be impossible to ignore. After a quick glance around to ensure no one had noticed, she rubbed the heel of her slipper over the spill, her motion swift and practiced. Satisfied that it was clean enough, she resumed her cautious trek—only to freeze when she spotted April.

April. *On the floor?* Behind the couch, of all places. The sight was strange enough to make Ilma hesitate. There was a momentary pause. Ilma's mind turned inward. Hiding behind the couch wasn't something she'd ever done—well, not in quite that manner—but she couldn't claim to be unfamiliar with avoiding people. She'd spent more time in bathrooms at parties than was socially acceptable, retreating to the solitude of a stall when the noise became too stimulating. And at the bar, whenever she did go out, ordering a drink was always an opportunity to delay the inevitable social interaction. A moment to breathe, to gather her strength before returning to the chaos. But even in all her avoidance, *hiding behind the couch* wasn't something she could rule out for herself in the future.

The guys' entrance seemed to snap her back into reality. After hearing about the cave and the man who had... whatever had happened there, she felt a deep, unsettling desire to numb herself. The drink had become a sort of lifeline, a way to blunt the sharp edge of the terror that had crept into the corners of her mind. She was grateful they'd told her, but part of her wished she could forget, wished she could return to the naïve days before the truth had shattered her fragile sense of safety.

She no longer worried about the spilled drink. With the only other witness—April—caught in her own awkward situation, Ilma moved forward, barely acknowledging the men's loud, chaotic entrance as she pushed toward her sanctuary.

The Library door hung open with an almost welcome finality. Inside, Ilma placed the bag of nuts and grapes on the side table next to her favorite chair, setting down the pitcher with exaggerated care as if placing a fragile artifact. The door slammed shut behind her with a definitive kick, and she spun the lock into place with a mechanical precision. The last thing she needed was for someone to wander by, see the door ajar, and mistake it for an open invitation. The locked door was her fortress, a message to the world that she craved privacy, solitude. The loud finality of the lock snapping into place was like her personal exclamation point.

The moment she sank into the chair, she took a deep, indulgent swig of the drink, the sweet, tart taste cutting through the tension in her throat. It was almost too much, but not quite—just enough to calm the creeping unease. She could feel her body beginning to relax.

CHAPTER THIRTY-NINE

The Challenge

When April crawled out from behind the sofa, her eyes immediately fixed on the trail of pink droplets snaking their way across the floor, leading into the hallway, and, she assumed, disappearing into the library's shadows. The droplets seemed to pulsate with a silent, ominous rhythm, each one a heartbeat echoing the room's sudden stillness.

Her gaze shifted toward the entryway, scanning for Jonah, but he was nowhere to be seen. Either he was outside parking the cart or had already bolted upstairs to check on Crystal. The absence was a nagging reminder that he had selfishly left her alone and incapacitated.

April glanced around the room, noting the lingering gazes of the remaining brothers. She felt their eyes tracking her every movement, their expressions a mix of curiosity and concern. Fighting the urge to panic, she raised a finger to her eye, mimicking the aimless motion of searching for a lost contact lens. She blinked deliberately, eyes darting upward as if battling an imaginary irritant.

She locked eyes with each brother in turn, her confidence building with every step she took toward them. Her charade had been a quick fix, a flimsy cover that wouldn't withstand scrutiny, especially from Ilma or Sean. Sean knew April didn't wear contacts, and Ilma had seen her ducked behind the couch like a coward.

Self-consciousness prickled at her skin as she became acutely aware of her attire—just a swimsuit clinging to her form. Despite her athletic frame and minimal body fat, the near-nakedness made her uneasy. Unlike Crystal, who flaunted her figure with ease, April preferred the comfort of a barrier. Grabbing a blanket from the couch, she wrapped it snugly around her midsection, transforming it into a makeshift beach towel.

"Going for a swim?" Will's voice cut through her thoughts, laced with a smirk that curled at the edges of his mouth.

April's mind raced, scrambling for a quick response. "Uh, yes," she replied, her tone light and teasing. "I was going to, but when I heard you guys were back, I remembered I hadn't challenged you to a game of pool yet." Her voice carried a hint of bravado, daring him to rise to the bait.

Will's eyebrows lifted, his expression shifting between intrigue and something darker, perhaps irritation. The playful banter they often shared seemed to carry an undercurrent today, a tension she couldn't quite place.

"You down, *Billy*?" she continued, infantilizing his name with a teasing tone, using the childhood nickname he had long since abandoned—except with Crystal, who remained oblivious to his wish to be seen as an adult.

Will's back straightened, his stance becoming rigid, adding an imposing inch to his height. The other brothers instinctively stepped back, as if sensing an impending storm and wanting to avoid the fallout. Thomas turned and headed upstairs, his retreat deliberate, while Sean lingered, his eyes flicking between April and Will with cautious interest.

Will's posture softened marginally as he finally answered, "Let's do it. I'll grab us drinks and meet you down there."

April watched him disappear into the kitchen, her body still tense. She shot Sean a quick thumbs-up, masking her anxiety with a forced smile before heading toward the basement stairs. Each step down felt heavier than the last, her mind replaying the moment, questioning why she had provoked Will in the first place. She needed the calming embrace of water to soothe her nerves, but instead, she was about to channel her tension into a pool game with her competitive brother-in-law.

CHAPTER FORTY

The Grooming

"Knock, knock," Jonah's voice floated in as he gently pushed the door further open, his head peeking around the corner with a tentative smile.

Crystal quickly stuffed her plastic bag of pills under her pillow, her movements swift but practiced. She leaned back against the headboard, her legs stretched out with her feet nestled on a pile of pillows, adopting her usual position before Jonah could suspect anything unusual. He had a knack for missing the subtle cues, oblivious to the latest fashion trends or the ever-shifting tides of social media. But one thing Jonah didn't overlook was her relationship with her pills. His eyes always seemed to linger a bit too long on the small plastic bags she used, his disapproval clear even without words. In Jonah's mind, a good husband would eliminate her need for any "uppers, downers, or in-betweeners."

Crystal's habit of splitting her pills into multiple baggies—one for the nightstand, another for her purse, one in the kitchen drawer—had always been about convenience. Yet, the downside was real: it became all too easy to lose track of a bag. This time, the nightstand bag had vanished without a trace. Panic had nearly set in when she awoke to find it missing, but a quick trip on her hands and knees to her suitcase and a rummage through the silky layers of her lingerie produced a spare bag, carefully hidden beneath her panties. She had scurried back to bed, erasing the telltale carpet marks that betrayed her path.

Jonah entered the room, his expression softening as he approached her side. He leaned in, placing a kiss on her forehead. "I brought you a drink," he murmured, holding out a glass. "Will made a fresh batch just for you. Apparently Ilma commandeered the other one."

Crystal took the glass, sipping delicately to avoid ruining her freshly applied lip liner and lipstick. She had hoped the makeup would add a touch of vitality to her otherwise pale face after her nap. Billy, intuitive as ever, would have known to bring a straw. Jonah, blissfully ignorant of all things beauty, wouldn't understand if she tried to explain the importance of preserving her look mid-tutorial. Instead, she offered a soft, appreciative smile. "Thanks, sweets," she purred. "Did you check on the pool stuff after the rain?"

Jonah stared at her, but didn't answer. "You know, the cushions, the awning, the umbrellas…"

"Yeah," he replied after a pause, rubbing his temples. "I know what you're talking about. There's just been a lot going on."

Crystal waited for him to volunteer more information or at least acknowledge her request, but he seemed distracted, his thoughts elsewhere. Instead, he shifted the conversation. "I'm going to jump in the shower real quick, then head back down. I hate leaving you, but I want to spend as much time with my brothers before everyone goes their separate ways."

"Don't worry about me. I'm just fine," Crystal reassured him, though she was well aware that any attempt to discuss her current activities would be lost on him. Jonah would never grasp the nuances of a makeup tutorial on lower face contouring. She imagined his mind translating her explanations into the garbled *wa wa* of a cartoon adult, a thought that made her giggle softly.

She closed her eyes, leaning back against the pillows, listening to the soothing cascade of water from the hot tub. Despite his cluelessness, Jonah had stepped up during this trip, taking on the host's duties with admirable dedication. She made a mental note to thank him properly later.

But the peace was shattered as Crystal's eyes snapped open, her heart pounding in her chest. Slowly, she turned her head toward the sliding doors leading to the terrace. They were wide open, the sea breeze and distant sounds of the ocean wafting in. Crystal knew with certainty that April had closed them before she left.

Chapter Forty-One

The Hallucination

From the window, Ilma could see the sprawling view of the estate, the peaceful landscape at odds with the tension tightening inside her. It was beautiful, yes, but the view only added to her unease. Her mind kept drifting back to the story of the cave, to the feeling that there was something, or someone lurking just beyond sight. The wind ruffled the trees outside, and every movement sent a jolt of paranoia shooting through her veins. Birds flew past, too quickly for her to really focus on, just blurs in the distance.

Unable to focus, Ilma drew the heavy velvet curtains closed with a huff, hoping the thick fabric would shield her from the world outside, if only for a little while. It wasn't just the birds; it was the feeling that someone was watching her. The possibility that a stranger could be lurking around, hidden from view. Her paranoia swelled.

Once the curtains were drawn, she flopped back into the chair, her body sinking into the cozy cushions with a quiet sigh of relief. She grabbed a handful of grapes, letting them roll between her fingers before popping them into her mouth, savoring the burst of sweetness. For a moment, she could pretend everything was normal—pretend she wasn't trapped in a house full of secrets, trying to escape from a reality that was becoming increasingly frightening.

The thought was so tempting: a day spent in this chair, reclined in peaceful solitude, fed grapes by some invisible servant. She laughed quietly to herself at the fantasy. *Of course, if there were a servant, I'd send them away too.* People. They were the problem. She'd rather sit alone with her drink and the hum of her own thoughts than be surrounded by anyone.

Ilma reached over to flick on the reading lamp beside her, but as she did, the room tilted unnervingly. A wave of dizziness hit her so hard, she dropped her head between her knees, clutching the armrest of the chair for support. The room spun, and her mind seemed to dissolve in a haze. Will really could make a stiff drink, she thought dazedly. Maybe too stiff.

Sinking back into the chair, Ilma rested her head against the back, letting her eyes close for a brief moment. She could just rest... just for a little while...

When her eyelids fluttered open again, the world around her seemed off, distorted. Her vision was clouded, as though she were seeing through a fog, or underwater. The edges of everything grew blurry, as though the world was stretching, warping. She could barely keep her eyes open, but she fought it.

And then, as she forced her eyes to focus, something in the bookcase caught her attention. The shelves—where once rows of books had lined the walls—were now *empty*. The panel that had once held them had vanished, leaving a gaping void of blackness.

How? How had it disappeared?

Ilma blinked, fighting to clear her thoughts. *Did I just see a person?*

Her mind raced, but her body wasn't cooperating. Was it someone outside? No, she had closed the curtains, hadn't she?

Before she could piece it together, her mind shut down as she lost consciousness, the dark nothingness swallowing her whole.

CHAPTER FORTY-TWO

The Failure

The Unwelcome Guest was growing far too comfortable navigating the maze of hidden passageways that snaked through the house. What had once been a cautious, methodical process—waiting by a door, listening intently for any stray sounds before daring to slip into the main house—had now turned into reckless abandon. He no longer hesitated. The doors were flung open with brazen confidence, each exit a gamble, each second spent in the open a flirtation with discovery. His lack of caution was beginning to catch up with him, as he nearly found himself face-to-face with The Bookworm—again.

It was a dangerously close call, especially after the debacle earlier when she had almost caught him staring in through the window. She had been mere seconds from opening the hidden door in the movie room, and he'd barely managed to retreat back into the shadows. But today was different—he had grown overconfident, underestimating her as she read in the library.

The library, with its vast collection of books and its air thick with ancient dust, held the most satisfying and well-concealed of all the secret passageways. The door swung open with a soft, practiced tilt of an old, leather-bound tome, its well-worn spine the perfect key to the hidden world beyond. The irony of it struck him sharply—the way the world of mystery novels, of carefully orchestrated murders and escapes, had always felt like a dream to him. *This* was his reality.

But the smell. Oh, the smell. It wafted out from behind the bookshelves like a thick, suffocating fog. Musty, stagnant, and heavy with the rot of time, the passage smelled of mildew and mold, a faintly acrid scent that clung to everything in sight. The library itself—no stranger to the scent of aging paper—could not compare. Here, there was no airflow, no relief. The air was thick, dense, and he felt as if it was pressing in on him, stifling him. He had heard The Bookworm speak fondly of the aroma of old books, but to him, it was revolting. The idea that a book could absorb the sweat, the grime, the residue of human hands and minds—it made his stomach twist in disgust. Public libraries, filled with the fingerprints and hair of thousands of strangers, felt like a nightmare.

His plan had been meticulously crafted. Each move had been calculated. Yet, somehow, his attempts on the women had failed. Well, not entirely. He had maimed The Supermodel—delightfully so—but the satisfaction was brief. And now, everyone thought The Runner was just paranoid. But The Bookworm? She was an enigma. He had known about her allergy, and yet he had bungled it, failed to finish what he had started. She wasn't a show-off like The Supermodel or an overachiever like The Runner. No, her only sin was being in his way. A small obstacle standing between him and his ultimate goal.

Stepping through the hidden door of the library's passageway, he should have been caught. The Bookworm was right there—laying on the chair, her eyes fixed, unblinking. It was a miracle he hadn't been seen. The hallway beyond the door was shrouded in darkness, and he had positioned himself just far enough back to remain unseen, an unseen shadow in the quiet space.

As he stood there, tension coiling tight within him, he almost laughed at the stroke of fortune that had landed in his lap. There, beside her, sat the pitcher—the fruity drink she had been sipping. The liquid seemed to taunt him, a reminder of his failed attempts. But this was different. He knew the path he was on was the right one. You couldn't have that much good luck unless you were *meant* to succeed.

She had been elusive. He had tried to trap her in an explosion. The mannequin under her bed? A cruel joke, but the shock on her face had been worth it. Watching her unravel in front of her family had been satisfying—almost. Her breakdown was inevitable, and he had done his part. But it wasn't enough. It never was. And now, with the drink, containing the crushed sleeping pills he'd added, the end was near.

He watched as her eyelids fluttered, slow and heavy, the result of the alcohol and the powder working their magic. His heart pounded as he waited for the final moment—the moment when her eyes would close completely. And when they did, he moved, his fingers closing the door gently, methodically.

His steps down the hall were quieter, but his heart was louder. It thrummed in his chest, exhilaration coursing through his veins like a drug. He had done it. He had slipped under her radar, and he would slip away just as easily.

Chapter Forty-Three

The Game

The entire basement floor reeked of burnt popcorn, the acrid smell clinging stubbornly to the air, making April's stomach churn. The scent turned her off from using the gym anytime soon—she doubted her nausea would mix well with her workout routine.

After tying the thin blanket around her body like a sarong, April began to rack up the pool balls, the familiar clatter comforting. Her dad had taught her to play pool when she was young, relishing the shock on the faces of grown men as she effortlessly bested them in smoky bars. People rarely suspected a little girl of being a pool shark, and fewer still dared to confront one after being outplayed.

Will entered the room, his gait confident as he made a beeline toward her, one of his signature fruity drinks in hand. She waved him off with a smirk. "No thanks, I need to stay sharp if I'm going to mop the floor with your ass."

Will shrugged, turning to place the drink on the bar, his neck cracking audibly as he stretched. April picked up a pool stick and a chalk block, absentmindedly rubbing the blue powder onto the tip of the stick while a curious thought flickered in her mind: why had Will brought her a drink from the kitchen when the basement bar was fully stocked? She could easily grab a beer from the fridge under the counter.

"Do you want to shoot for the break?" she asked, placing the chalk cube back on the table's edge.

"You can break," Will answered, leaning casually against the bar.

"Good answer, *Billy*." She couldn't resist, taunting him with the nickname he despised.

April circled the table, her movements deliberate as she placed the cue ball on the back quarter. A temptation to bend over suggestively crossed her mind, but it felt wrong. Will wasn't her brother, but after years of shared memories, he might as well have been.

"Can you step aside a bit?" she asked, standing just a foot in front of him. "I'd hate to hit you in the nuts. Accidentally, of course."

Will shifted, but only just enough to give her room. She bent over again, her fingers forming a bridge for the cue stick. With the release of a deep breath, she made the perfect shot, the cue ball colliding with the others, sending them scattering across the table. The satisfying thunk of a ball dropping into the leather corner pocket made her straighten, scanning the table to see which had gone in.

"I'm solids. You're stripes." April resumed her slow pacing around the table, eyes scanning for the best angle. She bent over a few times, considering her options, before finally deciding on a shot.

Will's exaggerated sigh broke the tension. "Ugh. Are you going to take your turn, or am I just going to sit here and watch you overthink in a game that should've been over by now?"

His tone caught her off guard. It wasn't the playful banter she expected but genuine irritation. The sight of him twisting his foot into the carpet in frustration made her stifle a grin. She loved seeing him squirm, even if it wasn't intentional.

Letting his comment slide, she leaned her hip against the table, lifting one foot off the ground as she swung the pool stick behind her back. "Three ball, corner pocket," she called out.

It was a challenging shot, especially for someone her height. She always thought the one-foot-on-the-ground rule was biased against short players. Despite this, her shot was flawless. The cue ball barely nudged the three-ball, sending it slowly rolling into the corner pocket with precision.

"Get comfortable, *Billy*," she called, her voice taking on a mock Southern drawl. "You may not even get a turn."

She laughed, watching his face redden in frustration. Winning always lifted her spirits. It was amusing how her mood could shift with the game—dominance made her feel invincible, and today, she was on fire. Standing at the far end of the table, she lined up her next shot, her eyes locking with his before she took a no-look shot, the thrill of the moment electrifying.

"Damn, boy. You had no idea what you were getting yourself into, did you?" April's voice carried a teasing edge, her grin wide with confidence.

"Do you ever shut the fuck up?" Will spat, his tone venomous.

The playful atmosphere shattered instantly. April's smirk faltered. She knew she had pushed too far, but the raw hatred in Will's voice was a shock. He wasn't in the mood for games, verbal or otherwise. As he pushed off the bar and stood tall, facing her, he seemed to transform before her eyes. Gone was the slightly awkward brother-in-law she teased; in his place stood a man whose rage contorted him into something more primal, more dangerous.

He squared his shoulders, standing straighter than she'd ever seen, casting off the usual slouch that seemed to symbolize his deference to his older brothers. His eyes locked on hers, burning with barely restrained fury, their intensity making her breath catch.

Instinctively, April took a step back, her grip on the pool stick tightening until her knuckles turned white. Her heart pounded in her chest, but she held his gaze, her mind racing for a way to defuse the escalating tension. Will's hand slowly reached out, his fingers curling around the cue ball on the table. He rolled it in his palm, a mesmerizing motion that contrasted sharply with the tension radiating from his frame. His right foot twisted against the floor, the motion hinting at barely contained aggression.

"You can't do anything for fun, can you?" Will's voice dripped with disdain. "How the hell does Sean live with such a competitive junkie?"

Before she could react, Will's movements shifted, his arm pulling back in a sudden, violent motion. For a terrifying moment, April thought he would hurl the ball at her face. She braced herself, muscles tensing, but instead, he pivoted and launched the ball across the room. It sailed through the doorway and into the gym, a sharp crash echoing as it shattered a mirrored wall.

The sound was deafening, the explosion of glass ringing through the basement. April's hands flew to her ears, her heart pounding in her chest. Fear gripped her, freezing her in place. That ball could have been aimed at her, and no amount of athletic training would have saved her from it. She felt exposed, vulnerable, utterly powerless.

Sean and Thomas burst into the game room, their eyes wide with alarm. "What the fuck happened?" Sean demanded, his gaze darting from the wreckage to April. One look at her, and he understood. His confident, fearless wife stood paralyzed, her eyes glistening with unshed tears. Without hesitation, Sean crossed the room and pulled her into a protective embrace, shielding her from whatever storm had just passed.

April trembled in his arms, her resolve cracking under the weight of the moment. She could feel the tears threatening to spill, her body shaking with the effort to hold them back. But Sean's warmth, his silent reassurance, broke her defenses. The tears came, unbidden and unstoppable.

Pushing against Sean's chest, she managed to pull away, covering her face with her hands. "I'm going for a swim," she mumbled, her voice choked with emotion.

Sean started to follow, his concern etched into every line of his face, but a single glance from April halted him. He needed to stay. She needed space. Brushing past Jonah, who was sprinting down the stairs, she shed the blanket sarong and bolted outside, seeking solace in the cool night air. Without pause, she dove into the pool, the water swallowing her cries as she found a private refuge to weep away her fear and frustration.

CHAPTER FORTY-FOUR

The Swim

April's hands sliced through the water, her legs churning steadily beneath her. Her breathing had settled, though it had felt erratic when she first plunged into the pool, teetering on the edge of hyperventilation. She loved the sensation of swimming, the way it engaged every muscle in her body, pulling her into a rhythmic dance of movement and breath. Stroke, stroke, stroke, breathe. The repetition became a meditative cadence, each stroke pulling her further from the emotional storm she had just weathered.

The cool water hid her tears, blending them seamlessly into the chlorinated depths. It was a small solace, but one she clung to. The image of Will's face, twisted in anger, haunted her. She had never seen him like that before—so consumed by rage, his eyes burning with something far darker than mere frustration. Deep in her bones, April felt it. The pool ball wasn't meant for the mirror; it was meant for her. He wanted to shatter her, not just the glass.

She tried to push the thoughts away, returning to the rhythm of her swim. Focus, she reminded herself. Stroke, stroke, stroke, breathe. But her mind rebelled, the intrusive thoughts clawing their way back in. She fought to regain her calm, repeating the mantra again and again, forcing herself into the monotony of the motion.

Stroke, stroke, stroke, breathe.

The calm was fleeting. A new humming noise began to echo through the water, jarring her from her trance. She assumed the pool pump or cleaner had kicked on and continued her swim, her eyes scanning the pool's bottom for signs of movement. But there was nothing—just the eeriness of still water and silence.

Suddenly, a sharp pain exploded at the back of her head. The world blurred as her skull throbbed, the pain radiating from the nape of her neck up to her forehead. She instinctively curled into herself, her body recoiling from the unexpected assault. But there was no time to process; she needed air.

April surged upward, desperate to break the surface, but her ascent was halted abruptly. Her head smacked against something solid—a surface blocking her escape. Panic surged as she opened her eyes wide in the dim underwater world. The pool cover was closing, and fast. Only a sliver of open space remained, a mere five feet at the deep end.

Adrenaline kicked in. She swam with all her strength, every muscle screaming in protest. She pushed off the bottom, her arms and legs working furiously to propel her forward. Her lungs burned as she reached the edge, gasping for precious air. Relief was short-lived.

A new pain struck her, more forceful and deliberate. Her head snapped forward, and she felt herself being shoved down into the water. Desperate, she looked up, squinting against the sting of chlorine. A shadowy figure loomed at the edge of the pool, clad in black, holding a pool net. He pressed the pole against her, driving her back under with alarming strength.

Within moments, the pool cover sealed the surface, plunging her into darkness.

CHAPTER FORTY-FIVE

The Brothers

"Bro, what the fuck?" Sean's voice cut through the thick tension in the room as he closed the distance to Will, his eyes blazing with disbelief and anger.

"It was really not a big deal," Will muttered, brushing past Sean with a rough shoulder-check that sent a clear message. His face was hard, unreadable, as he stormed out of the room, leaving the echo of his footsteps in his wake. "A ball jumped the table. You know how that happens."

Sean's gaze followed Will as he exited, his jaw clenched tight. "I hope you're going to get something to clean up this fucking mess," he called after him, though he doubted Will was listening.

Sean turned toward Jonah and Thomas, who stood frozen at the bar, their faces pale with shock. Their wide eyes mirrored the disbelief that churned in his gut. "Thanks for the backup, guys," Sean said, the sarcasm in his voice cutting through the silence. His brothers didn't respond, still too stunned to move or speak.

The shattered mirror in the gym caught Sean's attention, the jagged shards glittering ominously under the room's dim lights. He stepped closer, the crunch of glass beneath his feet sending a shiver up his spine. The cue ball lay amid the debris, a stark white orb in the chaos of broken reflections.

He turned back, his mind racing to make sense of the scene. The distance between the pool table and the gym seemed insurmountable for a simple misfire. "No way the ball went that far from a missed hit," Sean murmured, his eyes narrowing as he tried to reconstruct the trajectory in his mind.

"Dude, just drop it," Jonah finally broke the silence, his voice edged with forced nonchalance. He squared his shoulders, attempting to reclaim a facade of composure, though his unease was evident in the way he avoided Sean's gaze. "April's a big girl. She can take care of herself." Jonah's step toward the gym was hesitant, his body language betraying the lingering tension.

Sean's gaze flicked to Thomas, waiting for his younger brother to weigh in. Thomas shifted uncomfortably under the scrutiny, his eyes darting between his brothers before they fell to the floor, unwilling to meet Sean's steady glare.

"Seriously?" Sean's voice rose, a mixture of frustration and disbelief. "The whole brothers versus others argument doesn't apply when one of our wives is in the picture." His words hung heavily in the air, charged with the weight of unspoken rules and familial loyalty. "You know that, right?" He pushed for a response, his confidence waning in the face of Jonah's defiant stare and Thomas's continued avoidance.

"So," Will spoke up from the doorway behind Sean, startling all three of the brothers. "Two on two foosball?"

Without a word, Jonah and Thomas walked back from the gym and over to the foosball table. Although Will seemed to have composed himself after storming out moments ago, the two drifted to the same side and kept their eyes averted.

Sean scoffed, "Really?" Then with a quick look around at Will, "Where's the fucking broom? You need to clean that shit up."

"Give it a rest, Sean. Let's play, and I'll clean it later." Will walked over to the bar, pried open the sliding chiller door, and grabbed a beer. Using the side of the bar, Will held his beer with one hand, cap against the solid wood bar top, and with the other, banged his palm down, popping off the cap.

Sean watched as the cap flew into the air, then rolled on the ground like a quarter, coming to rest between Will and himself.

"Or, maybe I won't," Will continued after taking a long sip as he stepped over the bottle cap, leaving it on the floor. He pushed past Sean again, not bothering to walk around. "Looks like we're partners, *bro*."

The emphasis on *Bro* was like a mockery thrown in Sean's face.

"You coming?" Will said, looking back at Sean.

His three brothers stood at the foosball table, their expressions frozen in a mask of uneasy nonchalance as if nothing had happened. They looked at him, Will, as if the foundation of their bond hadn't just cracked beneath the weight of unspoken truths. Sean felt the weight of their stares like a physical burden, the awkward silence thickening the air between them. He blinked, trying to focus, but it was as if he were looking at Will through a fogged window, his image warped and indistinct.

Was this really his brother, or had the years created a chasm too wide to bridge? Sean couldn't shake the sense of disconnection. Will had been a different person since graduation, and their family gatherings had become rare, surface-level affairs. They hadn't shared a roof for more than fleeting visits in years, and now, on this isolated island, the fissures in their relationship were glaring.

Shaking off the dark thoughts, Sean joined the others at the table, gripping the blue handles. The silence was heavy, almost suffocating, until the familiar clatter of the foosball players filled the room. The brothers' laughter and shouts gradually eased the tension, masking the earlier confrontation like a thin veil over a brewing storm. If they avoided the gym and its shattered mirror, they could almost pretend everything was normal.

"Goal!" Will's triumphant shout shattered the tenuous peace as he threw his hands up in victory, his face flushed but alight with genuine joy. "Now, this is what it should always be like," he said, dropping the ball back into play.

The game resumed, the ball careening between the players in a chaotic rhythm. Thomas loosened his grip, casting a sidelong glance at Will. "Like what, Will?" he asked, his voice laced with cautious curiosity.

Will paused, wiping a tear before reclaiming the handle. "Just the guys. The brothers. No stupid wives to ruin our fun." The words hung in the air, stark and jarring.

Sean, caught up in the competitive fervor, didn't notice when Thomas's hands fell away from the grips. Seizing the opportunity, Sean scored another goal. "GOAL!"

But Jonah reached over, gently pressing Sean's hand to halt the next round. The touch jolted Sean, pulling his focus back to the room and the worried look on Jonah's face.

"Stupid wives?" Jonah repeated, his voice low and probing. "Our wives love you, Will. They're like sisters to you. Surely you don't mean that."

Will moved to the bar without a word, pulling out three shot glasses with a sharp clink against the wood. "Since you three got married, I've been an outsider," he said, his voice cold. "I feel like an unwelcome guest just being here. It's like you guys are in some special fucking club."

As he spoke, he withdrew a revolver from the back of his pants, setting it on the bar with a deliberate thud that sent a chill through the room. The brothers tensed, their eyes fixed on the weapon.

"It's too bad Crystal didn't jump into that hot tub," Will continued, his tone shifting to something darker, more menacing. "If I had to hear her call me Billy one more time..."

Will's hands trembled as he sorted through the liquor bottles, his rage simmering just below the surface. He grabbed his crotch, laughing bitterly. "If she saw my dick, she'd know I'm not a child anymore."

He poured the tequila with exaggerated care, his movements slow and deliberate. "Ilma's only crime was taking you away from me, Thomas," he said, his eyes locking on his brother with a mix of betrayal and longing. "We were the last ones unspoiled by marriage."

Will's voice cracked as he turned away, reaching for another bottle. "But April," he spat the name like a curse. "That fucking cunt always has to be the best."

The brothers sat in stunned silence as Will poured the shots, the revolver a grim reminder of the precarious situation. His rant continued, each word a knife twisting deeper into the fragile peace they had maintained.

"Fortunately, I controlled myself and flung the fucking ball away from April," Will said, his voice trembling. "Dumb bitch got locked under the pool cover."

He approached the foosball table, the shots in hand. "Brothers, here are three shots. To your three dead wives."

The sound of the cue ball hitting the back of Will's head echoed like a gunshot. His body crumpled, the tequila spilling across the floor. In the doorway, a soaking wet April stood, the cue ball clutched in her hand, her eyes blazing with cold fury.

CHAPTER FORTY-SIX
The Cue Ball

April and the three brothers stood frozen, their bodies stiff as statues, their eyes locked on Will's motionless form sprawled across the floor. The room was cloaked in a heavy silence, broken only by the soft, almost imperceptible sound of blood trickling from Will's head, pooling around him in a dark, widening circle. April's heart pounded in her chest, each beat a loud reminder of the violence that had erupted moments ago. Her hand trembled slightly, the adrenaline still coursing through her veins.

To her surprise, Thomas and Jonah exchanged a fleeting glance with Sean, a look heavy with unspoken understanding. Without hesitation, they turned and fled from the room, their footsteps echoing down the hall. Sean remained rooted, his eyes fixated on Will, his face a mask of conflicting emotions. His eyebrows furrowed, casting deep shadows over his eyes, while the lines etched between them spoke of inner turmoil. His mouth was a taut line, neither betraying sadness nor anger but a complex blend of both.

Was it sadness or disappointment that darkened his features? Sean's gaze lingered on his younger brother's bloodied form, and his thoughts spiraled into questions without clear answers. Was he mourning the injury Will had sustained or the betrayal that had cut deeper than any wound? Was he sorrowful that his brother had tried to harm April, or was he grieving his failure to foresee it? His shoulders sagged under the weight of guilt, unsure whether it was Will's actions or his own oversight that caused this.

When his eyes finally met April's, her calm nod sent a wave of relief washing over him. She was alive, unharmed, and in that moment, she gave him the silent assurance he needed to tend to his fallen brother. With a heavy sigh, Sean knelt beside Will, his hands shaking slightly as he reached out to feel for a pulse. His fingers pressed against the cold skin of Will's neck, searching for the faint beat of life beneath the surface.

"He's alive," Sean said, his voice barely above a whisper, thick with a mixture of relief and apprehension. "But he's bleeding pretty bad."

April wasn't sure if he was speaking to her or simply thinking aloud, but the words carried a weight that pressed down on both of them. The fear that had gripped her minutes earlier eased slightly, though the sight of Will's blood sent a shiver down her spine. She clenched her fists, trying to suppress the trembling that threatened to overtake her. Despite everything, the thought of having killed her husband's brother filled her with dread, an outcome she desperately wanted to avoid.

Sean tore his gaze away from Will, looking up at April with eyes that mirrored her fear and uncertainty. They both knew that the lines between family and foe had blurred dangerously, and whatever came next would test their bonds in ways they could never have anticipated.

Mere minutes ago, she had been floating in underwater darkness, disoriented, unable to tell which direction was up. With the last bubble of air from her lungs leaving her mouth and the burn in her chest setting in, she became awash with sadness. Sad that her husband would think her death was an accident. Sad that Sean had no idea what tragedy had befallen her. But mostly sad that the last face she would look upon was that of her brother-in-law. The now-grown boy she had watched over for years had looked at her with hate searing in his eyes as he had pushed her down with a pool net to what was to be her watery grave.

The sadness took over. Her body went limp, and she began to float. But rather than die a peaceful death, her buoyancy had carried her body upward toward the glorious half-inch of air between the water and the pool cover. The cool air brushed her nose, and she inhaled a long yet calm breath between her pursed lips.

She was suddenly propelled by a fierce will to survive, her mind sharp and her body ready for action. A profound sense of gratitude surged through her, gratitude for the isolation of the island that once felt suffocating. Thankful that the island's remoteness meant no internet or cell service. Ironically, it was this lack of connection that had driven her to pick up the God-damned Gold Book.

The hefty, three-inch-thick manual had been as dry as a technical white paper, dense with detail. Yet, its mundane pages now shimmered with significance. She had devoured the book cover to cover during a monotonous stationary bike session, save for the missing section—pages

121 to 134, mysteriously absent, their contents an enigma. But what she had absorbed had proven invaluable. The manual was a treasure trove of knowledge, meticulously detailing every appliance and feature of the house as though written by a seasoned professional organizer. Despite its intimidating bulk, it was a guide that could be a lifeline for any island guest.

While she had dismissed the intricate instructions for operating the jacuzzi in Thomas and Ilma's room as excessive, she was thankful she paid attention to the sections that detailed the fail-safe for the pool cover. It had seemed improbable that anyone could become trapped beneath the cover—it was fast, but unmistakable in its movement. Yet, here she was, a testament to the unforeseen. Whatever the logic behind including such a safety measure, April felt an overwhelming sense of relief and a silent thanks to the foresight of its creators.

She focused on calming her breath, each inhalation and exhalation deliberate and measured. The key was to keep her oxygen intake steady, to stretch the moments until the underwater safety system activated. With her eyes closed, she counted each slow breath, her internal clock substituting for seconds. One, two, three... at ten, a crimson glow illuminated the water around her. The red light was the beacon of hope, signaling the emergency system's engagement.

Without hesitation, April twisted her body, diving down to the pool's depths. Her limbs flailed purposefully, sending ripples through the water. The moment her presence was detected, the motion sensors triggered the mechanism, and the cover began its quick, mechanical retraction. The sound of the cover shifting was muffled underwater, but to April, it was the sweetest sound in the world—a promise of air, of survival.

As April hauled herself onto the pool's edge, every muscle in her body screamed in protest, her limbs trembling with exhaustion. Her lungs burned, greedily sucking in the cool night air. She longed to collapse on the concrete ledge, to surrender to the overwhelming fatigue that threatened to consume her. But a sharp, instinctual jolt pierced through her weariness, a primal need urging her to move, to flee.

The memory of Will's face, twisted with an unbridled hatred, flashed before her eyes. It wasn't just the frustration of a lost pool game. No, this was a hatred that had been festering, simmering beneath the surface for far too long. It wasn't just about her. Her mind raced, piecing together the unsettling puzzle: the sensation of being watched as she ran through the woods, the cave with its strange contents—the bag, the towels. She could almost see the missing pages from the Gold Book hidden there, but what secrets they contained eluded her grasp.

Her body ached, but the flood of memories brought a surge of adrenaline. The hot tub incident, the shellfish, the fire in the movie room—all pointed to a pattern, a chilling realization. Will hadn't just targeted her. He had methodically tried to hurt, maim, or kill all of his brothers' wives. The thought sent her heart racing, a cold sweat breaking out across her brow despite the water still clinging to her skin.

Ignoring the pain, April sprang to her feet, sprinting up the patio stairs into the living room. She couldn't afford to think about her own injuries. Crystal was trapped in her room, and Ilma was likely still in the library. Either—or both—could be in grave danger. But her first priority was Sean. Will's twisted love for his brothers made him unpredictable, capable of anything, even harming those he once held dear. After all, he had locked Thomas in the movie room without a second thought.

As she passed by Will's pink room, a shiver coursed through her. The bright pink walls now seemed grotesque, the once-innocent smiling dolls morphing into sinister figures, their glass eyes glinting with malevolence. It felt as if the entire room was watching her, mocking her with their frozen grins. She forced herself to look away, her feet carrying her toward the stairs to the basement.

April paused for a moment at the closed door to the library, her hand trembling as she tested the handle. Locked. Ilma would have to wait. There was no time to waste.

Halfway down the basement stairs, she halted, straining her ears to catch the faint sound of Will's voice. It no longer carried the carefree tone of the laid-back younger brother she once knew. It was wild, erratic—each word laced with a manic intensity that sent chills down her spine. He sounded like a madman, lost in a delusional spiral.

April's mind raced, knowing she couldn't simply walk into the game room without being seen. She needed another plan, another way to reach Sean without alerting Will. Slowly, cautiously, she crept back up the stairs, each step deliberate, her breath shallow as she tried to muffle the sound of her movements.

April ducked into Will's room, her breath hitching as she refused to glance at the dolls this time. Yet, even without meeting their lifeless eyes, she felt their gaze bore into her, tracking her every step as she crossed the room. The air was thick with an unsettling silence, broken only by her hurried movements. She reached the closet, her fingers trembling slightly as she opened the door and flicked on the light. The dim glow illuminated the rows of hanging clothes, but she wasted no time, shoving them aside to reveal what she hoped was there—the hidden passage.

The Gold Book had proven its worth again, despite the cryptic nature of its hints. One brief paragraph, just after the missing pages, mentioned a "door to the basement in the back of the Doll Closet." It had seemed nonsensical at first, a flaw in the otherwise meticulous guide. But now, as the pieces fell into place, April understood its significance.

When she opened the hidden door, she momentarily froze. This wasn't the dusty, cobwebbed passage she had expected. Instead, it was a sleek, high-tech maze, illuminated by faint, embedded lights along the floor. The adventurer in her wanted to explore, but urgency pulled her back to the reality of her mission. Time was slipping away, and Sean was in danger.

April sprinted down the hall, her footsteps echoing in the narrow corridor, and descended a metal spiral staircase, the chill of the railing biting into her palm. At the bottom, she cautiously cracked open the door, inhaling the distinct smell that confirmed her location—the pungent scent of burnt popcorn. It clung to the walls of the movie room, a memory of the chaos that had unfolded.

She pushed the door open, emerging behind the movie screen, and quickly moved toward the exit. The familiar layout greeted her: the wine cellar and stairs to the main floor on her right, the gym and game room on her left. Her eyes locked onto Will's back. He stood rigid, unaware of her presence, with the shattered remnants of the mirror wall behind him. The cue ball lay innocently on the broken glass, its surface unmarred despite the destruction it had caused. The entire scene felt surreal, the contrast between the ball's innocence and the devastation around it unsettling.

Jonah and Thomas stood like statues across the room, their eyes wide with terror. They didn't dare move, each breath measured as though the slightest blink could provoke their brother's wrath. April couldn't see Sean, but she knew this was her moment.

Her heart pounded as she tightened her grip on the cue ball. While she trusted her All-American Softball pitching arm, she didn't want to take the chance on a throw, so in three quick steps, she crossed the hall and hit Will square in the back of the head as hard as she could with the cue ball that was still clenched tightly in her fist.

A silent understanding passed between April and Sean, their eyes meeting briefly, each conveying the urgency of the moment without a word. While Sean knelt over Will's limp body, checking his pulse and noting the bleeding seemed to have stopped. April's gaze darted around the room, searching for something—anything—that could be used to restrain him. Her heart pounded in her chest, a rhythmic reminder of the precious seconds slipping away.

By sheer luck, she found a junk drawer in the bar, a chaotic mix of odds and ends—bottle openers, playing cards, pens, pencils, and crumpled scraps of paper. But it was the zip ties and duct tape that caught her eye, gleaming like lifelines amidst the clutter. She yanked the drawer open, snatched the items, and tossed the tape to Sean.

Sean quickly bound Will's hands, the silver sheen of the duct tape glinting in the artificial basement light.

The duct tape roll arced through the air as Sean tossed it back to April, who caught it with steady hands. She wasted no time, wrapping the tape around Will's feet in firm, tight layers. The adhesive tore with a satisfying rip as she pulled it taut, her mind racing with the urgency of their situation.

A low, guttural moan escaped Will's lips, causing them both to freeze for a heartbeat, their eyes snapping to his face. The sound, though faint, was a chilling reminder that time was not on their side.

The sudden clatter of footsteps on the stairs shattered the tense silence, the crunch of glass underfoot announcing the arrival of someone else. April and Sean turned in unison, their bodies coiled with readiness, eyes locked on the doorway.

Jonah stood there, red-faced and breathless, his eyes darting between April and Sean. He barely glanced at Will, still not yet fully conscious between them, his focus shifting quickly to the news he carried.

"Crystal and Ilma are alive. It appears that Will put something in their drinks but while Crystal only had a couple sips, Ilma drank so much, she threw up. Both seem to be okay, just groggy." Jonah said, his voice tight with concern. "Thomas is keeping an eye on them up in our room."

His gaze finally landed on his youngest brother, a deep, weary sigh escaping him. "You two go upstairs. See if you can figure out a way to contact the mainland. I'll keep an eye on him."

Without waiting for a reply, Jonah lowered himself to the ground, sliding his back against the bar until he was seated. His eyes never left Will, a silent vigil that spoke volumes of his inner turmoil. The room seemed to hold its breath as April and Sean exchanged one last glance before sprinting to their next mission.

Chapter Forty-Seven
The Early Checkout

Crystal's eyelids were heavy, but she didn't want to fall asleep. With Ilma sleeping the drugs off next to her and Thomas quietly pacing the room, she would be out before she knew it. Thankfully, April and Sean came tearing up the stairs and burst into the room, giving her a nice natural shot of adrenaline.

April had never been the touchy-feely type of girl, but she ran up to Crystal and pulled her into a giant bear hug. She paid no mind to Crystal's pained feet, Ilma snoring just feet away or the fact she was only wearing her bikini and her hair was still damp.

Crystal smiled at the emotional outpouring from her normally unemotional sister-in-law. Then the sight of Thomas and Sean embracing brought a tear to her eye.

"How did you get to Ilma? The door to the library was locked," April turned to ask Thomas.

"There are hidden doors and secret passageways all over the house," Thomas said with his head down. He looked ashamed for having kept the information to himself.

"I thought I was the only one who knew, but Jonah said the caretaker told him about it when she gave him the tour. He'd totally forgotten all about it until he saw me run to Will's closet, where a hidden door leads to a stairwell to the basement and a door hidden in the bookcases in the Library."

"I knew I saw someone walk out of the shelves," Ilma slurred, though her eyes never quite opened.

"There was a page in the Gold Book about a door in the *doll closet*. That's how I was able to sneak up behind Will." April took a deep breath, unable to believe the words coming out of her own mouth.

"Sean and I will go check the cave. If Will was keeping things there, maybe we'll find the flares," April said with a newfound sense of purpose.

But, as she stepped forward in Sean's direction, her knees nearly gave out beneath her. "Oh, my God. Whose body was that in the cave?"

Chills ran over her body, and the hairs on her arms stood up. As much as the others doubted her over the last few days, they looked just as scared as she was. No one else had seen the body, but they no longer doubted that there was one.

Sean held out his hand to her. "We will figure that out later. Let's find a way off the island."

April extended her hand and let him pull her close.

CHAPTER FORTY-EIGHT

The Flare

Even with April's ankle throbbing from her earlier injury and her running shoes missing, she and Sean chose to jog to the cave instead of using the electric cart. Sean didn't want to waste time searching for the keys or go back down to the basement to ask Jonah; besides, April needed an outlet for the turmoil simmering inside her. The rhythmic pounding of her socked feet on the path was a small reprieve, a desperate attempt to channel the storm of emotions coursing through her.

Her body still trembled from the traumatic events that had unfolded earlier. She had never struck anyone or anything before—except for a punching bag in the gym—and the experience had left her shaken to the core. She knew she was strong, but the resilience of a human skull had caught her off guard. When she had brought the cue ball down on Will's head with all her might, she had half-expected her hand to shatter under the force. The movies made it seem effortless to knock someone unconscious with a crowbar or the butt of a gun, but reality had proven otherwise.

Despite the sheer power she had exerted, Will had only been out for a few minutes.

At that moment, as she swung the cue ball, she had wanted to kill him. The desire for revenge burned fiercely within her—for locking her under the pool cover, for nearly boiling Crystal alive, and for terrifying Ilma to the point she might never eat again. The staged accidents of the past week flashed through her mind like a macabre slideshow. And there was still the body in the cave she hadn't yet confronted. By the time she had emerged from the pool cover and raced to the basement, her intent had shifted from self-defense to a dark desire to end the threat Will posed.

Running side by side with Sean now, the flashlight beam bobbing between their evenly paced strides, she stole glances at him. His jaw was set in a rigid line, clenched tightly, his teeth forming a slight underbite he only displayed when he was seething with anger. His eyes, usually soft and kind, were narrowed and distant, fixed on a point ahead that seemed to hold all his rage. A tear escaped down her cheek, and she swiftly wiped it away, pretending it was only sweat. She was grateful that she hadn't killed Will, but the revelation of what she was capable of haunted her. She had come perilously close to taking a life, and the knowledge was suffocating.

Could she live with herself knowing that under the right circumstances, she could kill another human being—even someone she loved? The weight of that realization pressed down on her, heavier than any burden.

When the two reached the cave, it only took a few minutes for Sean to locate the flares. April stood outside and couldn't even bring herself to look into the dark maw.

Sean stepped out of the opening pulling his cinch bag tight and throwing it over his shoulders. "I have the flares and a couple of other things."

He held up her running shoes for her, and she snatched them out of his hands. "I knew it," she shouted in victory.

April sat on the ground and pulled on the shoes, embarrassed at her celebration over being right. Boasting was a hard habit to break, even in questionable circumstances.

"Um," she started as she tied the laces. "What else was in there?"

"Paper, a baggie of pills," Sean paused.

"And, let me guess," April interrupted. "A scarf and a bookmark?"

She fought the urge to smile as she stood up, and the two took off for the dock.

The moon hung high in the velvet sky, casting a silver sheen over the dock, bathing everything in an ethereal glow. Its light was ample, allowing April and Sean to navigate without the flashlights they'd used earlier in the woods and cave. As their frantic pace slowed to a walk, the air between them was thick with unspoken thoughts. Sean reached into the bag and pulled out a flare, the cylinder glinting under the moon's gaze. In the lunar light, he looked almost otherworldly—his tan muscles rippling beneath the soft, unbuttoned fabric of his shirt, his every movement exuding a rugged, primal grace.

April's gaze lingered on him, appreciating his chiseled form in a way she often overlooked amidst the routine of their lives. In the gym, surrounded by sculpted bodies, his looks blended into the backdrop of their profession, but here, under the stars, he stood apart. His usual gym attire, the expected tank tops and protein shakes, seemed worlds away from this moment of raw survival. The idea of him, her husband, transformed into some sort of survivalist, sent a strange mixture of admiration and unease coursing through her.

Sean strode to the dock's edge, his steps sure and steady, and with a practiced hand, aimed the flare gun toward the mainland. The flare shot into the night, a brilliant streak of red slicing through the darkness before bursting into a brief, fiery bloom. The sky momentarily blazed with its light, then dimmed, leaving only the ghost of its glow lingering on their retinas. The mainland, a mere three miles from the small island, seemed to stretch into the infinite void, the distance amplified by the shadowy expanse of water.

April's eyes were fixed on the horizon, the dark line where sea and sky merged into a single, indiscernible mass. In her mind, the events of the past week played on an endless loop, each scene more unsettling than the last. Her thoughts spiraled—*when had Will found the time to slip away to the cave? What had he done with the body after she had discovered it? Was the victim a random misfortune, or had they been an accomplice, ensnared by Will's malevolence?* The possibilities clawed at her, each more sinister than the last.

The silence between her and Sean was a chasm, filled only by the soft sounds of the waves lapping against the dock's supports. April longed to bridge the gap with a touch, a gesture to reaffirm their bond, but the weight of everything they had endured held her back. Sean's deep sigh broke the quiet, a sound heavy with the burdens he carried, but April couldn't bring herself to ask what was on his mind. She feared what she might learn, wary of any new revelations that could shatter the fragile equilibrium she was struggling to maintain.

She shifted her weight, a nervous habit bringing her fingers to her mouth as she bit at her nails and cuticles. The anxiety gnawed at her, exacerbated by the uncertainty of their rescue. The flare felt like a desperate plea, a cry into the abyss, and she wondered how long they would wait before they saw a sign of acknowledgment from the mainland. The thought of remaining on the island for three more days, isolated and vulnerable, was suffocating. Crystal needed medical attention, Ilma's recovery from the drugs was uncertain, and they all needed relief from the psychological torment they had endured.

The breeze carried the salty tang of the ocean, a scent that would usually bring comfort, now tainted by the night's tension. Each minute stretched into eternity, the familiar sounds turning into a soundtrack of dread. *Should they fire another flare once the sky darkened completely? How many flares would it take before they received a response, if any?*

Just as she turned toward Sean, prepared to voice her concerns, a small red flash flickered on the horizon. It was faint, barely perceptible against the creeping darkness, but unmistakable—a glimmer of hope cutting through the oppressive night.

CHAPTER FORTY-NINE

The Betrayal

Will sat slumped against the cold, unforgiving wall, his back pressed into the rough plaster as though it were the only thing keeping him tethered to reality. His gaze was fixed, unwavering, on a small imperfection in the wall across from him—a bump, barely noticeable, yet it became his focal point. It was easier to concentrate on the irregularity than acknowledge Jonah's presence looming nearby. He wouldn't give his brother the satisfaction of seeing him broken, begging, or even acknowledging him.

His hands and feet were bound tightly with duct tape, restricting any movement and leaving him in a state of helpless discomfort. The pounding in his head was relentless, a throbbing reminder of the blow he had taken. Leaning back slightly, he winced as the pain intensified, confirming the exact spot of impact. A dark thought flickered in his mind: was it a cruel coincidence or an intentional gesture that he was placed directly beneath the dartboard? The irony was not lost on him. He could almost imagine his brothers standing there, taking aim, their betrayal sharp as the darts they might throw.

He didn't have to look at Jonah to feel the weight of his brother's disappointment and confusion. They had all sworn a blood oath as children, a bond they believed to be unbreakable. The memory of pricking their fingers, mingling their blood, and vowing eternal loyalty burned in Will's mind. Yet here he was, tied up and abandoned, the once sacred bond shattered by the very people who promised to uphold it.

His thoughts drifted to the past, to the time when Jonah had first brought Crystal into their lives. Initially, Will, along with Thomas and Sean, had teased Jonah mercilessly, the way brothers do, not realizing how quickly Crystal would become entwined in their family dynamic. But Crystal wasn't a brother. She wasn't bound by the same unspoken rules. One by one, his brothers had succumbed to the allure of their wives, forsaking the bond that once defined them.

Will's jaw tightened, his resentment simmering just beneath the surface. In his mind, he was the last one standing, the only one who hadn't allowed a woman to come between them. His brothers had faltered, blinded by love, or perhaps lust. And now, their betrayal was laid bare. This vacation was meant to be a testament to their unity, a reaffirmation of their brotherhood. Instead, it exposed their fracture, a chasm that Will believed he could mend by eliminating the distractions—the women who had seduced them away from their blood pact.

But his plan had failed spectacularly. Crystal's constant complaints, April's suspicions, Ilma's tantrums—they had all driven wedges deeper between the brothers, not removed them. Will felt the weight of their collective grievances pressing down on him, suffocating and inescapable.

Jonah's voice broke through Will's internal storm, soft and pleading. "What happened?" he asked, his tone trembling with desperation. "Please, Will. Please. Tell me what happened. Why did you do this?"

Will didn't flinch. He kept his eyes locked on the wall, determined not to give Jonah an inch. He could hear the emotion in Jonah's voice, the way it cracked under the strain, and he knew his brother was near tears. He refused to be moved by it. Jonah's sniffles and the rustling of fabric as he wiped his nose on his sleeve were the only sounds in the otherwise heavy silence.

"Will!" Jonah's voice rose, filled with an urgency that made Will's heart beat just a fraction faster, though his outward demeanor remained unchanged. Jonah stood, his shadow casting a long stretch over Will's face as he moved to block his brother's view.

"Are you even sorry? You could have killed them," Jonah whispered, his voice now barely more than a broken whimper. "You could have killed Crystal. She has been like a sister to you."

Will's eyes flicked slightly in reaction, a subtle roll before he locked them back in place. *A sister I want to fuck, who just wants me to be her personal chef, is more like it,* he thought bitterly, a sneer forming at the corners of his mouth.

Jonah's voice softened, "What did you think was going to happen? Did you think we would all just move on together like nothing happened?"

Will's once-defiant stare fell to his lap. The truth was, he had no endgame. All he could see were the obstacles between him and his brothers' love. He would have done anything to turn back time—to when they would drop everything to be there for their baby brother. He had been the center of their world. Until he wasn't.

Jonah took in several deep breaths, his chest rising and falling as he fought for composure. Eventually, he sank back under the bar, the weight of his despair pulling him down. And in that silent, shared moment of defeat, Will recognized the finality in Jonah's posture. His brother had given up on him.

CHAPTER FIFTY

The End

Crystal watched as the ferry crept closer to shore. Rather than smiling hand-in-hand with Jonah, she sat in the electric cart and watched as Jonah talked to the police, whose boat had arrived that morning. Jonah spoke with one detective while Billy stood with another officer close to the boat. The uniformed man didn't engage him, and Billy just stood and stared out to sea.

She'd only seen Jonah for a few minutes before they rode the cart out to the pier. In fact, with the police questioning all of them, she'd hardly seen anyone.

Jonah had spent the entire night sitting on the floor next to Will. Or so he said. He told her he hadn't been tired, but she knew he felt responsible. It was a trip *they* had planned. It was supposed to be perfect. Plus, Jonah was the oldest and had always felt the need to protect everyone else. He said it was an older sibling thing, but Crystal's older sister was perfectly content to sit aside and let Crystal plan family parties or shop for holiday gifts while she swooped in to sign the card.

April had sat up with Crystal most of the night. They talked about Billy. They talked about their husbands. They occasionally woke Ilma from a nightmare and got her back to sleep. April's presence had been a balm, her careful attention to Crystal's needs a small comfort in the storm of uncertainty.

Crystal's stomach growled when Jonah popped in to take the luggage down to the electric carts.

"Want me to get you something to eat?"

"No, thanks. I think I'll wait until I am away from any food Will has handled," she stopped herself. Momentarily feeling bad for voicing what she had been thinking all night long. "I think I'll feel better eating and drinking when we're off the island."

Jonah didn't respond. He just stood staring down at their pile of bags April had so carefully packed for them.

"So, did he talk to you?" Crystal asked softly.

Jonah shook his head slowly. "Not a word," he sighed. "Not that I tried that hard. I wanted something, anything. Some kind of reason or answer or excuse. He gave me nothing. I pretty much stared at the space between us and wondered how it got so big."

The statement made her heart hurt. He had always looked after his family and those who he loved; even seemed to carry some bizarre responsibility for their happiness. Crystal had been a part of the family for over a decade and had witnessed countless examples of him putting his family first. What she dared not think of was how this betrayal made *her* feel. There were moments when she let her mind go to what Billy had tried to do to them... to her. It was too painful. As soon as the thought popped up, she pushed it back down. She didn't want to unpack that again until she was in her therapist's office.

Just watching Jonah standing near Billy on the pier was more than she could handle. With his initial conversation with the detective now wrapped up, Jonah leaned in toward Billy as if he were going in for a hug but pulled back, dropped his head, and walked away. Away from his brother, away from the police boat, and out to the end of the pier.

The electronic hum of the approaching electric cart gave her something to look at other than the emotional scene unfolding before her. Sean pulled the cart to a stop with Thomas riding shotgun and their wives in the back. The four looked on with mixed emotion. Only Thomas stood and walked toward the dock. His shoulders and face were drawn as if gravity were tugging them downward. His expression was sad and somewhat solemn, but his eyes were full of anger. In the time it took Crystal to glance back at the others still sitting in the cart, Thomas had made up ground, let out a blood-curdling scream as he ran up behind Billy, and, with pure adrenaline and emotion-fueled strength, flung his brother's body like a ragdoll into the ocean.

Thomas stood broken on the dock with tears pouring down his face as he stared at the bubbles where Billy fell in. His breath hitched, and his chest heaved, bordering on hyperventilation.

Crystal nearly leaped to her feet which would have been horribly painful but stopped when she saw Jonah jump into the water. The water was likely under ten feet deep, but being handcuffed by the police surely restricted Billy's ability to swim. Jonah yanked his baby brother up above the water by his neck and pulled him to shore, dumping him unceremoniously on the edge of where the water met the sand.

The taller of the two officers pulled the defeated, sandy, and drenched Billy to his feet and roughly placed a life jacket over his head; a necessary precaution after watching Billy sink to the bottom of the ocean without even putting up a fight. The second officer joined them, and the two guided Billy onto the boat without further incident.

After a brief, subdued conversation with one of the detectives remaining on the island, the boat was untethered from the dock. For a few moments, it floated silently, adrift in slow motion, like a ghost slipping away from the world of the living. Then, with a roar that shattered the stillness, the engine came to life, and the boat began its journey out to sea, the sound fading into the distance like a departing spirit.

Only when the police boat was no longer visible did the ferry captain hesitantly maneuver into the dock. His eyes flicked momentarily toward the departing vessel, a shadow of recognition crossing his face, but he remained expressionless as he attached the dock lines with practiced ease. He offered a solemn nod to the detective left behind, then turned his attention to his task.

The detective's steps echoed on the wooden planks of the dock as he made his way toward the shore. Crystal, perched stiffly in the cart, had managed to wipe away the evidence of her tears, but the emotional storm still brewed beneath her composed exterior.

"May I start loading your luggage, ma'am?" the young captain asked, his voice gentle, almost as if he sensed the fragility of the moment.

"Yes. Thank you," Crystal replied, her tone polite but distant.

The captain nodded and approached the cart's rear, where he hefted two large designer suitcases with a practiced efficiency. Crystal's gaze drifted to Jonah, who remained standing at the water's edge, his back to her, his eyes following the distant police boat until it was no more than a speck on the horizon. When he finally turned around, he removed his sunglasses and wiped them on the hem of his shirt, revealing the redness and puffiness around his eyes. Even from where she sat, Crystal could see the lingering moisture, glinting in the sunlight like tiny shards of glass. Jonah quickly replaced the sunglasses, hiding the vulnerability they betrayed, before walking past the captain with a silent nod.

Crystal's heart ached to comfort him, to hold him and chase away the darkness clouding his eyes. But she knew his pain was a fortress not easily breached.

Sean and April disembarked from their cart with steely determination, their faces set in expressions of cold resolve. They moved with the efficiency of soldiers, gathering as much luggage as they could carry without uttering a word. Sean hoisted one of Thomas's duffel bags over his shoulder, balancing two more under each arm, his silent strength a stark contrast to the visible collapse of Thomas and Ilma.

Thomas remained on the dock, staring into the distance with a vacant, haunted look, as though he were seeing something only he could perceive. His eyes, unblinking, were fixed on some distant point, while his body seemed paralyzed by an invisible force. Ilma, seated in the back of the other cart, mirrored his catatonic state. Her posture was rigid, her eyes wide with silent screams, her face a mask of fear frozen in time.

Crystal's breath caught as she took in their broken forms. They were teetering on the edge, suspended in a free fall, and she feared they might never find their way back to solid ground.

Sean and April's methodical work paused briefly when a third boat approached the dock. Sean straightened, his chest puffing out in a defensive stance, one foot ready to step onto the gangway like a pirate guarding his treasure. But as soon as he recognized the crew was simply a group of groundskeepers and maids, the tension melted away, and he returned to his task without a word.

With the carts unloaded, Thomas finally moved toward Ilma, extending a hand to help her out. She flinched at his touch, as if his hand were a burning brand. Crystal imagined invisible quills bristling around Ilma, a protective barrier against the world that had become too harsh, too unforgiving. Slowly, hesitantly, Ilma reached out, her hand trembling as it met his, and allowed him to escort her to the boat.

The tension between them was evident, a cord stretched too tight, on the verge of snapping. They had all been through so much, and Crystal knew the trauma had carved deep rifts in their hearts. Young love, so often resilient, now faced a trial that threatened to break them apart. They needed each other more than ever, but the distance between them loomed like an insurmountable chasm.

Crystal struggled to keep her frustration in check as she watched the delay unfold, knowing she would be the last to board the boat. Her patience frayed further when Jonah, about to return to fetch her, was intercepted by the detective, who pulled him aside for a hushed conversation. Though the words weren't meant for her ears, the detective and Jonah stood only a few feet away, and it was impossible not to overhear fragments of their exchange.

Despite the turmoil swirling within him, Jonah maintained a composed exterior. He had shifted into business mode, his voice steady and controlled, even as his hands betrayed him, wringing behind his back in a nervous rhythm.

"Look, there's not much I can tell you," the man admitted, his tone apologetic yet firm. "It's not that I don't want to; we just don't know much yet."

Jonah inclined his head, a picture of understanding. "I understand, detective. Are there any details you can share?"

The detective rubbed his chin thoughtfully, eyes flickering with hesitation. "We have officers at the house collecting evidence and are preparing to interview the crew later today. I'll be heading to the cave shortly to search for any signs that might provide clues."

He pulled a small, ragged notebook from his breast pocket, flipping it open with a practiced motion. Jonah waited silently, his patience a mask for the anxiety gnawing at him.

"We'll examine the cameras, the cause of the fire, and the hot tub tampering. Several of you mentioned the secret passageways. I'll have the caretaker walk me through those later." The detective's eyes met Jonah's briefly before returning to his notes. "We'll ship any evidence to the lab and hope for a quick turnaround. There's also a search boat on its way to patrol the ocean-side cliffs."

Jonah nodded, the slight movement barely concealing the tension coiling within him.

"The caretaker mentioned one of her employees was missing, so we're looking into that as well. She and the owners have been cooperative. We've questioned everyone in your party and have all the necessary contact information. If anything comes up, we may reach out with more questions."

The detective shifted his weight, cleared his throat, and glanced down at his notepad again. "Your brother, Sean, found a few items in the cave when they went to recover the flares—a bookmark, shoes, a scarf, and a little plastic baggie of pills."

Jonah stiffened, the change in his posture imperceptible to most, but Crystal caught it. She knew, almost certainly, that the pills were hers. The knowledge settled heavily between them, unspoken but understood.

As the conversation wound down, Crystal leaned back in the cart, closing her eyes to feign disinterest, though every word had imprinted itself on her mind. The sound of parting pleasantries between Jonah and the detective drifted into the air, followed by the soft crunch of loafers on the rough sand as Jonah approached.

The cart rocked gently as Jonah settled into the driver's seat beside her. Crystal opened her eyes to find him staring down at his lap, his head shaking slowly, burdened by the weight of unspoken thoughts.

"Do you remember when you first brought me home to meet your family?" Crystal's voice was a quiet murmur, barely loud enough to reach him, yet it cut through the silence like a lifeline.

A faint smile tugged at the corner of Jonah's mouth, his gaze remained downcast. "Will was crazy about you."

"He followed me around like a puppy, always wanting me to sit with him at the dinner table." Crystal's lips curved into a bittersweet smile. "He was so disappointed at our wedding, being the ring bearer. I think he truly believed I might choose to marry him instead."

Jonah's eyes finally lifted to meet hers, the vulnerability in them unmasked. "And when we moved away, it was never me he wanted to talk to on the phone, was it?"

Crystal shook her head, a tear slipping down her cheek. "He was only seven when we met, but no matter how much he's grown, he'll always be that sweet, shaggy-headed little boy to me."

Jonah nodded, his gaze drifting toward the ocean where the police boat had vanished. The horizon stretched endlessly, a somber reminder of the distance between their past and the present chaos.

Thomas approached to help Jonah lift Crystal. Though her slight frame made it unnecessary for both men to assist, their joint effort was a comfort rather than an insult. As Jonah met her eyes once more while they walked down the dock, Crystal noted the tear slipping from beneath his sunglasses, the silent testament to the storm raging within him.

The passenger ferry eased away from the island, the once-dreamlike retreat growing smaller with each passing second. While the others watched the mainland draw nearer, Crystal turned her gaze back, her heart sinking with the receding shore. The rolling waves stirred her nausea, and she prayed the sea sickness medication she'd taken would take effect soon, offering her a brief respite in sleep.

The cool ocean breeze swept through her hair, a fleeting comfort as her eyes grew heavy. Just before sleep claimed her, Crystal glimpsed the shadowy maw of a cliffside cave, its darkness a chilling reminder of the mysteries left behind, staring back at her like the dead, unblinking eye of a corpse.

Thank You for Reading

If you enjoyed THE UNWELCOME GUEST, please consider leaving an honest review on your preferred platform.

Your feedback is invaluable and helps other readers discover new books and authors.

If you didn't love it... sorry it wasn't your jam.

Thanks for giving me a try.

Want more?

In **Making a Killing** by Cori Nevruz, Natalia thought she had finally escaped her mother's suffocating grip, only to be drawn into a web of dark family secrets. A quirky misfit, she heads to New York City, driven by the discovery of a stepbrother she never knew—Daniel. Desperate for love and acceptance, Natalia carefully molds herself into the perfect sibling he expects. But her hidden life tells a different story.

By day, Natalia works for Stuart, an eccentric corporate powerhouse, covertly eliminating retired pension recipients. With a knack for making each hit seem accidental or natural, she rationalizes her deviant actions by focusing on her victims' flaws. The pay is good, and her skills sharpen with each job, but the weight of her dual life starts to wear thin.

As Natalia spends more time with Stuart, his enigmatic wife, and a budding romantic partner, her carefully constructed facade begins to crumble. Daniel's growing suspicion forces Natalia into a dangerous balancing act. Can she maintain the illusion, or will her true identity be revealed, setting off a chain reaction that could shatter her newfound connections?

Making a Killing is a gripping tale of deception, identity, and the deadly cost of living a double life.

Left Without Answers by Cori Nevruz plunges readers into a heart-stopping journey of grief, mystery, and unyielding determination. After the sudden and unexplained loss of her son Hank, Alice is consumed by a relentless need for answers. The vibrant spirit of her boy couldn't just vanish without a trace—there must be more to the story.

As Alice reaches out to Hank's best friend Arnold, she's met with a chilling resistance. Arnold, like everyone else, insists she move on, urging her to let the past rest. But Alice's motherly intuition is a force that cannot be silenced, especially when she begins finding cryptic notes from Hank. Could Hank be reaching out from beyond, or is something more sinister at play?

Alice's quest leads her deep into Hank's hidden life, unraveling a web of betrayal, bullying, and secrets darker than she ever imagined. Each revelation threatens to tip her over the edge of sanity, as she battles the terrifying truths lurking in the shadows.

In a race against time and her own fears, Alice must uncover the truth behind her son's death. But as the specters of Hank's final moments haunt her, Alice faces a chilling realization—some secrets are meant to stay buried. Will her search for answers bring justice, or will it plunge her into a nightmare from which there is no escape?

About the Author

Cori Nevruz

Cori Nevruz is a suspense and thriller author known for her gripping narratives and psychological depth.

Cori resides in Wilmington, North Carolina [USA], where she balances her writing career with family life alongside her husband, three sons and two dogs, Chumpy and Munch. When she's not crafting thrilling stories, she enjoys reading and passionately following her favorite sports.

Visit her website at http://CoriWroteABook.com.